W9-CFC-719

"We need to talk," Kane said, his deep voice serious.

"I'm coming to understand that there's a lot more to you than I or anyone else realizes."

"I warned you I was messed up." Lilly tried to keep it light, failing miserably. "Fifteen years of captivity will do that to a person."

He took her hand, stunning her into temporary silence. "It was more than just captivity, I know. You mentioned they experimented on you."

Her nod was the only answer she could manage.

"Lilly, I need you to tell me what happened to me when you sang."

Once she would have hung her head. But this was not her fault. So she lifted her chin and looked Kane directly in the eyes.

"I don't know how or why, but apparently when I sing, my voice is like the mythical sirens, compelling men. As it did you."

Narrow-eyed, he stared. "Then why can't I remember? Even if you could make me do something, you shouldn't be able to make me forget."

"I don't know. But you kissed me." Her face heated, which meant she was most likely a fiery red.

Books by Karen Whiddon

Harlequin Nocturne

*Lone Wolf #103
*Wolf Whisperer #128
*The Wolf Princess #146
*The Wolf Prince #157
*The Lost Wolf's Destiny #167
*The Wolf Siren #181

Silhouette Nocturne

*Cry of the Wolf #7
*Touch of the Wolf #12
*Dance of the Wolf #45
*Wild Wolf #67

Harlequin Romantic Suspense

The CEO's Secret Baby #1662
The Cop's Missing Child #1719
The Millionaire Cowboy's Secret #1752
Texas Secrets, Lovers' Lies #1773

Silhouette Romantic Suspense

*One Eye Open #1301
*One Eye Closed #1365
*Secrets of the Wolf #1397
The Princess's Secret Scandal #1416

Bulletproof Marriage #1484
**Black Sheep P.I. #1513
**The Perfect Soldier #1557
**Profile for Seduction #1629
Colton's Christmas Baby #1636

*The Pack
**The Cordasic Legacy

Other titles by this author available in ebook format.

KAREN WHIDDON

started weaving fanciful tales for her younger brothers at the age of eleven. Amid the Catskill Mountains of New York, then the Rocky Mountains of Colorado, she fueled her imagination with the natural beauty that surrounded her. Karen now lives in north Texas, where she shares her life with her very own hero of a husband and three doting dogs. Also an entrepreneur, she divides her time between the business she started and writing. You can email Karen at KWhiddon1@aol.com or write to her at P.O. Box 820807, Fort Worth, TX 76182. Fans of her writing can also check out her website, www.karenwhiddon.com.

THE WOLF SIREN

—

KAREN WHIDDON

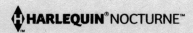

If you purchased this book without a cover you should be aware that this book is stolen property. It was reported as "unsold and destroyed" to the publisher, and neither the author nor the publisher has received any payment for this "stripped book."

Recycling programs
for this product may
not exist in your area.

ISBN-13: 978-0-373-88593-0

THE WOLF SIREN

Copyright © 2014 by Karen Whiddon

All rights reserved. Except for use in any review, the reproduction or utilization of this work in whole or in part in any form by any electronic, mechanical or other means, now known or hereafter invented, including xerography, photocopying and recording, or in any information storage or retrieval system, is forbidden without the written permission of the publisher, Harlequin Enterprises Limited, 225 Duncan Mill Road, Don Mills, Ontario, Canada M3B 3K9.

This is a work of fiction. Names, characters, places and incidents are either the product of the author's imagination or are used fictitiously, and any resemblance to actual persons, living or dead, business establishments, events or locales is entirely coincidental.

This edition published by arrangement with Harlequin Books S.A.

For questions and comments about the quality of this book, please contact us at CustomerService@Harlequin.com.

® and TM are trademarks of Harlequin Enterprises Limited or its corporate affiliates. Trademarks indicated with ® are registered in the United States Patent and Trademark Office, the Canadian Trade Marks Office and in other countries.

Printed in U.S.A.

Dear Reader,

I wrote *The Wolf Siren* during one of the most difficult times of my life. My mother was declining after a nearly two-year battle with pancreatic cancer. She passed away a few weeks after turning this story in. Nevertheless, as my brilliant editor Patience Bloom pointed out, sometimes writing—like reading—can be an escape. Tagging along with Kane, whom I fell in love with when I first met him in *The Lost Wolf's Destiny,* and Lilly, who might have been considered damaged beyond repair, helped me through a lot of worry and grief. As I wrote about the healing power of their love and as I watched Lilly find her own inner strength, I was able to come to a sort of peace with my own rapidly approaching loss. Because love heals, and love is eternal.

Karen Whiddon

To Patricia Ann Corcoran, 5-2-35 to 9-27-13. You were many things in the 78 years you lived in this world, but to me you were first and foremost my mother. I will always miss you.

Chapter 1

"You look…" The tall, dark-haired man stared, his silver gaze intense. "A thousand times better than the last time I saw you."

Clutching the door handle and peering out through the six-inch crack, Lilly Gideon tried hard not to tremble. Belatedly, she realized she never should have opened the door. But then, she hadn't known this man had been coming up the sidewalk.

Or had she? Something, some inner restlessness, had given her the urge to step out onto the front porch. Surely, she hadn't been going to meet this stranger who talked as if he knew her. He had a confident air of masculine authority and the sheer strength of his muscular body overwhelmed her.

She struggled to speak, to summon up some sort of relatively normal response. She was safe, she told herself over and over like a mantra, ignoring the shiver of dread working its way up her spine. Finally safe. Her brother, Lucas, his wife, Blythe, and her daughter, Hailey, were in the kitchen and would come running at the slightest sound. All she had to do was call. But staring at the handsome stranger, still she couldn't seem to force words past her closed-up throat.

"Lilly?" he asked, the deep dustiness of his voice striking a chord inside her, as if her soul recognized him. "It's me, Kane McGraw. Don't you remember me?"

Pushing away the panic, she struggled to simply breathe. The chiseled planes of his rugged face did seem achingly familiar, but with her tangled confusion of memories, she didn't know if this was a good thing or bad. He wore his dark hair short, spiky, a bit longer than military style, which added to his self-confident appearance. Once again, she found him intimidating.

Despite her best effort to appear brave, she let her hand creep up to her throat and dredged up words. "I…no. I don't remember you."

Her twin brother, Lucas, must have had a second sense, too. Something that told him she needed him right now. "Lilly?" he called, appearing in the arched opening that led to the foyer. "Are you all right?"

Relief flooding her, she turned her panicked gaze toward him, imploring silently for help.

"What's wrong?" Lucas strode toward her, putting himself in front of her even as he yanked the door all the way open.

"Kane?" Despite hearing the joy in her brother's voice, Lilly stepped back, taking refuge in the small space between the door and the wall. She hated the way terror still consumed her, but for now she didn't yet have the strength to overcome it. Maybe someday, but not just yet. She only hoped that with time…

"Lucas!" The two men gave each other the quick shoulder hug used by men.

"That was fast," Lucas said, the sun making his brown hair appear blond. He glanced at Lilly, and then back at their visitor, grinning. Lilly envied her brother's carefree attitude. Newly married and in love, his clear blue eyes radiated happiness. She kept hoping some of it would rub off on her. So far, she hadn't been so blessed.

Kane laughed, a throaty chuckle, drawing her attention. "As soon as you told me what you needed, I dropped everything. My vacation days were piling up unused anyway. I think the Society of Pack Protectors was shocked that I wanted to take them."

Though the deep rumble of this stranger's voice chased away the chill inside her, she kept herself utterly still, hoping she wouldn't draw any attention to herself. Of course, her brother noticed immediately.

"Lilly?" Lucas held out his hand, waiting until she'd slipped her fingers into his before continuing. "Don't you remember Kane? He helped us rescue you."

The reassuring sincerity in Lucas's expression calmed her enough to enable her to look at the other man. "I'm sorry," she murmured. "My memories from that time are all blurry."

Kane's smoky gaze held hers. "That's understandable. You've been through a lot."

She nodded, although fifteen years of torture, clinging to the edge of life, had been more than a lot. She was damaged, broken in more ways than one. Though she was eager to purge that time from her memory and heal herself so she could stride with confidence into the world, first she had to shake the paralyzing terror that dogged her every move.

Before she could run, she needed to walk. Before she could walk, she'd have to manage a crawl.

"Come on in," Lucas said, pulling Lilly toward him so he could fully open the door. She yanked her hand free, fighting the awful tide of panic rising in her throat. Though she wanted to flee, to tear down the hall toward her room, where she could close herself in and feel safe, she kept herself still, legs rooted in the carpet. She hated her fear and used this to find the strength to stand her ground. Her hands were clenched into fists, but despite that, she managed to lift her head and study Lucas's friend.

"Welcome," she said, trying to remember how to sound warm.

At her greeting, he smiled. Not just any smile, but a devastating curve of the mouth that heated her and inexplicably sent her pulse racing. Before, she'd thought him good-looking, in a muscular, dangerous sort of way. But now, feeling the pull of his grin, she realized he was more than that. He was beautiful, like a dark angel who'd recently tumbled from heaven.

She shivered. She'd had enough of angels and prophets, thank you very much.

"Blythe will be happy to see you." Lucas strode toward the kitchen, calling his wife's name as he went. Blythe met him halfway, her long blond hair pulled into a neat braid. As she moved toward them, she appeared to dance on her bare feet. Her bright green eyes lit up when she saw Kane.

Lilly watched, as detached as if she were separated from the others by a thick sheet of glass. Blythe, hugged Kane as if he was a long-lost brother, then her daughter, Hailey, squealed with delight as she threw herself at the tall man's legs.

Once the greetings and hugs were finished and things quieted down, Lucas led the way into the kitchen. He waited until everyone else had disappeared inside before returning to retrieve Lilly, who still stood frozen, unable to make herself move.

"Are you coming?" he asked, the concern in his voice making her feel guilty.

Rather than answer, she shook her head, sending her long hair whipping around her. Wrapping her arms around herself, even though the movement gave her no comfort, she swallowed. "I'm not feeling well," she told him. "I'm going to go lie down."

His expression sharpened, letting her know he didn't entirely buy the lie. But then, as she'd known he would, he nodded. "I'll bring you something to eat later then, okay?"

Angry—both at herself for lacking the courage to join them and, unreasonably, at him for cutting her so much slack—she nodded. Then, without another word, she spun on her heel and marched away to her room.

Once there, she didn't dissolve into tears and throw herself on her bed. She supposed that would have been progress, at least. Instead, she went to the small desk she'd placed in front of the window, and took a seat, gazing outside and marveling once again at how green everything was here. As she'd learned to do while trapped in a dank, basement cell, she let her mind separate from her body. She wondered if she'd ever stop wanting to curl up and die.

Following Lucas and Blythe into the kitchen, Kane fought the urge to turn back and go after Lilly. His wolf had once again reared his wild head the instant he'd inhaled Lilly's fragile and feminine scent. On the long drive from Texas to Seattle, he'd thought about this reaction, which had stunned him the first time he'd seen her, half-dead in a concrete cell. Then, he'd wondered if it had been a fluke. Now he knew it hadn't. The question was, what was he going to do about it?

Though she no longer looked like a broken rag-doll, Lilly was still clearly damaged. Kane would have to be careful, especially since he'd just agreed to act as her full-time bodyguard.

"Does she know why I'm here?" Kane asked, taking a seat at the oak-planked, country-style table and accepting the beer Blythe brought him.

"Just a minute." Lucas cast a warning look at Hailey, which Blythe picked up on.

"Hailey, why don't we watch one of your DVDs," Blythe said, taking her daughter's hand and leading her from the kitchen.

Kane sipped on his beer. Lucas waited until the sound of the television came on before speaking. "No. Despite therapy once a week, she spends most of her time in a state close to terrified anxiety. I thought it better if she didn't know." He got up, crossed to the fridge and snagged his own beer.

"About any of it?"

Lucas's troubled expression gave Kane his answer. "I've been trying to shield her as best I can. She isn't aware of the break-in attempt. I had Blythe and Hailey take her out for ice cream when the police came to make their report."

"And you're confident they weren't after Hailey?"

"Yes." Lucas clenched his jaw. "They broke in through Lilly's window. This might have been a coincidence, except they never left her room. They tore it apart like they were looking for something."

"You also said someone tried to abduct her?"

"Yes. Someone tried to grab her when she and Blythe were leaving therapy, but Blythe pretty much convinced her that the guy was trying to rob them."

"How sure are you that he wasn't?"

Dragging his hand across his chin, Lucas nodded. "First

off, he didn't try and get their purses. Second, he left Blythe alone. The SOB went right for Lilly."

Kane nodded. Both he and Lucas had dealt with the crazy cult members who'd belonged to Sanctuary, Jacob Gideon's pseudo-religious organization. They'd worked together, along with The Society of Pack Protectors, to take them down. In the process, they'd not only rescued Blythe and her daughter, Hailey, but they'd saved Lilly, Lucas's sister, whom he'd believed had been murdered fifteen years earlier.

"Most of the cultists are locked up," Kane mused. "Though we've been made aware of a few others who weren't there the day the raid went down."

"You know how determined those bastards are." Lucas didn't bother to hide his bitterness. "My sister suffered for years because of them."

"I think I should take her out of here," Kane said. "And quickly."

Lucas stared at him in shock. Of course, Kane had known getting Lucas to accept his plan wasn't going to be easy.

"Hear me out."

After a moment, Lucas finally nodded. His guarded expression made it clear he wasn't happy with the idea. "Go on."

"You want me to keep her safe." Kane leaned forward. "I can do that. I'm good at my job. But…"

The word hung in the air. Lucas took a long drink of his beer, waiting for his friend to finish the statement.

"She needs to go into hiding."

"You really think you can protect her better away from here?" The low pitch of Lucas's voice told Kane he recognized the truth, whether or not he liked it.

"Don't you?"

Grimacing, Lucas gave a reluctant nod. "Where are you planning to take her?"

"I think it's actually better if you don't know."

"Then she's not going anywhere." Lucas's emphatic answer came without hesitation. "I lost her once before. I won't do so again."

This Kane could understand. He nodded. "Fine. I want to take her to my hometown. Leaning Tree, New York."

From Lucas's frown, it was clear he'd never heard of it. This was one of the reasons Kane had chosen the small town. "Is it Pack?"

"Mostly. It's pretty remote, tucked away in the rolling Catskill Mountains. My entire family lives there—parents, siblings, aunts and uncles, cousins." He shrugged. "I haven't been home in a few years. My parents own a resort—actually, it's an old-fashioned motor court. With separate cabins. They're pretty secluded and there's only one road in and out. I'm thinking Lilly and I will stay there."

Lucas narrowed his eyes. "You've got this all planned out, don't you?"

"Yes." Kane smiled and then rolled his shoulders, trying to release some of the knots he'd incurred on the long drive northwest. "I'm damn good at what I do. That's why you called me, isn't it?"

Instead of answering, Lucas pushed to his feet. He strode to the doorway and peered out into the den, his expression softening noticeably. "Blythe, could you come here for a minute? I need to get your opinion."

Instantly, Blythe appeared, sweeping her silky, brownish-blond hair away from her face.

"Kane wants to take Lilly away," Lucas said. "He feels he can keep her safer if he does."

Blythe's bright green gaze locked on her husband's as they linked hands. She and Lucas appeared to communicate silently. Watching them, Kane pushed away a sharp stab of envy. Not everyone in the Pack was fortunate enough to find their mate like their wild cousins. Human Shape-shifters only mated once. Kane had been privileged to be present when Lucas and Blythe had realized they were meant for each other. Witnessing this had only increased Kane's intense and private hunger to join with a mate of his own someday.

"How do you feel about that?" Blythe finally asked, a soft frown of worry creasing her smooth brow. Kane noted she didn't ask whether Lucas felt Lilly would be safer some-where else. She knew her husband well and understood how tightly Lucas wanted to hold on to the sister he'd believed to be dead fifteen years gone. Kane got this, too, but he knew what he wanted to do was ultimately the best way to keep Lilly safe.

Hands linked, Lucas and Blythe turned to face Kane. "Do you promise to keep us in the loop? We want frequent updates, texts and pictures, all of it, you know," Blythe said.

"As much as I can," Kane answered. "As long as it doesn't compromise Lilly's safety."

Still Lucas hadn't spoken. Kane waited, arms crossed. He needed to be sure he had Lucas's 100-percent approval or his plan was a no-go.

Finally, Lucas gave a slow nod. "Fine. Let me get her and we'll tell her now. When do you want to leave?"

"As soon as possible."

Lucas jerked his chin and turned. Blythe's hand on his arm stopped him. "Let me fetch her," she said softly. "You and Kane need to present a united front in this."

Though Lucas nodded, Kane saw Blythe's comment perplexed him. Clearly he hadn't considered the possibility that his sister wouldn't go along with his plans.

A moment later, Blythe returned. Behind her came Lilly,

a quiet wraith of a woman, strands of her long, honey-blond hair drifting around her shoulders as she moved. She slipped into the room, the graceful way she seemed to glide making Kane think of a dancer.

"You want me to what?" she said, as soon as Lucas finished explaining to her. Her bright blue eyes appeared to glow in her delicate oval face. "That makes no sense. Why would you think I'd want to take a trip with a man I barely remember?"

That stung, though Kane kept the same pleasant expression he always wore when around her. Since the first time he'd seen Lilly, emaciated and filthy, huddled in a heap of rags in a dark and dank cell, she'd haunted his every thought.

Lucas exchanged a glance with Blythe and Kane knew they were deciding whether or not to tell her the truth. While this wasn't his call, at least not yet, he felt he had to make his position known. "I'm not going to lie," he warned the other man, his arms still crossed. "I don't see a reason to."

"Lie?" Frowning, Lilly looked from Kane to Lucas and back again. "What are you talking about? Is there something you're not telling me?"

Judging from Lucas's clenched jaw, he wasn't happy. Yet when he spoke, his tone was soft and soothing. "We think a few of the doctors from Sanctuary are still at large."

Suddenly, Lilly's entire demeanor changed. Kane watched as all the animation disappeared from her face and she…shut down. That was the only way he could describe it. All the light simply vanished from her eyes.

"And you think they're going to try and take me back." Not even a question, she delivered the statement in a flat, emotionally dead voice.

Kane found himself aching to reach out and comfort her, but of course he couldn't.

Having no such compunction, Blythe wrapped Lilly in her arms. "It's okay," she murmured. "We've got your back."

Lilly stood like a statue, neither returning nor rejecting the embrace. Finally, she stepped away from Blythe and faced her brother. "Why didn't you tell me?"

"We didn't want to stress you. You've already been through so much." Lucas's voice broke as he tried to explain. Lilly continued to wait, her gaze unblinking, while Lucas struggled to find the right words to express his concern without completely terrifying her. A difficult task.

Finally, Kane took pity on him. "Your brother is worried about you. Rightly so. That's why he asked me to come help. I promise, you'll be safe with me," he said, the certainty in his tone meant to let her know she needn't be anxious.

"Will I?" Just like that, with one sweep of her eyes through impossibly long lashes, she let him know she'd rather stay. "No offense, but I think I'd rather take my chances here, with my brother and his family."

Lucas shook his head, his gaze full of pain and regret. "That's not an option, Lilly. Much as I'd like it to be."

Lilly glanced from her brother to his new bride, and then toward the living room where a newly healed five-year-old watched television. Kane saw the moment the realization came to her. Both hurt and understanding flashed across her fragile features before she gave a wooden nod.

"I understand," she said, her flat tone letting them know she'd retreated to that place inside herself that made her feel safe. "When do you need me to be ready?"

Steeling himself, Kane glanced at his watch. "How about in one hour?"

Ignoring the instant protests by both Lucas and Blythe—

their voices merging together as they insisted Kane stay for dinner or better yet, the night—Lilly jerked her chin in a simple nod and glided out of the room.

Kane waited until she was gone before lifting his hand. "Enough."

Just like that, they fell silent. "I'm leaving tonight. She's getting ready. The sooner we get out of town, the better. I don't want whoever is watching her to get a make on me or my vehicle."

Blythe frowned. "You think they're watching the house?"

Careful to appear casual, Kane gave a nonchalant shrug. "It's possible. One thing I've learned over the years is to always expect the worst."

Though Lucas nodded, agreeing with him, Blythe's frown deepened. "If that's the case, when they see you leaving with her, they're going to follow."

"I've already considered that." Fishing in his backpack, he pulled out a plastic bag containing one of the wigs he'd purchased before leaving Texas. "Have her put this on. The color and style are similar to yours. Also, it'd help if you lend her one of your outfits. Something you wear often, that might be easily recognizable as yours."

Accepting the wig, she finally graced him with a small smile. "You think you can make them believe Lilly is me."

Again he shrugged. "People generally see what they want to see. They'll have no reason to think otherwise. But to make certain, I'd like you to put on this." Again he dug in his bag, bringing out a second wig. "This is as close as I could get to her hairstyle."

Taking this wig, too, Blythe laughed, the musical sound making both Lucas and Kane smile. "You really have thought of everything."

Still smiling at his wife, Lucas clapped him on the shoulder. "I told you he's good."

Before Blythe could respond, Lilly appeared in the doorway. "I'm ready," she said quietly, holding a small overnight bag. Though she wore a determined look, she couldn't manage to banish the trepidation in her eyes.

"Is that all you're bringing?" Blythe crossed to her and took her arm. "Would you like me to help you pack a few more things?"

"No." Lilly's gaze found Kane's. He felt a connection sizzling along his nerve endings. "I don't need much," she said.

He nodded. "And if she needs more, I can always buy something for her. Now," he continued, his tone brisk. "The two of you go in the bathroom and change clothes and put on the wigs I got you."

"What?" Lilly appeared thoroughly confused. "I don't—"

Blythe took her arm, steering her in the right direction. "I'll explain while we're changing."

After the two women had gone, Kane turned to find Lucas eyeing him. "Don't worry. I'll take good care of her," Kane said.

"You'd better." Lucas's harsh tone spoke of deep emotion. "I don't want to lose her again."

"You won't." Kane uttered the two words fiercely. They both knew he'd given an oath. Nothing would happen to Lilly Gideon while on his watch.

When the two women reappeared, he eyed them critically. Up close, he could tell that the wigs were cheaply made, but even through binoculars they'd do the trick. Blythe's clothing hung on Lilly's too-thin frame, but again, the disguise should serve its purpose.

"Are you ready?" Kane asked Lilly, holding out his hand. Though she nodded, she stepped back rather than touch him. Which was okay, for now. Eventually, he hoped she'd trust him enough to welcome his touch.

And more, his inner voice whispered. He banished the thought as soon as it occurred to him. Life was messy enough without unnecessary complications.

Lilly waited until they were on the highway before speaking. "More than anything," she said, sounding softer than she would have liked, "I wish I could be like everyone else."

"Really?" A smile curved Kane's hard slash of a mouth. "How's that?"

She shrugged, hurriedly glancing away from him. "Normal." Hesitating the space of a heartbeat, she resolutely continued. "Sane. I'm not, you know."

Though he had to realize she was, in all fairness, trying to warn him, Kane didn't appear concerned. His chiseled features still radiated masculine confidence, as if there was no problem she could throw his way that he couldn't handle. "Don't be so hard on yourself. You've been through a lot. You're stronger than you think. Not too many women could have survived an ordeal like that."

Rote words, the kind of meaningless phrases her therapist was fond of throwing around. The anger surging through Lilly startled and surprised her. "You don't even know me." Her even tone gave no hint of the resentment simmering just below the surface. She'd learned the hard way how to impose an icy self-control, to pretend a confidence she didn't feel.

Even now, having finally gained both her freedom and her brother, she felt as if she walked under the shadow of her father's madness. He'd hurt and abused her, all in the name of love. After fifteen years of living as his captive, trying to hang on to the rapidly diminishing spark that made up her inner self, she no longer knew how to interact with others. Especially not men. Most particularly men like Kane, the kind that embodied all that was male.

"You'll be fine," he said, smiling, looking like some dark angel who ought to frighten her, but instead intrigued her way too much.

"Don't," she ordered, the catch in her voice contradicting its sharpness. "Don't patronize me."

"I wasn't," he said firmly. "Believe me, Lilly Gideon. That's the last thing I want to do with you."

She didn't dare ask him what the first was. Though she knew he didn't do it on purpose, the underlying sensuality in his husky voice made her shiver. If that was, in fact, what sensuality sounded like. She, who knew everything about how to endure torture and experiments and pain, knew absolutely nothing about a healthy relationship between a man and a woman. The closeness she'd experienced with her brother and his wife had been her first experience in fifteen years with anything remotely resembling love.

If that's what it was. With the ground constantly shifting under her feet, she didn't feel certain about anything. After all, she'd just begun to feel comfortable around her new-found family, and now she was being sent away with a man she barely knew.

"For your own safety," Kane said, making her start and wonder if she'd said what was in her head. She hoped not.

"Did I...?" she asked, waving her hand to indicate what she meant.

"Speak your thoughts aloud? No." He shook his head. "But you didn't have to. Believe me, Lucas loves you. He only wants to keep you safe."

"I understand." Again, she thought she sounded cool and confident, the opposite of how she felt. Everything about this man made her feel unsettled. Even the throaty rasp of his voice danced along her nerve endings like a silk edged sword soaked in fire.

How did one respond to that?

"What's in this for you?" she asked, more to distract herself than any real curiosity.

Instead of answering, he laughed. While she stared at him with a weird mixture of annoyance and trepidation. "Not everyone is completely self-serving. Some of us do things because it's the right thing to do."

She wanted to ask him to explain this cryptic message, but wasn't sure how. Instead, she turned and pretended an interest in the passing scenery.

He didn't speak again, which should have relieved her. Instead, her discomfort grew, making her fight the urge to squirm in her seat. Finally, she gave in and glanced at him. "Where are we going?"

"Someplace safe." Though he barely looked at her, one corner of his mouth lifted to take the sting off his words.

"How far away?" Again she had to quell her own uneasy restlessness. She hated—no, *despised*—this weakness within her. She'd felt unsafe for so long she'd begun to wonder if she even knew how to be strong. Even with her brother, she'd found herself jumping at the slightest sound and battling the urge to crawl into her bed and take refuge under the covers.

"Across the country. It'll take us four days to get there, if we travel easy."

Again she nodded, keeping her face expressionless while she wondered what the hell was wrong with her, that she could don a mask of normalcy while inside she struggled with a maelstrom of conflicting emotions.

"And then what?"

He cocked one eyebrow, looking devilish and dangerous and a thousand other things that all made her want to wrench open her door and leap from the vehicle. Only the knowledge that she'd promised her brother—sworn to Lucas that she'd let Kane keep her safe—made her stay in the car.

"Once we arrive at our destination, we'll work on beginning to teach you to protect yourself."

Even trying to understand his cryptic pronouncements fatigued her. In fact, weariness slammed her with a force nearly as strong as one of her father's blows. Too exhausted to fight any longer, she relaxed and gave in to it, closing her eyes and willing herself to fall asleep.

Chapter 2

Kane nearly grinned as Lilly closed her eyes and pretended sleep, as if by doing so she could shut him out. Whether she liked it or not, and she'd made it quite clear she did not, they were going to be spending a lot of time together.

The first few miles were awkward, as Kane had suspected they'd be. He drove in silence, giving her the space he knew she needed, trying not to let her scent make him dizzy. Her breathing slowed and evened, and he realized she truly had dropped off to slumber. Oddly enough, he felt honored. The fact that she could do so meant she trusted him, even on a subconscious level.

Either that or, in her years of captivity, she'd learned to take her rest when she could.

Though he couldn't get a read on her inner wolf, his own beast had gone into an adrenaline-fueled high alert. Kane couldn't figure out why, unless it was reacting to Lilly's unusual aura. The visible aura was the way all Shape-shifters identified their own kind. Most were a subtle glow of color, pleasing to the eye.

Not Lilly's. Hers pulsed a violent purple, so dark it appeared black. Such an unnatural color, the Pack doctors had said, could mean madness or even…death. None of them had seen anything like it.

Naturally, this worried Lucas and Blythe. Now that Kane had seen it, he understood their concern. He hoped with time he could help Lilly regain her confidence and perhaps bring her fractured inner wolf some kind of healing.

She dozed for a little over an hour, giving him time to work on relaxing, as well. It surprised him, this antsy restless feeling. In his work for the Protectors, he'd been in lots of dangerous situations. He and his wolf had always been in accord—none of the warring between the two halves of himself, as he'd heard happened with others.

But now, when there was no apparent danger, at least at this exact moment, his inner beast couldn't be calmed.

Finally, Lilly stirred. Stretching, she smiled sleepily and opened her eyes. When she speared him with her bright blue gaze, the catch in his heart nearly made him recoil. What the hell?

An instant later, when Lilly realized where she was and who she was with, her smile vanished. Turning away, she resumed staring straight ahead, her entire body stiff and tense.

He put on a CD of old-school country music classics, believing that even the most die-hard introvert couldn't sit quietly through Johnny Cash, Loretta Lynn, and Dolly Parton.

Eventually, even though she never looked directly at him, she began tapping her foot, proving him right.

Good. An outward sign she was finally relaxing.

Again she glanced sideways at him, and then looked

away without speaking. He didn't ask her if she had a question or needed something. Not yet. Since it would be a long drive cross-country from Seattle to upstate New York, he had the luxury of taking things slow.

Her stomach rumbled, causing her to flush red.

"Are you hungry?" he asked quietly.

"I could eat," she admitted, careful to keep her eyes firmly fixed on the passing terrain. "What did you have in mind?"

An image flashed before him. He saw himself, as vividly as if it were happening, slanting his lips over hers, plundering her mouth with his tongue.

Swallowing hard, he blinked to dispel the picture. "How about a burger?" he managed. "I'm sure we can find a fast-food place."

She made a noncommittal sound that he chose to take as agreement. He stifled the urge to smile. After speaking to Lucas and agreeing to help, Kane hadn't been sure what to expect. While he knew Lilly was emotionally and physically fragile, he hadn't realized he'd have to continually fight the urge to pull her into his arms and swear to her he'd give his life to keep her safe.

This was a given, even though she didn't realize it yet. Maybe she never would. None of that mattered. She was his to protect, no matter the cost. As a Pack Protector, recruited at an early age, he always took his duties seriously. Even in his real job as a veterinarian, he considered himself dedicated. His clients and their pets—his patients— loved him for it. They'd even understood when he'd taken a leave of absence from the veterinary clinic to help Lucas protect Lilly.

"How often do you shape-shift?" Though she asked the question casually, the intent way she fixed her sky-blue eyes on him told Kane it was important.

Since he knew she wanted him to think it wasn't, he lifted one shoulder in a shrug. "As often as I can. How about you?"

"I'm the opposite. I'd be happiest if I could figure out a way to never shift again."

He'd expected this. Lucas had mentioned that Lilly had issues with shape-shifting. After what she'd been through, Kane could well imagine.

"There." She pointed at a sign for a well-known fast-food restaurant. Obliging her, he took the next exit and parked close to the entrance.

Her question pleased him. It showed a bit of natural curiosity, a spark of life, a quality he'd feared he'd have to help Lilly completely rebuild.

After they'd both eaten and freshened up, they got back on the road. Kane had barely driven thirty miles before Lilly fell asleep again. Eyeing her, he couldn't resist a smile.

She slept well for several hours. A good, clean rest, he thought. She didn't appear to suffer from nightmares or even dreams. Apparently she had no bad associations from riding in a car.

He drove until dusk, then a bit farther. His neck hurt, his hands were stiff from gripping the wheel and he needed to stretch his legs. In the passenger seat, Lilly had begun to stir, blinking sleepily and looking around her with the barely awake curiosity of the truly innocent.

"Where are we?" she finally asked, her voice rusty.

"Nearly to Billings, Montana. We're going to stop in a little bit."

"Okay."

Relief flooded him, though he was careful not to show it. Driving so long with only his own thoughts had made him wonder how she would do in a hotel room alone with him. He'd calculated they'd need to stop three times and they'd have to share a room each time. No way was he letting her out of his sight, not even to sleep. While he'd make sure they'd have separate beds, she'd be spending the darkest part of the night with a virtual stranger. Apparently, she wasn't concerned, which was much better than he'd expected. He nearly smiled at her. Only the notion that it would probably scare her kept his face expressionless.

With classic country music wailing away in the background, they continued on. He pulled off I-90 in Billings, figuring ten hours on the road was enough for the first day. Truth be told, since Lilly had slept for several hours, he could have gone farther, but having recently made the trip from Texas to Seattle, all that driving had begun to catch up with him and he needed to rest.

After stopping in the office and paying for one night, he returned to the car holding the plastic key card. They drove around to the back side of the building, looking for Room 149. Parking in front, he glanced again at Lilly and then killed the car engine. The exterior of the hotel appeared a bit shabby, but hopefully the rooms would be clean. He slid his key into the sensor and opened the door. Lilly drifted along behind him like a ghost.

Kane turned on the lights, inhaling the slightly musty scent, and looked around. Two beds, check. Worn carpet that had seen better days. But a working window air conditioner. The bathroom was large and had obviously been redone. There were four white towels, a bit thin but clean and serviceable. Exactly what he expected to find for thirty-nine dollars a night.

"After you," he told Lilly, gesturing toward the bathroom. "I don't know about you, but a hot shower would feel really good right now."

Though she dipped her chin to acknowledge him, she didn't comment. Instead, carrying her overnight bag, she brushed past him and closed the bathroom door behind her. A moment later, he heard the shower start. When he did, something that had been clenched inside of him relaxed. Odd, but he hadn't even realized he'd been so tense.

He took to roaming the room, stopping occasionally at the single window and peering out through the middle of the closed curtains. Not that he expected to see anything—he was 100 percent certain they hadn't been followed—but old habits were hard to break. Plus, during his twice-yearly stints working for the Protectors, he'd come to appreciate the value of being overly vigilant.

The shower cut off, drawing his attention to the closed bathroom door. Though he knew it might be a bit of a cliché, he was a man and couldn't help but picture her reaching for a towel, her pale and creamy skin glistening with water.

A few minutes later, she emerged, a towel piled high on her head. Her long legs were bare under a soft black T-shirt that skimmed her knees. She barely glanced at him, claiming the bed farthest from the door. He watched her pull the ugly, patterned bedspread down and fold it neatly, before she slid under the worn sheets.

"Here," he said, tossing the television remote on the bed near her. "I'll just be a few minutes."

Still keeping her profile averted, she ignored him.

Since he could well understand her nerves, he moved past her, careful to act as if everything was perfectly ordinary. He hoped she'd be able to relax once he closed himself in the bathroom. Maybe find something banal on television to help lull herself back to sleep.

The hot, as close to scalding as he could stand, shower improved his mood 100 percent. He dried off, dressing in loose gym shorts and an old T-shirt even though he preferred to sleep naked. After brushing his teeth, he opened the door, listening for the sound of the TV. Instead, only silence greeted him. Not completely unsurprised, he saw she hadn't turned it on. Instead, she lay curled into a ball, her long lashes fanning the curve of her cheek. She didn't move as he quietly approached her, though he could tell from the uneven rise and fall of her chest that she only pretended sleep. Even so, she was still the most beautiful thing he'd ever seen.

Then, while he stood drinking in the sight of her, she began trembling. A horrible, violent shivering, reminding him where she'd been and what a man looming over her bed most likely meant to her.

Horrified, he stepped back. His inner wolf snarled, evidently unsettled by the sudden, sharp ache just below his heart. Moving carefully, he crossed over to his own bed and pulled back the covers. A quick glance over his shoulder at her revealed her shaking hadn't abated in the slightest. Poor Lilly was clearly terrified.

His chest tight, he considered his options. Deciding, he snagged his car keys from the dresser. "Be right back," he murmured, even though he knew she wouldn't acknowledge his words.

Unlocking his car, he reached into the backseat and retrieved his battered guitar case. While he was out there, he did a quick scope of the parking lot, reassured by the emptiness of the well-lit area. Even the highway seemed quiet. Not a lot of activity on I-90 near Billings at night.

Back inside the room, he bolted the door behind him. Lilly continued to lie in the same position, her slender body still wracked by shudders. Cursing under his breath, he sat down on the edge of his bed and fumbled with the latches on his case, careful not to look too long at her.

Once he had the old acoustic guitar out, he considered. He needed something soothing, not the rollicking bluesy-country music he generally favored. His entire family played one instrument or another. One of the first things he'd learned on the guitar was the old Beatles song "Let It Be." Perfect.

She gave a reflexive jerk of her shoulders when he strummed the first chord. Ignoring this, he continued softly playing, singing the words in his low voice. While he sang, his wolf tried to sense hers. So far, even though such a thing was common among Shape-shifters, he hadn't been able to do this with her, not even the most minute fraction of contact. Kane couldn't understand why her wolf seemed to be locked away most of the time, though he guessed this was the result of the torture and experiments she'd suffered while locked away in the basement of Sanctuary. He had hopes that eventually, with the passage of time, she'd be able to return to a semblance of normalcy.

So he continued to play music for her, and for her wolf. He'd learned music not only calmed the savage beast, but provided a soothing balm to troubled souls.

Gradually, her trembling appeared to lessen. Encouraged, he began another song. This time the old Bob Dylan tune "Blowing in the Wind." Though several artists had done covers of this song, in Kane's head he always heard Bob Dylan's gravelly voice. Kane knew all the words to this one, too, and he sang with his heart, quietly paying homage to a beautiful woman who should never have had to endure what she had.

Midway through this second song, Lilly opened her eyes. She turned her head and, after a moment of silent scrutiny, she pushed up on one elbow to watch him.

Progress. He barely managed to suppress an encouraging smile. Instead, pretending not to notice, he launched into some old Judy Collins, refusing to reflect on how every soothing song he could think of was from four or five decades ago. What could he say? He'd always liked oldies.

Once the last notes of the music died away, he placed the guitar on the chair next to his bed. "Good night," he told her, inclining his head in a sort of salute before reaching up and quickly extinguishing the light.

As he lay in the darkness, his heart inexplicably pounding in his chest, with his wolf wanting to howl mournfully, he listened. The faint sounds of the nearby interstate were muted, and the rest of the motel was quiet. But these things barely registered in his consciousness, because he attuned every fiber of his being to hearing her.

At first, there was nothing, as if she was frozen in place. But then Lilly must have accepted the need to sleep or resigned herself to the inevitable. He heard the slight rustle of her sheets as she tried to make herself comfortable, the soft sigh that escaped her lips. And finally, her breathing slowed, became even and deep.

The tightness eased in his chest. She'd fallen asleep. Why he should feel as if he'd accomplished a victory, he couldn't say. This drive would take four long days, with three overnight stops. They'd made it through the first. He could only hope the next two would be easier for her.

Eventually, he drifted into a restless slumber of his own.

Lilly came awake sometime in the dark of the night. As was her habit, she held herself utterly still while she gathered her bearings. The even breathing of the man in the bed next to her told her he was out, safely locked in the throes of REM sleep.

Kane. He looked like a fallen angel, or at least how she'd always pictured them when her father had ranted. Maybe not Lucifer, but one of the others caught in the fallout. She thought this because she detected no malice in those amazing silver eyes of his.

Everything about him affected her. Her experience outside of Sanctuary was too small for her to know why. She couldn't understand her reaction toward him. Lucas had told her she could trust him, and she took what her twin brother told her as gospel. But the effect Kane had on her wasn't like fear. He exerted some kind of magnetic pull on her, the way a candle attracts a moth. She wasn't sure what it was exactly. An odd combination of trepidation and fascination, maybe. The latter worried her.

Of course, it seemed as if everything made her anxious these days—ever since gaining her freedom, something she'd once hoped for but had given up on. Now she wished for normalcy, to understand how to interact with others without the crippling sense of trepidation. Lucas had said she needed to be patient, to give it time.

But she couldn't lie, not to herself. She suspected that the fear would always be with her. Even in Lucas's home, she couldn't control her immediate reaction if someone inadvertently startled her. The first few times that she'd dropped into a feral crouch and bared her teeth had been humiliating, to say the least. She'd just begun to try to train herself to relax when Kane had shown up and she'd learned she'd have to travel.

Among the many things she was working on was trying to blur her memory of the years of her captivity. Sometimes, she held out hope that she could be successful, but then the dreams would come and she'd wake panicked, believing herself to be still shackled to a bed, a helpless prisoner while nameless people shoved needles into her or hooked her up to machines that brought nothing but pain.

At such times, she'd learned the trick of leaving her body, a sort of disassociation that allowed her to travel far, far away. It was this ability, she now knew, that had enabled her to hang on to the last shreds of her sanity.

Had this been a good thing? Often, she found herself

wondering. She certainly hadn't expected life after captivity to be so painful. Sometimes she thought life might have been easier if she was mindless and drooling.

Pushing aside her dark thoughts, she wondered what the followers of Jacob Gideon and his church of Sanctuary found so valuable about her that would make them continue to hunt her. As far as she knew, none of the multitude of experiments they'd performed on her had been even remotely successful.

The man in the bed next to her, Kane, made a sound, low in his throat. More like a growl than a snore, even though she knew he was still deeply asleep. She wondered if he knew she sensed his wolf and how much such a thing terrified her. The only other wolf she'd ever been able to be aware of was her twin brother's. And even that had been before the man who'd called himself their father had discovered that they were abominations.

His music… She smiled to herself in the darkness. She'd never heard anything like it—or hadn't in at least fifteen years. The *thing* inside her, the abomination, had actually gone quiet for once.

Should she tell Kane this? Or would doing so somehow give him a weapon to use against her?

Trust, no matter what her brother said, had to be earned. As of yet, she trusted no one. Least of all herself. Unable to sleep, she lay awake waiting for sunrise, listening for any sounds that might mean danger had found her.

Once the sky began to lighten and Kane began to stir, she sat up, pushed back the sheets and padded to the bathroom, where she brushed her teeth and got dressed. When she returned, Kane sat on the edge of his bed with the television on. Some sort of daybreak news show played.

"Mornin'," he drawled, the kindness of his smile making her feel warm all over. Struck speechless, she could only dip her chin in a nod.

He didn't seem to notice. "My turn." Pushing off from the bed, he headed for the bathroom, closing the door behind him.

With nothing to do but wait, Lilly sat down to watch the television. A commercial about laundry detergent wrapped up, and then the perky woman anchor appeared, her hot-pink suit matching her bright voice.

"Breaking news," she exclaimed. "Police in Maine have rescued two women who have been held captive for twelve years. This is eerily similar to the case in Ohio, where two girls were abducted as teens and held for ten years."

Lilly froze. There were others like her? As the women's photos appeared on the screen, first the older ones from Missing posters showing them as teens, and then shots of them as they emerged from the house that had been their prison, she wrapped her arms around her waist and her eyes filled with tears. She knew these women, not personally but in spirit. In their sad gazes, the tightness around their mouths, and the way they walked, shoulders rounded as if they expected a blow, she recognized herself.

She barely heard Kane emerge from the bathroom. Engrossed in the story, she didn't look up. Nor did she make a move to wipe away the tears streaming down her face.

"What's wrong?" He sounded alarmed. When she didn't respond, he dropped down onto the bed next to her and put his arm around her shoulders. "Lilly?"

Gathering her shredded composure, and überconscious of his arm, she gestured at the TV, where they were wrapping up the segment. Then she whispered, "Those women were held captive for twelve years. And they mentioned there were others, held somewhere else for ten."

"Yes." He hugged her. She wasn't sure whether to stiffen,

push him away or simply accept the comfort he offered. In the end, she stayed where she was.

"You're not alone," he continued.

Enough of this wallowing in emotion. "They told me that in therapy." Pushing to her feet, she swiped the back of her hand across her wet face. "Are you about ready to go?"

Watching her carefully, he nodded.

"Give me just a minute." And she hurried to the bathroom, where she blew her nose, splashed some cold water on her face and shook her head at her image in the mirror.

They ran through a drive-through and grabbed breakfast sandwiches and coffee. In a few minutes they were back on I-90, heading east. Something about the motion of the car made her sleepy, and she accepted this as a gift. When she opened her eyes again, she saw several hours had passed. They stopped for lunch and this time when they got back on the road, she felt jittery and wide-awake.

Noticing this, Kane turned down the radio. Stomach sinking, Lilly glanced sideways at him. He was going to ask questions. She recognized the signs.

"You know, I'll never forget when we found you," Kane said. "All those years, with both you and Lucas believing the other one dead."

She nodded. Lucas was the only one with whom she'd spoken honestly. As twins, their emotions usually were mirror images of each other's. But Kane had been kind to her and he was her brother's friend. Trying like hell to calm her jangled nerves, she took a deep breath and braced herself for his curiosity.

"Seeing my brother was the highlight of my life," she told him honestly. "At first, I thought I was dreaming. I'd carried the knowledge of his death for so many years."

"What was it like?" Kane asked, his casual tone not fooling her one bit. "You don't have to talk about it if you don't want to, but I can't imagine…. It must have been pretty awful."

"Awful doesn't begin to describe it." She gave a rueful smile, settling back in her seat and folding her hands in her lap. This, discussing her captivity, was something she'd actually grown accustomed to. After all, she'd been dutifully attending therapy sessions twice a week ever since she'd gotten out of the hospital. And before that, she'd had to tell her story numerous times to the police, the FBI and the media.

She had gotten quite adept at giving details without revealing any of her inner turmoil.

Glancing at the large man behind the steering wheel, she launched into the standard, memorized description she'd given so many times before.

"You saw where he kept me," she said, grimacing. "Dark, cold, isolated. Exactly where demons should be kept, according to him. Sometimes I was left alone for days at a time. They fed me just enough to keep me alive. I craved water more than food, maybe because that was doled out sporadically. I had a large bucket to use as my bathroom. It was rarely emptied and stank, but after a while I didn't even notice the smell."

Rote stuff. She'd said it a hundred times in exactly the same way. Usually, it was enough. She raised her eyes to find him watching her. The observant look in his narrowed gaze told her for him, it wasn't. Somehow, he knew.

Such a look… The sharpness of it might have stripped another woman naked. But Lilly had been through much worse. Though the slightly guilty pang she felt inside surprised her. She didn't care what he thought. Or she shouldn't. It was all so puzzling.

Confusion exhausted her. Instead of continuing, she closed her eyes and tried to pretend he wasn't making her remember, making her hurt. In fact, she tried to act as if he didn't exist.

"Are you okay?" The gentle tone in his whiskey voice made her insides quiver.

"Yes." Short answer, total untruth. Keeping her eyes closed, she averted her profile, hoping he'd take the hint.

"If you don't want to discuss it, that's fine," he said. "But don't feed me all that bullshit you rehearsed for the press. I saw the interviews. I read the news magazine reports. If I could find one right now, it'd probably show you parroting the same exact thing you said then. Why is that?"

Was that *anger* vibrating under his words? She took a moment, mulling over the fact that she felt no fear, instead a sort of baffled curiosity.

She understood what he was saying, even if it made absolutely no sense. Kane barely knew her. Why did he want so badly to know the inner her? She'd shared that with no one, including her own twin brother. Though she suspected Lucas had a good idea, not only since they were so much alike, but because he too had briefly suffered at the hands of their father.

At her lack of response, he gave a slow shake of his head. "If you don't want to talk about it, all you have to do is say so."

Clenching her teeth, she swallowed. "I. Don't. Want. To. Talk. About. It."

"Fine." His jaw appeared as tight as hers. "Let me know if you need anything." And before she could even consider replying, he turned up the radio and began singing along to the music, some country-western song about something called a redneck.

Mystified, she turned away and faced the window. She decided to practice her deep breathing, something her last therapist claimed would help calm her but which hadn't worked so far. To her complete amazement, with Kane singing happily in the background, this time she felt tranquility washing over her. But it had nothing to do with her breaths and everything to do with Kane's deep, melodic voice. The night before, she'd thought it was the guitar, but she realized now she'd been wrong. The instrument was only part of it. The rest was him. Something about the way he sang reached deep inside her, into her bones and her blood.

Chapter 3

Foolishness. Or so Lilly quickly told herself. That didn't stop her from enjoying the respite from the constant buzz of trepidation that usually swirled inside her, mingling with the fear. Abstractly, she knew she wasn't supposed to be so uneasy, but the queasy feeling that there was danger all around her persisted. She didn't know how to stop it. Therapy was supposed to help, but it hadn't.

In fact, she could count on the fingers of one hand the moments of calm since she'd been freed from captivity. Last night and right now—this was huge. Allowing herself a small smile while making sure Kane couldn't see, she sighed. She closed her eyes and let herself slide into sleep.

She'd slept a little, and then they'd stopped for lunch and stretched their legs, and gotten right back on the road. They didn't talk much, which to her surprise felt comfortable.

That night, they stopped in Sioux Falls, South Dakota. When he pulled into the small motel's parking lot, asking her to wait in the car while he got them a room, anticipation filled her rather than dread. Because later, surely he'd sing. Stunned, she realized she craved this, the same way she'd once craved water.

After checking into their room, which oddly bore a close resemblance to the previous one, Kane suggested they walk across the parking lot to the small, brightly lit café.

"Okay." She didn't even have to consider her answer. The fast-food they'd consumed hours ago for lunch had long since been digested and she felt hollow. Which meant she was hungry. Not a new sensation by any means, but her body had once been accustomed to being starved. Allowing herself to want food, to actually anticipate the flavor on her taste buds, was yet another thing that should have brought her happiness, but instead stressed her out. She couldn't shake the certainty of believing if she allowed herself to enjoy one thing—anything—it would be promptly taken away from her. Conditioning, her shrink had said. Whatever it was, it was a part of her that she now hated.

He stayed close to her side as they crossed the well-lit motel lot into the café. The place was bright and crowded, and the scent of hamburgers cooking made her mouth water.

"Heaven," she breathed, before realizing what she'd done and immediately trying to shut the instant of pleasure down.

"Don't," he said quietly, as if he understood. And then, shocking her, he took her hand. When he closed his large fingers firmly around hers, she struggled against a sharp stab of panic.

"I…" Tugging, she stopped when she saw the kindness in his eyes. "Sorry."

"Don't apologize." Instead of releasing her, he continued to hold on to her hand while they waited for the hostess to gather menus. As they followed the woman to their booth, Lilly wondered when Kane planned to let her go.

He released her when they reached their seats, sliding into the booth on the side facing the door. Studying him, she thought he appeared relaxed. Which was good, as that would mean they weren't in any immediate danger.

She wished she could relax, as well.

"Are you always so jumpy?"

As if to underscore his comment, she started at his words. "Yes," she answered, refusing to sugarcoat it. "As I'm sure you noticed, I'm pretty messed up."

"That's understandable." No censure, only compassion in that wonderful, rich voice of his. He opened his menu, to her relief. "What are you in the mood for?"

"A burger," she blurted, her mouth starting to water, "and fries."

He nodded. "Sounds good. I'll have the same."

With a start, she realized the waitress stood nearby, ready to take their orders. Lilly'd been too lost in her thoughts to notice.

"And two milkshakes," Kane continued, handing the menus back.

"What flavor?" the waitress asked.

Kane's silver eyes met Lilly's, causing a spark to flare low in her belly. "Are you a chocolate or vanilla person?"

"Do you have banana?" she blurted, forcing herself to meet the waitress's gaze.

"Yep."

"I'd like that."

"We'll take two," Kane seconded, grinning so broadly Lilly wondered if she'd made some sort of public mistake.

Once the waitress moved away, Kane reached across the table and lightly touched her cheek, pretending not to notice when she flinched. "You know what you want," he said, his tone vibrating with praise. "I like that."

To her befuddled amazement, she felt her face heat at the compliment. "Thanks."

When their food arrived along with the milkshakes, huge burgers next to a mound of crispy fries that looked every bit as good as they smelled, she froze. After shooting Kane a quick glance, she snatched hers up and sank her teeth into it. The flavor exploded in her mouth, making her hum with pleasure.

Half the thing was gone before she realized it. Glancing at Kane, she saw he watched her while he ate his own, much more slowly. Sheepishly, she put her burger down and made herself take some of her fries.

"You look like you're enjoying that," he said, smiling.

"I am." Careful not to talk with her mouth full, she took a long drink of her shake, almost purring out loud at the sweet banana deliciousness as it slid down her throat.

He laughed, a sound of genuine pleasure. "I take it you like your milkshake, too."

She nodded, swallowing one last sip before answering. "This is great." Looking up, she met his laughing gaze. With a sense of shock, she realized Kane was damn near beautiful when he smiled. The thought made her full stomach hurt. Careful to look away, she tried to think of something else.

As seemed to be his wont, Kane came to the rescue. "Didn't Lucas feed you back there in Seattle?"

"He did." She tried to think of a diplomatic way to explain. Since there was none, she went ahead and told the truth. "Food is another one of my...neuroses. I have a lot. Too many to count, actually." Her lame attempt at a joke fell flat. Once again, she felt her face color.

When he didn't respond, she glanced up at him. He appeared to be engrossed in devouring the remains of his meal. With a feeling of relief, she did the same.

After they'd finished, Lilly declined dessert, even though the apple pie the waitress mentioned made her mouth water again. Amusement flickering in his eyes, Kane asked for the check. As they got up to leave, she half expected him to reach for her hand again. When he didn't, she marveled at her feeling of disappointment.

Still, full and sated, she noticed an unusual lightness in her steps as they walked side by side to the motel.

Back in the room, as soon as he closed the door, the familiar uneasiness swept over her. She knew she should try to fight it. After all, they'd spent two days driving in the car together. Intellectually, she knew he meant her no harm, but some kind of rationality based on past experience made terror grab her by the throat and refuse to let go. Paralyzed, she tried to regain control, to push back the dizziness, to slow her rapid heartbeat.

Deep breathing, deep breathing. She would be strong. She *was* strong. Purposefully avoiding looking at the bed, where she longed to crawl under the covers and curl into a protective ball, she headed for the bathroom and a hot shower.

When she emerged, instead of sitting on the edge of the bed waiting for her, Kane had stretched out, still fully dressed, and fallen asleep. Padding over on her bare feet, she studied his strong profile. Even asleep, she saw the inherent strength in his hawklike features. Emboldened, she let her gaze travel over the rest of him, his impossibly long, black lashes, high cheekbones, and firm yet sensual lips. An unfamiliar warmth began inside her. He really was dangerously beautiful. Tendrils of his thick dark hair curled on his tanned forehead, and his broad shoulders and muscular arms made him look virile in his T-shirt. Even his bare arm silky with hairs and his long fingered hands fascinated her. The same way one would marvel at a great work of art, she told herself. Nothing more.

Sleep had muted the air of isolation she'd sensed in him and identified with, making him appear unexpectedly vulnerable. If not for the power she sensed coiled within him, making his aura pulse with potent masculinity, that is.

Aching to touch the heat emanating from his flesh, she cleared her throat instead. Oddly enough, she felt more at risk now than she did when he was awake with his quiet confidence filling the room.

At the sound, he opened his eyes. His silver gaze locked on hers, making her catch her breath.

"All done?" he asked, sitting up. Momentarily struck dumb, she nodded.

"Great." Pushing himself off the bed, he smiled at her. "I'll only be a minute or two. Go ahead and sleep if you want."

An instant of panic clawed at her. Unreasonable, but still… "Will you," she began, trying to bring the words up a suddenly tight throat. "Will you play and sing again tonight?"

He went so still she wondered if she'd offended him. But his expression appeared neutral when he looked her way. "Do you want me to?"

Nodding, she glanced down, aware she'd begun twisting her hands together. "I would like that," she managed.

"Then I will." His easy tone made her think he hadn't noticed her uneasiness. But then she was coming to realize he pretended not to notice a lot of her weirdness in order to put her at ease.

"But first, I want a shower." Turning, he headed toward the bathroom.

"Thank you," she said, right when he closed the door

behind him. She wasn't sure he'd heard her, but at least she'd tried.

Carefully she removed the bedspread, folding it neatly at the end of the bed. Then, peeling back the sheets, she slipped in between them, trying to lie on her back, propped up with a pillow, or on her side, stretched out like normal people. In the end, she gave up and curled up into her usual, comforting ball and lay inflexible and rigid.

She'd give anything to have the ability to drift off to sleep. Just close her eyes, and let herself get carried away to the land of dreams. Instead, she lay absolutely still, her heartbeat fast, her mind racing.

Though she'd tried to school herself against it, she stiffened the instant the door opened. Keeping her eyes closed, she felt his presence fill the room. Damn it. No reason for fear, no reason at all. But helpless against instinct, she couldn't stop the dread from filling her. A few minutes later, the familiar shivers started. Clenching her jaw, she tried to keep her teeth from chattering.

"It's okay," he said, his deep voice calm and sure. "I'll get my guitar. Just a minute." She heard the sound of him unlocking the dead bolt, then the door opened and closed as he went outside.

Her jaw began to ache as she waited.

After what seemed like an eternity, but in reality was probably only a moment, he returned. Eyes still closed, she held herself rigid, hating that she felt so tense. She listened as he moved around the room, heard the click of the fasteners as he opened his guitar case, the rustle and creak of the bed next to her as he settled on it. She could barely contain her impatience.

And then finally, he strummed the guitar. As the soft notes filled the room, she loosened her iron grip on herself, letting them pull some of the tension from her. When he sang, his husky voice low and sensual, and just exactly right, she heaved a great sigh, willing herself to become unknotted.

One song ended—she wasn't even sure of the words—and he began another. As the music filled her, releasing her from the iron grip of her damaged psyche, she smiled. Muttering a slurred thank-you, she let herself fall toward the blessed oblivion of sleep.

Kane kept playing, long after he'd watched Lilly fall into slumber. Though exhaustion made him unsteady, he knew he had to keep playing or he might do something he'd regret. Like touch her.

Hell, the aching need to lay a hand on her had only intensified the longer he was around her. Only the certain knowledge of how badly such a thing would freak her out kept him from giving in to the craving. He'd been surprised as hell when she'd let him hold her hand earlier. And pleased, more than he should have been.

Four songs in, as the last notes died away, he made himself stop. Moving slowly, his body uncomfortable and aching, he returned the guitar to its case. He then went to bed, hoping he could get to sleep. He had another full day of driving tomorrow.

When he opened his eyes again, the grayish light told him dawn had nearly arrived. He sat up, glancing over at Lilly, who still slept. Heading toward the shower, he braced himself for yet another long day of driving. South Bend, Indiana, here we come.

Though this was only their second morning together, Kane considered it odd the way he and Lilly seemed to have developed a routine. In less than forty-five minutes, they were on the road, both having showered and dressed. After running through a drive-through for breakfast, they hit the highway. Once again, Lilly was silent, so he again located a country-music radio station and turned up the volume.

Several hours later, fueled by two large coffees, he debated trying again to engage her in conversation. She was a quiet little thing, though her slender, wild beauty lit up the interior of his car. He knew she had no idea of her impact on him, though everything about her fascinated him, from the apricot cream of her soft skin to the long lashes framing her clear blue eyes. He struggled against the temptation to taste her lush mouth, to tangle his fingers in her careless tumble of thick, honey-gold hair.

Even the first time he'd seen her, emaciated and filthy, huddled on a cold stone floor with nothing but rags to keep her warm, he'd seen the light of her beauty shining through her damaged exterior. For the first time in his life, he'd wanted to kill another human being, to find the one who had done this to her and wrap his fingers around his throat.

Since he couldn't, he'd managed to hold himself in check. The bastard, one Jacob Gideon, a prominent religious leader of a church called Sanctuary, had been arrested. The worst part of it was that Lilly'd believed Jacob to be her father. It'd turned out Jacob had killed her parents back when she and Lucas had been infants.

Shaking off his thoughts, he focused on the road. When she finally spoke, he nearly missed it.

"What's your story?" Her soft-voiced question had him hurrying to turn down the radio. "How'd you get into the bodyguard business?"

He couldn't help but smile at her description. "I'm actually a veterinarian. I work at a veterinary clinic in Fort Worth. I also work for The Society of Pack Protectors."

To his amazement, she smiled back, making an ember smolder inside him. "Lucas told me about the Protectors. They…you helped free me and the others from Sanctuary. He said you're sworn to keep safe others of our kind. Shape-shifters."

Since he knew she'd believed her and her brother to be freaks of nature and hadn't realized there were others, her calm acceptance now made him make a mental note to call Lucas and thank him for teaching his sister so much in such a short period of time. At least she knew some of her heritage.

"Exactly. The Protectors recruited me when I was still in high school. They paid a full scholarship to Texas A&M University and then to the veterinary program. In exchange, I have to work for them a few times a year. It's similar to the military reserves here in the United States."

"And you just finished up working undercover at Sanctuary." She glanced sideways at him. "Since you're an animal doctor, then how are you able to do this for Lucas?"

"And you," he added softly. "I took a leave of absence, the same way I always do when I go work for the Protectors."

She nodded and turned to look out the window.

By the time they made South Bend, he had to force himself to stay awake. Aware of the danger, he took the first exit with a motel sign and pulled in and parked in front of the dingy window with the red, neon vacancy sign.

Half turning in his seat, he dragged his hand through his hair. "I'm sorry, but I'm beat."

She nodded without looking at him.

"Wait here." Getting out, he went inside the office and procured them a room.

Which turned out to be yet another carbon copy of the previous two.

Dropping his gear on the floor, he didn't even have the energy to hit the shower. "You go ahead," he told her, lying back on to the bed and closing his eyes. "I'll take mine in the morning."

That was his last conscious thought before sleep claimed him.

Overnight bag still in hand, Lilly stood and watched as Kane dropped off into a deep sleep. She felt a flare of panic that he hadn't even brought his guitar case inside.

She shook her head at her own weakness and took her bag with her into the bathroom. She made the water piping hot, and took her time, trying to summon up the courage to let Kane sleep undisturbed. The poor man obviously needed his rest. He'd been driving for a solid three days, and since she didn't know how to drive she couldn't even spell him.

But though she knew her thoughts were selfish, she couldn't help but wonder what kind of a night she'd have, alone with him in a small hotel room, without even his music to soothe her. Telling herself to stop thinking of herself, she toweled off and put on her soft sleep T-shirt.

When she emerged into the room, Kane's deep, even breaths told her he was still deeply asleep. She moved quietly, went through her familiar routine of folding the bedspread and slipped into the still tucked sheets. Only once she had, she realized she'd forgotten to put out the light. On her way to do so, she once again found herself entranced by Kane. A sudden image of what it would feel like to slide into his bed next to him, wrapping herself around him, made her gasp in shock and confusion.

What the... Staggering back, she managed to click off the light and hightail it back to her own bed.

Once there, she curled up in her familiar ball, but couldn't relax enough to get comfortable. Again she briefly considered waking Kane up and asking him to sing to her, but she hadn't the heart. So far, he'd been nothing but accommodating to her. She couldn't be such a selfish person to keep such a man from his well-deserved rest.

If she didn't manage to get to sleep tonight, she always had the car during the drive tomorrow. He'd promised it would be their last day of driving. And then they'd be... Grimacing, she realized she didn't even know their destination. She told herself she needed to be more proactive, to take charge of her own destiny, or at least try.

And with that thought, somehow she must have fallen asleep, because when she next opened her eyes, it was morning. Kane's bed was empty. Sitting up, she heard the sound of a shower going and smiled.

She'd done it. Gone to sleep alone in a room with a strange man, who wasn't really a stranger anymore. Still... Baby steps, as her therapist had been fond of saying.

He gave her a curious look when he emerged from his shower, his dark hair still damp. She smiled at him, which appeared to shock him, since he froze, though he didn't speak as she continued past him. Her smile held, even as she disappeared into the still-steamy bathroom.

When she came out, dressed and ready, he'd taken a seat in the chair by the door. "I've already loaded the car and turned in the key."

Though she wondered at the impersonal tone to his voice, she simply nodded.

As usual, they got breakfast on the road. She waited until they'd both finished eating their egg sandwiches, turning the questions she wanted to ask around and around in her mind. For the past two days, she'd been wanting to ask, but hadn't summoned the energy or the nerve. Finally, with her usual lack of finesse, she just blurted out the first one. "Where are we going?"

Kane's smile told her he approved of her curiosity.

"Leaning Tree, New York. It's upstate, in the Catskill mountains. My entire family lives there."

"Your family?" She hadn't anticipated having to meet anyone else. Somehow she'd thought Kane was taking her to some sort of remote safe house where she'd live alone with him until it was safe to return home.

"Yep. Both my parents, two brothers and a sister, along with their respective spouses and a bunch of nieces and nephews." He said this so cheerfully she could tell he expected her to greet this news with enthusiasm.

Damned if she didn't hate to let him down. But she had no choice—she could barely master her own emotions yet, never mind try to summon up fake ones.

"Are we…" Licking her lips nervously, she tried to sound upbeat. "Are we going to be living with them?" Which would be close to a nightmare as far as she was concerned.

"Sort of." Then, apparently noticing her crestfallen expression, he reached over and lightly squeezed her shoulder. "Don't worry, you'll still have your privacy."

Though she didn't see how, she didn't pursue the questions any further. In fact, she wished she'd never asked. Now that she knew, her anxiety had rocketed sky-high.

She couldn't imagine what Kane's family, his no-doubt nice, normal family, would make of her, so clearly damaged and one short step away from crazy.

"Are you sure you want to impose on them?" she hesitantly asked. "Maybe we should find alternative lodging."

He laughed. "They'd never forgive me if I did that. I haven't been home in three years or more. Work got crazy and somehow I never made it. I owe them a nice long visit."

Crud. Settling back in her seat, she swallowed the huge lump in her throat and tried again to concentrate on her breathing.

"Hey." His voice softened. "My father owns a motel. It's

actually more of an old-fashioned motor court. There are separate cabins. I've asked to use the most remote one. It's on the other side of a meadow and small lake. I promise, you won't be crowded in with anyone."

She nodded, wishing she could quiet the roiling turmoil inside her. Squaring her shoulders, she tried to reach inside her, to that dark, violent and often empty space, hoping she might find strength. Once or twice, she actually had, but that was years ago. Lucas and Blythe had talked often about their inner wolves, but Lilly was pretty sure hers had gone mad a long time ago. One thing she knew for sure, she could no longer touch her inner beast. Her father had believed this meant she'd conquered the demon he claimed lived inside her.

She knew better. The demon waited, crazed and hungry, ready to devour her the instant she gave it a chance.

"I've never seen anything like your aura," he said. "Just now it went from black to gray, then swirls of purple started exploding, like fireworks. It's unreal."

Yet one more thing different about her. Sometimes she couldn't help but believe Jacob Gideon had been right. She wasn't normal, nor would she ever be. A few times she had actually considered the possibility she might be better off dead.

"My aura?" Again she said the first thing that came to mind. "I can't see it, though Lucas told me it was…special. Can everyone see their own?"

From his crestfallen expression, he seemed to realize he'd hurt her. "I meant no offense. I'm sorry."

Lifting her shoulder in a casual shrug cost her more than he'd ever know. "None taken." She swallowed, steeling herself to meet his gaze. "Please, I'd really like to know. Can you see your own aura?"

"No." He held her gaze for a second, and then turned

his attention back to the road. "We can only see each others'. Oh, every now and then, if I'm walking by a mirror, I might catch a glimpse of the light surrounding me, but when I look full-on, it's gone."

Frustrated, she nodded. "That's what I thought." Once again, she glanced his way. "Yours looks a lot like Lucas's. I figured mine looked more like Blythe's. I'm guessing it doesn't."

A shadow crossed his face. Though she hadn't exactly asked a question, she'd been hoping for confirmation. Blythe's aura was gorgeous, bright and golden, exactly like her. In the short time Lilly had gotten to know her, she'd come to see the woman her twin brother loved with all his heart was beautiful both inside and out.

From the way everyone reacted to Lilly's aura, she guessed now her own must be dark and twisted, full of holes and ugly mashes of color, like the ones inside her head.

Just like that, her faintly hopeful mood evaporated, and a crushing sense of doom settled down on her. Since these feelings frequently descended on her for no rhyme or reason, she knew there was no way to dissipate the blackness of her mood. She had to ride it out.

Turning her head away from Kane, she closed her eyes and waited for him to turn up the radio. When he didn't, she reached out and did it herself.

Kane saw the first billboard when they were still thirty miles out from Leaning Tree. "Wolf Hollow Motor Court Resort, only thirty miles to paradise!" the sign proclaimed, along with a picture of a wild wolf howling at a full moon. Years ago, Kane's father had decided to adopt an advertising strategy of using six billboards, five miles apart. Since the slogans never changed, Kane could recite all six of them from memory, even though he hadn't been home in three years.

Lilly stirred in her seat, opening her eyes and leaning forward. "Do you feel that?" she asked, her low voice thrumming with emotion.

Kane went absolutely still, using both his human senses and his wolf. "No," he finally said, regretful. "What was it?"

She settled back in her seat, shaking her head. "A feeling…intuition…I don't know. Never mind. It was probably just my imagination."

But he could tell it hadn't been, not to her. Absurdly, he felt as if he'd let her down. "You've been asleep awhile. We're almost there."

Now she looked at him full-on, her blue eyes clear and wide-awake. "We made it here without any trouble."

"Yes." Entranced, he wondered if it was possible to drown in her gaze.

"No one followed us or tried to intercept us. I think it's possible my brother was worried for nothing."

Glad of the distraction, he dragged his gaze away from hers and flashed a grim smile. "No. All this means is we got away without them realizing it. Once they know you're gone, they'll be searching all over for you."

Her vivid gaze didn't waver. "Do you think they'll find me?"

"Not yet." At the stark fear flashing across her features, he almost swore, though at the last minute he bit back the words. "Bad choice of words. I don't think they'll find us. Not here."

"That's not what you said." Cocking her head, she made a face, evidently downplaying her own fear. "But you think eventually they'll track us down?"

He bit back a curse at his own carelessness. "It's possible. Look, anything can happen. You know that. But it won't be for a while, I promise. It'll give us time to prepare."

"Prepare how?"

Another billboard flashed into view. This time the wolf faced north, the direction they were heading.

Kane ignored it. "Lilly, in the time you spend with me, I'm going to teach you how to be strong, how to defend yourself. By the time we're done in Leaning Tree, you should be prepared to take on any comer."

Chapter 4

He'd surprised her, Kane realized. Her eyes widened and she opened her mouth, though no sound came out. He'd wondered how she'd react. Now, he was about to find out. What she said next stunned him.

"Good." Her lush lips twisted in a semblance of a smile. "I don't ever want to be a victim again. I'd like that. Very much."

They were approaching another sign. "Look," he urged, pointing. "My father's idea of a brilliant marketing plan."

She read out loud as they drove past. "Wolf Hollow? Is he—" she waved her hand vaguely "—like us?"

Kane appreciated the way she now lumped herself in with him and other Shifters. Lucas had told him that at first she'd been so terrified of being associated with her own kind, she'd tried to deny their existence.

Apparently, in the month she'd lived with her brother, Lucas had managed to convince her that she wasn't a monster. Good.

"Yes." He smiled at her, hoping to take away some of the sting. "Both my parents are Shape-shifters. Most of the town is Pack."

A tiny frown creased her forehead. "Seriously? There are that many of us?"

He wasn't surprised Lucas hadn't fully educated her. In her situation, it made no sense to deluge her with too much information. He decided to keep things light. He'd give her more info later, when she was ready for it.

"Yes, there are millions of us, scattered all over the world. We exist alongside humans, living the same sort of lives they do. We also organize ourselves into Packs, but on a much broader scale than our wild brethren. Similar to the government, we have a national Pack, state Packs and local city and county ones."

She nodded, clearly unimpressed. "I suppose that's a good thing."

Unable to suppress a grin, he nodded. "It is." He liked this about her, this faint edge of prickliness. Much better than the reclusive shell of a woman he'd half expected. After what she'd been through, he considered any signs of a fighting spirit a good thing.

When he'd seen her reaction to the news story about the other women who'd been held captive, he'd seen sorrow, but not righteous rage. Quite honestly, he would have preferred the second.

Still, she'd come a long way. And he planned to be around to help her go the distance.

They pulled into Leaning Tree as the sun was beginning to set. The time of the gloaming, he'd heard it described once. The place looked just the way it always did in his mind; not much had changed since he'd lived there as a child. Huge leafy oaks and maples spread their thick green branches over the buildings on Main Street, shops and restaurants and a small Dutch Reform church that had been built in the early 1700s and had been lovingly restored.

Unlike downtown areas of most small towns, in Leaning Tree, cars still filled the parking lots and pedestrians strolled on well-lit sidewalks. Outdoor cafés did a bustling business—they passed full tables under umbrellas with tiny white lights. The scene could have been a postcard or the cover of a travel brochure. In fact, he thought it probably was.

"It's beautiful," Lilly breathed. Her eyes glowed as she took in her first glimpse of the place where she'd be living for the next few months.

He couldn't help himself; he grinned. After the flat, Texas landscape with its sparse trees, Leaning Tree looked like heaven.

"My family's motel is on the other side of town," he told her. "Part of it borders on New York State forest preserve land."

And just like that, she shut down. He grimaced, aware that the mention of his family had made her nervous again.

In fact, once they'd driven through downtown and taken the turnoff, following more strategically placed signs to Wolf Hollow Motor Court, she withdrew even further.

Refusing to acknowledge her tension, he knew the only thing he could do was express his own anticipation at seeing his family again. But how? As a man unaccustomed to sharing his feelings, he wasn't sure what to say.

In the end, he decided to go with the truth.

"Every time I come for a visit, my mother goes on a baking binge," he confided. "She's a great cook, and I can't wait to see what she's made. Her apple pie melts in your mouth and no one can make chocolate chip cookies the way she does."

When Lilly turned to look at him, a reluctant gleam of interest flickered in her eyes. "Cookies?"

He nodded. "And pies, cakes and whatever else she feels like making. We usually have a huge family dinner. Since I haven't been home in several years, I imagine she's gone crazy with the cooking."

At least Lilly'd stopped twisting her hands in her lap. "What's your father like?"

"He's like a big, gruff bear." He smiled to take the sting off his words. "But a kindhearted bear."

"I see." Though she nodded, he could tell she had no idea what he meant.

"My sister and my brothers and their spouses will probably be there for a welcome-home dinner," he told her, aware it would be better if she were prepared for a crowd. "They can be a bit...boisterous."

She swallowed hard. "Do they have children?"

"Yes. I have three nephews and two nieces. They range in age from four to twelve."

Her smile seemed less wobbly. "I like children."

"Good." The road changed from pavement to gravel. "Here we are. Right around this bend."

They pulled up in front of the main house, a low-slung, stone-and-wood creation with lots of glass that his parents had designed and built over thirty years before. As he coasted to a stop and killed the ignition, the door opened and his family began to spill from inside.

As they surrounded the car, Lilly made a low sound. Seeing the terrified look in her eyes, he squeezed her shoulder before opening his door and climbing out. "I'll fend them off and then we'll introduce you, okay?"

He didn't hear her answer in the chorus of glad cries that followed as he was engulfed by family. His mama wrapped her plump arms around him, squeezing happily while raining kisses on his cheeks. She still smelled the same, like gardenias. She wore her long, gray hair in the same neat braid.

His brothers chimed in, thumping him on the back in glad "guy hugs." His dad, a bald giant of a man, stood back, watching with a happy grin as he waited for his turn. Kane had nearly made his way over to him when his sister, just emerging from inside, squealed and launched herself at him, hugging and laughing and babbling happy words of welcome.

Meanwhile, all the kids swarmed around, playing and yelling and doing the hundred loud and endearing and annoying things small children do. Finally, Kane's father tired of waiting and moved toward him, enveloping him in a bear hug. The scent of pipe tobacco and spearmint tickled Kane's nose. Home. Finally, he was home.

Turning, he took note of his guest. Through all this, Lilly sat quietly in the car, not moving, as if by being still, she hoped not to draw attention to herself. He could only imagine what she thought of the uncontrolled chaos outside the car.

Clearing his throat loudly, Kane gestured for silence. His family ignored him, too caught up in the joy of seeing him. Next he tried clapping his hands and asking them to calm down. Again, this had no result.

Finally, he put his fingers in his mouth and whistled as loudly and ear-piercingly as he could.

Everyone went silent.

"Thank you," he said, pitching his voice so that everyone could hear him. "As I mentioned to Mom and Dad, I have a guest with me. She's been through a lot."

Jostling each other to get a look at the passenger side of the car, some of them starting talking. Kane glared at the offending teenagers, and they instantly stopped. "As I was saying, Lilly Gideon is here with me. She's not used to the organized craziness of our family, so I need to ask you to give her a little bit of space. Can you do that?"

He thought his serious tone must have registered, because the younger family members looked at their feet. Of course his parents, siblings and their spouses all nodded solemnly.

"Thank you." He felt all eyes on his back as she crossed to the passenger side of his car and opened the door.

Lilly's wide blue eyes stared up at him.

"It's okay," he said, and held out his hand. "I won't let anything happen to you. You're safe with me."

She barely hesitated before sliding her fingers into his.

Helping her out of the car as if she was royalty, he kept his body close to her side as they turned to face his assembled family.

"These heathens," he said fondly. "Belong to me. Lilly, meet the McGraws."

As she bravely attempted a smile, he watched in gratified amusement while his normally boisterous family mumbled subdued hellos.

Then, Lilly lifted her chin and murmured hello back.

The instant she spoke, his family's tenuous grip on propriety shattered. Chattering all at once, the female members, young and old alike, surrounded Lilly, touching, patting, smoothing back her hair. Kane held on to her hand, and felt her suddenly go rigid. Still, he didn't interfere—he wouldn't unless she asked him. She'd have to get used to his family sooner or later. Might as well jump in the deep end and learn how to swim.

Of course, the gentle pressure of his fingers on hers let her knew he'd always be her life preserver. Always.

While the women made a fuss over Lilly, the masculine contingent regarded Kane with a mixture of awe and disbelief.

"She's beautiful," his brother Kyle said, cuffing him on the arm.

"Damn." His other brother Kris breathed, barely taking his gray eyes off Lilly. "How'd you rate a woman like that?"

Kane's father chuckled, rubbing his shiny bald head. "Boys, he already told you he brought her here to keep her safe. He's her bodyguard, nothing more."

As one, both of Kane's younger brothers turned to look at their father, disbelief plain on their rugged faces. "You're telling me you believe him?" they asked in unison.

The elder McGraw shrugged. "Guess we'll just have to wait and see."

Before Kane could respond, Lilly squeezed his hand, hard, letting him know she'd reached her limit of endurance.

Without hesitation, he turned away from his father and brothers and gently began moving his mother, sister, sisters-in-law and cousins aside. "Come on ladies, give her a little space. We've been driving for four long days and she's exhausted. Let me take her to our cabin so she can rest up."

Lilly shot him a grateful look before her long lashes swept down to hide her eyes.

"But you'll still be coming tonight for dinner, won't you?" his mother asked, self-consciously patting her long gray braid. Kane gave a reassuring nod. If he knew her, and he did, she'd spent the past ten hours cooking. His mouth watered at the thought.

"Here you go, son." His dad tossed him a set of keys. "I had cabin nine made ready for you, just like you requested."

Catching the keys, Kane grinned his thanks, then shepherded Lilly back into the car. Once he'd closed the door behind her, he crossed to the driver's side. "See you later," he said, lifting his hand in a wave.

Once he closed the door, cutting off the noise outside, he started the engine. "You all right?"

"Yes." The wobbly answer told him she wasn't, not exactly, but he knew she'd be fine.

"They mean well," he told her.

"I know," she said, her slight smile curving her lips surprising him. "And even though they're Shifters, they don't bite."

A joke? Was she making a joke? Just in case she was, he grinned back at her.

"Where are we going?" she asked.

"Our cabin. It's the most isolated one, and also the most difficult to get to. There's only one way in, at least by road."

The gravel road crunched under their tires as they passed the first four rental cabins. Made of wood and surrounded by towering trees, these were clustered around a parklike garden, complete with wild rose bushes in vivid colors, a vine-covered arbor and a wood-and-metal bench. A stone wolf statue occupied a place of honor in the middle, as if it had been meant to be a shrine of sorts. At one time in his family's long history of owning this land, Kane supposed it had been.

"That's beautiful," she breathed. He couldn't tell if she meant the garden or the statue or both. Either way, though the land and the place glowed with earthen beauty, none of it could hold a candle to her.

"Yes," he answered, his heart full. The road curved ahead of them, steadily climbing through the untamed forest. The next four wooden cabins sat in a semi-circle to the right, situated around a small, spring-fed lake. A doe and two fawns looked up at their approach and vanished into the woods.

At the sight, Kane's inner wolf snarled, reminding him that soon they'd go hunting. Maybe even tonight after the big meal if they followed tradition. He'd have to make sure Lilly knew and offer her the choice to join them or retreat to their cabin.

"I've counted eight," she said, leaning forward to peer into the forest. "How many are there?"

"Nine. Ours is my favorite. It sits up at the top of a rise in the land, with a pretty good view of the entire acreage." Not to mention it was pretty damn near impossible to approach the cabin from any direction without being seen.

A slight frown creased her brow. "Exactly how isolated is it?"

"Not too far." They climbed in earnest now. "We're almost there."

One more curve in the road, and the cabin came into view. Unlike the others, this was made of stone. Two giant oak trees sheltered it. "This one is older than the others," he told her. "Originally, this was where my ancestors lived."

Though she nodded, he didn't tell her the significance of this. His entire family spoke of the power lingering in the ancient stones. In addition to being easily defensible, Kane had the vague hope that cabin nine might help Lilly heal.

They crested the hill, parking next to the covered porch. He killed the engine, pocketed the keys and climbed out. He'd made it halfway around the car, meaning to open her door, but she beat him to it. She unfolded her long and shapely legs and climbed out of his low-slung car. Stretching, she cocked her head and studied the house.

"I feel it again."

He understood what she meant. "It's a ley line. The strength of the earth, made manifest."

A shadow crossed her pretty face. "Are you sure you don't mean demons?"

Cursing the man who'd caused her to think something so natural was evil, he shook his head. "No. It's good energy. Beneficial. Since our kind has such close ties to the earth and the sky and moon, we appreciate and honor such places of power."

Holding utterly still, she considered his words. "Places? Are there more than one?"

"Yes." Relaxing again, he took her arm and steered her up on the porch. "I've been lucky enough to feel several of them."

Unlocking the door of the cabin, he flicked on the light switch. "After you. This will be our home for the next several weeks."

Gliding past him, she inspected the interior, from the weathered wood of the old plank floors to the cast-iron stove. The windows were double-paned and new, and over the years, different parts of the cabin had been updated. The most recent renovation had been to the bathroom.

He watched as she walked all around, wondering if she could sense the history trapped inside the old stone walls. Sometimes, late at night, he almost felt the ghosts of times long gone drifting up from the rocks.

Finally, she looked up and met his gaze. A reluctant smile hovered at the edge of her lush mouth. "Very nice." She swallowed, her cheeks turning pink. "But there's only one bed."

"I know." He indicated the couch. "That makes into a bed. I'll bunk there."

Relief palpable, she nodded.

He glanced at his watch. "We have about an hour until they'll expect us back at the main house for dinner. Do you want to freshen up or take a nap or…"

"What are you going to do?"

"I'm not sure." If he'd been alone, he'd already have

turned and headed back to the house to be with his family. But since he knew this would be rough enough on her as it was, he wouldn't ask that of her. Nor would he leave her alone. Until the missing Sanctuary members were arrested, he didn't plan to let Lilly Gideon out of his sight.

"I think I'd like to take a walk," she said, surprising him. "After so long in the car, my legs could use a bit of a hike."

"Sounds like a plan." Crossing to the door, he held it open. "After you."

She didn't move. "If you don't mind, I'd like to be alone."

Compassion warred with common sense. "I'm sorry, but right now that's not a good idea."

He expected her to argue. Or maybe just challenge his statement. Instead, she dipped her chin in a sort of resigned acceptance and moved past him. He fought the urge to take her arm, and only the knowledge that she wouldn't have made it so long if she wasn't a fighter, kept him from demanding she try harder for what she wanted.

"How about I stay a bit behind you?" he offered. "Give you some space without leaving you completely alone?"

All the light had faded from her eyes, leaving them as dark as a storm. "Suit yourself."

So he did. Since she hadn't indicated a preference, he remained right by her side. Unspeaking, yet close enough to touch.

They'd barely gone a quarter mile when she stopped and rounded on him. "I understand you take this guarding me thing seriously," she began, "but I barely know you."

"You will," he said softly. "And, yes, I do take keeping you safe very seriously."

Her expressive face revealed a combination of frustration and determination. "I'm used to being alone. Even when I was staying with Lucas and Blythe, they were kind enough to give me some space."

"No worries. You'll have your liberty again, once those last three Sanctuary people are caught. Until then, I'm afraid you're going to have to put up with me. I'll be keeping you very, very close."

Jerking her head in a stiff nod, she turned and walked briskly away. He almost laughed, well aware of what she was trying to do. She didn't realize his long stride would enable him to effortlessly catch up to her without him having to run. If he wanted to, that is. He'd offered to give her as much space as he could, and that's what he intended to do. At least for right now.

So he dropped back, keeping his distance, and tried to ignore the enticing sway of her hips as he followed behind.

Lilly fumed, hating the way that once again, she had absolutely no control over her life. Even though she couldn't help but admire Kane's steadfast determination and his attempt to give her a small modicum of privacy, his refusal to let her walk alone angered and frustrated her.

Of course it didn't help her mood that she'd be paralyzed with terror if he actually did set her loose.

So she strode off, her fast pace practically daring him to keep up. A few offhand glances over her shoulder revealed he didn't seem to be having any trouble. She walked and walked, at first thinking she'd go until the path ended. Eventually she realized the trails apparently crisscrossed the woods for miles. Defeated yet again, she spun around and motored on past him, refusing to look at him even though she knew she was acting childish. After all, none of this was his fault.

Back at the cabin, she found herself still jumpy and out of sorts. She'd thought a good hike through the woods might soothe her—nature often did. But instead, she'd been ever conscious of the large man walking behind her, ready to rush to her side at the slightest threat and defend her. Her conflicted emotions about this didn't do anything to help improve her state of mind.

Part of her liked the way having him near made her feel protected. But part of her hated the necessity. She liked that he'd said he'd teach her to protect herself. As soon as they were settled in, she'd demand he make good on that promise.

Meanwhile, there was the dinner with his family to get through.

She didn't know why she felt so nervous about everything. The jangling rawness angered her, made her wish she could be a different person. After all, these were just regular people. They weren't going to shackle her to a machine and send volts of electricity coursing through her system. Having dinner with Kane's family shouldn't matter—a simple meal would be minor compared to the numerous atrocities she'd suffered at the hands of her father's minions in her fifteen years of captivity.

Thinking this helped. She squared her shoulders, dragged a brush through the tangle of her long hair and headed out into the living area where Kane waited.

He gave her a long look, and then offered his arm. "Are you ready?"

Forcing herself to move forward, she hesitated, just short of touching him. "Are we walking?"

"We can." His cheerful smile struck a chord of warmth inside her. "Though we might need a flashlight to make it back. There are no streetlights here, just cabin lights."

She frowned, trying to decide.

"Or we can drive," he added. "Whichever is easiest on you."

"Let's walk." More time to get herself psyched. "I don't

mind a flashlight later." And she took his arm, the warmth of his skin sending a flush of warmth into her hand.

The woods were beautiful, a leafy canopy through which slashes of sky teased the eye. The gravel crunched under their feet as they made their way back toward the main house.

They'd just rounded the last turn, passing by the first four cabins, when a childish shout rang out. Kane shot her a rueful smile. "We've been spotted."

She couldn't help but tense. Her unease must have communicated itself to him through her hand.

"It's okay," he said. "They're only children."

The words had barely left his mouth when they were surrounded by kids of all ages and sizes.

"Uncle Kane!" They attached themselves to Kane, full of a joyous exuberance that made Lilly smile. One of the little girls, seeing the smile, shyly tugged on Lilly's shirt.

"Hi, I'm Candace," she said. "I'm five. Are you Uncle Kane's girlfriend?"

"Um, no." Despite herself, Lilly blushed. "We're just friends."

"You're a girl. If you're friends, then you must be his girlfriend."

Grinning, Kane ruffled Candace's mop of red hair. "It's hard to argue with logic like that," he said, winking at her. Seeing that, some of the tightness eased off Lilly's chest. Just some, but at least now she could breathe.

With children dancing around them as if they were some sort of pied pipers, they reached the main house. A knot settled low in Lilly's stomach. She had zero practice with any kind of social situations. After all, the only interactions she'd had in the past fifteen years had been with her captor and the doctors who'd tortured her in the name of Sanctuary.

She felt as if she was about to take a blind leap off a cliff. Which she knew was foolish—this was only dinner, after all—but she couldn't help herself.

"It's going to be okay," Kane murmured, his breath tickling her ear. "I promise."

And then he pulled open the door and they went inside.

Her first impression was the chaos and the noise. A blur of activity—people and food and music—so much the swirl of energy overwhelmed her. She took a step back, forgetting Kane still had her hand engulfed in his.

"Come on." Smiling in reassurance, he tugged her into the middle of the maelstrom. As she tried to hold back the rising tide of fear, the creature inside her raised its bruised and battered head and curled its lip in the beginnings of a snarl.

The beast. *Her* beast. No. Not now. Fear changed to horror, to panic, to terror. She froze as the thing within her stretched, flexing its claws, making a garbled, sorrowful song low in its battered throat.

All around her, in the middle of the noise, people began looking around, sniffing the air, as if they somehow sensed the struggle being waged inside her. Maybe they did, perhaps this was a Shifter thing, but she knew whatever the creature inside her might be, it wasn't the same as theirs.

If she had her way, her beast would never again see the light of day. She'd vowed this, no matter the cost. She had to save the rest of the world from its awful vengeance, even if she had to die trying.

Kane turned to look at her, at the same time tightening his grip on her fingers. Something must have shown in her face. Using his body to block her from their sight, he shepherded her away from the others.

Chapter 5

"Come with me." The deep rumble of his voice sent a shudder through her. She felt as if he'd tossed her an invisible lifeline. Grateful, she went where he led, ashamed of the way she clung to him, yet unable to do more than that.

Inside her, the creature still stirred, wary now.

He took her down a long, narrow hallway and into a small room that had apparently once been a bedroom but had been converted to a craft room/storage space/office. Once inside, he kicked the door closed behind him.

"Are you all right?" Cupping her face with his other hand, he tilted her chin up, making her look at him.

Cautiously, she took a deep breath. She'd been lying to everyone, including her twin brother, and she knew she couldn't be truthful now, to Kane. She had no choice. He'd never understand. Whatever had been done to her had made her different than the rest of them. No one could help her deal with this. She had only herself and hoped to tap into some inner strength that so far had been conspicuously absent.

"I think so," she managed, the answer to his question coming a heartbeat too late.

Hand warm under her chin, he studied her, his silver eyes missing nothing. Her entire body flushed. Slowly, moving her head, she gave him no choice but to let her go. Though their fingers were still linked, she backed away, putting just enough space between them so she could once again breathe.

"Are you going to tell me what that was?" he asked.

For a second, she considered feigning ignorance, but since it appeared that everyone in the room had sensed her internal battle, or some aspect of it, she knew this would be futile. "I'd rather not. At least not right now."

Eyes narrowing, he nodded. "Are you going to be all right to rejoin my family?"

For now, her beast had gone quiet again. She didn't know what had set the monster off; whatever triggered it seemed to follow no pattern that Lilly could see.

"I think so." She tried for a smile, partially succeeding.

"Good." Opening the door, he led her back down the hallway toward the kitchen.

The organized chaos stilled the moment they reappeared. Kane broke the awkward silence by sniffing and grinning as he made a broad gesture toward the pots simmering on the stove. "Something sure smells good. What's cooking?"

Just like that, everyone went back to what they'd been doing. Bemused, no longer terrified of them, though she wasn't sure why, Lilly let Kane tug her along by the hand, while he joked and teased his family.

"Go ahead and get seated," the elder Mrs. McGraw ordered, already bustling from the kitchen to the dining room, carrying steaming bowls of food. She wore a brightly colored apron and her plump hands were adorned with rings, one on every finger.

Judging from the scents wafting from the bowls, she'd made some kind of roast, along with vegetables, and home-made bread. Lilly's mouth began to water.

Everyone seemed to rush at once to take their seats at a long table. Lilly stopped counting at twelve chairs, amazed as she realized there was another table set up for the kids.

"Here you go." Kane pulled out a chair for her. Once she'd taken her seat, he dropped into the one next to her. Someone to his left good-naturedly jostled him, almost causing him to knock over his water glass. He saved it with another grin.

Once everyone had taken a seat, they began passing around the bowls. Lilly had never seen so much food in her life. Amazed, she accepted one bowl after another, spooning a little on to her plate, afraid she might offend Kane's mother if she didn't sample everything.

Watching, she noticed no one started eating. Apparently they were waiting until everyone had gotten everything. She waited, as well, even though she felt hollow from hunger.

Finally, Kane's father stood and tapped on his glass with his knife. He flashed a friendly smile at her before glancing around the table. "Today, in honor of Kane's guest, I'd like to say a little prayer."

At his words, everyone bowed their heads. Confused, Lilly glanced at Kane, only to realize he too had closed his eyes and dropped his chin.

Unnerved, she also bowed her head, though she kept her eyes open so she could watch Kane through her lashes.

"Higher power, we thank thee for your blessings. This food, our company, the love we have for one another and, finally, our good health. In your name, we salute the earth, the sun, the stars and the moon."

The moon? She frowned, thinking of the kind of prayers Jacob Gideon and his followers had prayed with such fervor. They'd invoked a lot of retribution and hellfire, and nothing about thankfulness or love. Then and there, she decided Sanctuary and Kane's family didn't share the same God.

Once the prayer was finished, everyone dug in. Bowls were continually passed as people took seconds, even thirds. Lilly tried, but she couldn't even finish everything on her plate.

"Wonderful meal," Mr. McGraw boomed, patting his ample stomach. "Leave the dishes, hon. Me and the boys will get them."

Once again, Lilly could scarcely believe her ears. In the world where she'd been raised, Sanctuary, all the men had treated the women as little more than serfs. And that had been in the best-case scenario. Once more she was forcibly reminded that the rest of the world wasn't like Sanctuary.

As the men pushed back from the table and began gathering the dishes, Kane touched her shoulder. "You'll be all right? I shouldn't be gone more than a minute or two."

Slowly, she nodded. He grabbed her plate and his, and moved to the other side of the table, picking up silverware. Lilly noted some of the other women pretending not to watch her. She offered Kane's mother a tentative smile, relieved when the older woman smiled back, genuine laugh lines creasing her light blue eyes.

With the background noise of silverware and plates clattering in the kitchen, chatter flowed easily among the women. Lilly didn't participate, but she listened, marveling at the feminine camaraderie. A swift stab of yearning filled her. The closest she'd ever come to having a friend had been one of the female doctors at Sanctuary, who'd exploited Lilly's loneliness. Dr. Silva had pretended friendship in order to make it easier for her to perform experiments on Lilly.

The first time Lilly had begged her to stop, her so-called friend had ignored her and tightened the screws instead.

Since that day, Lilly no longer believed in friendship.

But the camaraderie among these women, who were joined by blood or by marriage, felt different. None of them appeared to have anything to gain, no private agenda as they joked and laughed, teased and commiserated. Lilly made a note to watch them while she was here, and see who tried to exploit whom.

The men returned a few minutes later. They too seemed in high spirits, jostling one another, bumping shoulders and fists. Kane seemed slightly embarrassed, side-stepping when his two brothers tried to get him in a headlock. His gaze locked on hers, sitting so quietly, as if he knew she thought herself a weed among blooming flowers.

"You're beautiful, you know," he murmured, holding out his hand to help her up.

Shocked, she couldn't respond. As her face heated, she gripped his fingers and allowed him to help her up.

A loud whistle made everyone go silent as they turned their attention to where the elder McGraw stood at the head of the table. "After such a fine meal," he began, bestowing a grin on his wife, "I can think of nothing better than all of us heading to the woods to shift. It's been a long time since Kane was home for a family hunt."

At his words, a subtle change occurred in the atmosphere. While Lilly stared blankly, several of the others' auras changed, going from light to dark and back again. An invisible energy charged the room, like the low thrum of electricity just before a lightning strike.

Shift. He wanted them all to become their wolf selves. The thing inside Lilly reacted violently. Taking her by surprise, the monster tried to break out, using claws and teeth and some sort of dark magic. Caught by the figurative throat, Lilly fought back. Because of the battle inside herself, she stood stock still. Though she bared her teeth, she made no sound.

The room grew quiet as the others somehow sensed her inner struggle.

"Lilly?" Kane's voice, strong and steady, gave her strength. Blindly, she held out her other hand, asking him to grip it. When he did, she clung to him like a lifeline. She'd fought this battle before and almost always won. The few times she hadn't, she couldn't bear to think about. Though these had been during her captivity at Sanctuary and induced with drugs, the end result had been bloodshed and terror.

Never, ever, would she willingly allow her beast out again. Especially not now, surrounded by these good, innocent people.

"Come on." Kane pulled Lilly away from the others, hustling her toward the front door. Though his father called him, he only shouted a quick apology and an order that no one follow them.

Once he had her outside, he let go of her hands and pulled her close, wrapping his strong arms around her as if he could will away the monster.

Even as the thought occurred to her, she felt the beast falter in the middle of its onslaught. Taking advantage, she forced the thing back into a mental cage, slamming imaginary iron bars down.

Only then, was she able to relax her guard, and allow herself to sag in relief.

As she began to take note of her surroundings, she realized with some shock that Kane still held her. And she had no desire to push him away.

He felt…good. Warm and muscular and safe. As she had when he'd played his guitar, she felt the awful weight she carried 24/7 momentarily slip away from her shoulders.

Even as she let herself enjoy the temporary peace, she began gathering strength to push him away. Because she knew if she let him become involved with even the smallest aspect of what snarled and paced inside her, she'd risk him becoming infected with it, too.

Later, after Kane had gotten her into the cabin and made her drink some hot tea, Lilly claimed she wanted to sleep, even though the sun hadn't yet set. Before he could even respond, she fled to her room without meeting his gaze.

Once she'd closed the bedroom door, leaving him alone in the living room, he eyed his guitar case and debated playing a few notes. But the last night on the way here, he'd been so proud of Lilly when he'd realized he'd fallen asleep and she hadn't woken him to ask him to play.

She'd overcome her fears. Damned if he'd give her back the crutch she'd managed to kick to the curb.

He wanted his family, but wasn't up to the endless questions he knew they'd have. They'd decided to postpone the family hunt, and he'd had to promise them he'd participate as soon as things improved. By things, he meant Lilly. Truth be told, he had no idea when that might be.

His wolf grieved at the missed opportunity to change. For half a second, he entertained the idea of shifting and hunting solo. Only the thought of his family's disappointment and Lilly's shock dissuaded him. Instead, he left and walked the woods, taking care to always keep the cabin in his sight. Walking was like meditation for him. He'd tried to empty his mind, refusing to dwell on anything beyond the sound of his feet hitting the ground and the crackle of the leaves underneath.

By the time the darkness was complete, he must have walked several miles, picking his way over rocks and sticks, guided only by moonlight and sheer luck. Despite this, his unease and concern was no better than it had been when he'd begun.

Finally, he returned to the cabin. Two handcrafted rocking chairs sat to the left of the front door. He took one, staring out into the dark woods, listening as the sounds of the nocturnal creatures, which had grown silent at his passing, began again.

Something had happened earlier. Though they hadn't discussed it, he knew his entire family had sensed it. Something to do with her inner wolf, though he wasn't sure he could call the animal he'd sensed inside Lilly a wolf, exactly.

But what the hell else could it be? Despite rumors or myths to the contrary, he'd never heard of any other kind of Shape-shifter. Not bear or leopard or lion. As far as he knew, there'd never been a documented instance of such a thing.

And even if there had been, this wasn't possible. Not with Lilly. Kane knew her twin brother, Lucas, pretty well. He'd seen the other man shift, had been nose to nose with his wolf. Lilly's brother's beast had been perfectly normal.

Which meant something had been done to her, some poison injected or worse, during the experiments performed on her while she'd been her so-called father's prisoner.

Kane wanted to put his fist through the wall. He hated that Lilly had been suffering alone. He'd sensed her strength, her iron will and fierce resolve as she'd battled the misshapen thing that had once been a wolf. Was this fixable? Curable? He'd have to put a call in to the Protectors and have them ask the Healer.

He also needed to talk to Lucas to find out what the other

man knew about his sister's wolf. He hadn't thought to ask if Lilly had shifted at all since getting out of the hospital, making the obviously erroneous assumption that of course she had. It had been several months, after all. Most Shifters couldn't go that long without changing into their wolf form. Those who tried were often known to become mad.

A chill ran through him. Not Lilly. He'd vowed to protect her from whatever dangers might threaten her. Even though he hadn't known one of those would come from within her, he didn't care. His oath remained unchanged. He would help her. No matter what the cost.

Pushing up from the chair, he walked a short distance away from the cabin before turning on his cell phone and locating Lucas's phone number, the one that went to the disposable phone they'd purchased for this purpose. Since it was three hours earlier in Seattle, he knew Lilly's brother would still be up.

"What's wrong?" Lucas asked upon hearing Kane's greeting. "Has something happened to Lilly?"

"No, nothing like that," Kane hurried to reassure the other man. "I was calling because I had a question. Has Lilly shape-shifted that you know of since she got out of the hospital?"

Lucas took time to consider the question. "Now that you mention it, no. I asked her if she wanted to a couple of times, but she said she wasn't well enough. Why?"

"It might be nothing…"

"No." Lucas wasn't having any of that. "If you're taking the time to call me, it's something. What happened?"

"I'm not sure. We had dinner with my family tonight, and several times over the course of the evening, she clearly struggled with her inner beast. Everyone noticed it."

"So?" Lucas sounded incredulous. "That's not unusual, you know that. Lots of inexperienced Shifters fight that same battle. It takes time and ease of practice before they can control it."

"I know. But that's not it. Have you ever seen her wolf?"

"I told you, not recently. In fact, the last time we shifted together was over fifteen years ago."

Briefly, Kane closed his eyes. "That's what I was afraid of. I don't know what they did to her while she was a captive, but something's happened to her wolf."

"What do you mean?"

"I'm not sure. You've noticed her aura. I think that's tied in with her beast."

Lucas cursed, low and furious. "I'd like to wrap my hands around Jacob's throat for what he did to her."

"Me, too."

"What are you going to do?"

Dragging his hand through his hair, Kane exhaled. "I don't know yet. Right now, I'm going to stick with my original plan. Teach her self-defense, instruct her in firearm use and keep an eye on things."

"Promise me you'll keep me posted."

Kane promised and ended the call. Then, heart inexplicably heavy, he went inside to try to get some sleep.

He woke just before sunrise and made coffee, carrying a cup outside to sit and watch the sun come up. He'd barely taken a couple of sips when the door opened and Lilly emerged, cradling her own steaming mug in her hands. Her disheveled hair tumbled over her shoulders, looking as though she'd just gotten out of bed. He felt a sudden urge to bury his hands in it, to see if the silken strands were as soft as they looked. Surprised, he shook his head, belatedly realizing she'd think he was warning her away.

"Good morning." She flashed an uncertain smile, already taking a half step back. "Do you mind company?"

"Mornin'." Patting the arm of the chair next to him, he smiled back. "I'd love some company."

Her gaze clung to his, before she nodded and lowered herself into the other rocker. For a moment, birdsong was the only sound as they each drank their coffee.

Someone rounded the corner, heading their way on foot. Kane stiffened, then saw that it was his sister, Kathy, her thick brown hair in a braid like their mother's, carrying a covered dish. This meant his mother had cooked something and sent Kathy to deliver it. His mouth began to water. He hadn't even realized he was hungry until right that instant.

Beside him, Lilly pushed to her feet. "I'm going inside," she said, her voice distant, her hands trembling.

He pretended not to notice. "Would you mind bringing me another cup of coffee?" He held up his mug, an excuse to get her to come back out.

Staring at him, her blue eyes wide, she finally took his cup and jerked her head in a nod.

"You might wait a second," he continued, ignoring her agitation. "My sister might want coffee, too. If she does, I'll get it."

She wanted to run, he could tell. Her face had the look of a startled doe caught in the headlights.

"Don't be afraid," he told her softly, holding her gaze. "She doesn't bite."

She blanched. "I'll go now," she said, rushing inside.

Lilly barely pulled the front door closed. A sudden image of a wolf, powerful jaws open, flashed through her mind. She blinked, breathing hard. She actually had to catch her breath. Automatic footsteps carried her into the kitchen and toward the coffeepot, where she inhaled the calming scent of Seattle's most popular coffee. Her brother had packed several bags for her to take with her, telling her just because she was traveling to the other side of the country, didn't mean she had to give up good coffee.

Lucas. If she tried really hard, she could remember the time before. Before their father had learned they were Shifters, before something so natural and beautiful had been made to seem ugly and evil. Closing her eyes, she attempted to remember his wolf. She thought she could see it, a vague gray shape in her mind's eye. But years of conditioning, years of being told what she'd seen was hideous and repugnant, dimmed her memory.

Opening her eyes, she filled Kane's mug, then her own. She rummaged in the cabinet, located one more cup and filled it, too. She found a tray, a plastic container of powdered cream, and some little packets of sugar and artificial sweetener. Lastly, she added a couple of plastic spoons. Then, squaring her shoulders, she turned and walked back outside, determined to face her foolish fears with her head held high.

Kathy looked up and smiled, genuine pleasure lighting her eyes, a lighter gray than Kane's, just like Kris and Kyle. "I brought over breakfast," she said, her smile widening as she spotted the tray and the three mugs full of steaming coffee.

"Coffee!" Drawing out the word and sounding ecstatic, Kathy set her covered dish down on the table. "Thank you, thank you, thank you."

"I take it you haven't had your morning caffeine fix?" Kane drawled, grinning at his sister as she waited, looking about to pounce, while Lilly placed the tray on the table next to her dish.

"I've been cutting down on caffeine." Grimacing, Kathy waved away the coffee as Lilly tried to hand her a cup. "Eliminating it, actually." She sighed. "And I won't have any now. I haven't had real coffee in two weeks. I've been drinking decaf."

"Decaf? Why even bother?"

She blushed. "I'm pregnant."

Kane whooped, hugging her. Watching, Lilly noted the siblings had nearly identical smiles.

When Kathy pulled away, she was still grinning. "But you can't tell anyone. Tom and I want to wait to announce it until after the first trimester."

"Understood." Glancing at Lilly, he gestured at his sister. "I'm going to go make some decaf. Will you be all right out here?"

Slowly, Lilly nodded. Kane disappeared inside the cabin.

An awkward silence fell now that the two women were alone.

"Congratulations on the baby," Lilly finally managed, pleased at how even her voice sounded.

"Thanks!" Kathy's gaze seemed friendly. "So how are you feeling this morning?"

Lilly blinked. She might be a tad bit socially awkward, but the question confused her. "Fine."

"I'm glad." Leaning forward, Kathy continued, her tone earnest. "We were all pretty worried last night. Kane never mentioned you being sick, but since it's clear you are, we're all willing to help any way we can."

Somehow, Lilly's reaction to their inner wolves anticipating a change had registered as illness. Which, if she thought about it, in a way it was. "Thanks," she replied, hoping that would be the end of it.

Instead, Kathy touched her arm. "If you don't mind me asking, what's wrong with you, exactly? Is it a terminal thing or something minor?"

Kane's arrival saved Lilly from answering. He handed Kathy a cup of decaf, lowering himself into his chair and snagging his own mug from the table. He took a long, deep drink before looking up. "What'd I miss?"

Kathy squirmed. "I was just asking Lilly about her health."

Frowning, he gave her a long look before glancing at Lilly. "Her health?"

Pretending a sudden interest in her mug, Kathy blushed. "After what happened at dinner...you know."

Kane's frown deepened. "Kath, I know you mean well, but—"

"It's all right." Eager to smooth things over, Lilly interrupted. "She's just curious. If I were in her place, I'd wonder too."

Though Kane's gaze sharpened, he simply nodded.

Meanwhile, Kathy leaned forward, her eyes sparkling with curiosity. "Are you going to tell me?"

Slowly, Lilly nodded. She'd have to choose her words carefully since she had no doubt Kathy wouldn't waste any time repeating what she learned to all the others.

"I'm recuperating," she finally said. "You may have seen my story on the news. I'm the woman who was rescued in Texas after being held captive for fifteen years by a religious cult called Sanctuary."

Eyes wide, Kathy looked to Kane for confirmation. When he nodded, she jumped to her feet and threw her arms around Lilly, hugging her close. "I'm so sorry," she murmured.

To her surprise, Lilly's eyes filled with tears. She stood frozen in place, unable to move, even when Kane's sister released her and stepped away, murmuring what sounded like a cross between an apology and a desire to hear more.

"Are you all right?"

Lilly nodded. "I am. Now."

"Oh, my gosh. How awful it must have been to go

through that." Again, Kathy appeared to be on the verge of rushing her for another hug. In fact, Kane's grip on his sister's arm might be the only thing that prevented her from doing so.

Fighting an overwhelming urge to flee, Lilly forced herself to stay put, legs rooted in place. "It was," she said softly.

Glancing from Kane to Lilly, Kathy opened her mouth to ask more questions. "Did you—"

"Not now," Kane said, his voice firm as he took his sister's elbow and turned her back in the direction from which she'd come.

"But…"

"Congratulations on your news," Kane said smoothly, effectively cutting her off before she could begin asking more questions. "Now please, go on back to the house. And I'll have to ask you to keep what you know about Lilly under your hat for now. There are still a few of those Sanctuary people on the loose looking for her."

Finally, Kathy nodded. "Of course," she said, her gray gaze landing softly on Lilly. "If there's anything I can do…"

"We'll let you know," Kane finished. "See you later."

Lilly watched in silence until the other woman disappeared around the bend in the road.

"Does your entire family think I'm ill?" she asked, not entirely sure why she found the thought so upsetting.

Head cocked, Kane drank his coffee before replying. "Their inner wolves could tell something's wrong. When you started battling your beast, ours knew and reacted."

Horrified, Lilly swallowed. To disguise her shock, she reached for her own mug and drank, grimacing at the taste of cold coffee. "Can they… Can they *see* the thing inside me?" she asked, her voice quivering.

"No. No one can. Not until you actually change."

At this, she was able to release a breath she hadn't even

known she'd been holding. "Good," she managed. "What's on the agenda for today?"

His smile took her breath away. "Nothing. Rest up, regain your strength and get used to the place. Tomorrow, if you feel up to it, we'll take a drive and go into town. But as far as today goes, enjoy doing nothing."

Though she nodded and tried to look pleased, she felt even more uneasy. Kane couldn't fathom how much of the past fifteen years of her life had been spent locked up in a concrete cell or chained to some machine in the lab at Sanctuary. Doing nothing was the absolute worst he could wish on her.

"I'm assuming you plan on being around?" she asked, mindful of his refusal to let her out of his sight for very long.

If anything, his smile widened. "Of course."

"I'm going for another hike," she told him, almost defiant. "Exercise helps me think."

Without waiting for an answer, she started off down the road, once again heading in the opposite direction of the main house. Despite the beauty of the forest, the massive trees blocked too much of the sky. She felt uneasy here, hemmed in by nature, trapped. Though she hadn't been allowed out much at Sanctuary, every so often Jacob Gideon had recognized her need for sunshine and fresh air. In the old days, her handlers had shackled her to keep her from running. She would have, too, especially believing Lucas dead.

The last few times, they had to wheel her in a chair, she'd grown so weak. Still, she'd relished the open landscape, the sky so huge she could pretend to change into a mockingbird and fly away from her private hell. She'd never forgotten that the mockingbird was the Texas state bird. It made sense, because they knew how to adapt.

Conscious of the big man shadowing her, she looked around. Here, not only were the birds different but she seldom saw them. There were no large grassy areas, no expanse of bright blue sky for them to fly into. The weight of the tree canopy felt heavy, as if made of glass. Or so she told herself, aware her finding fault with such beauty made little sense.

But it did, to her. Because the real reason she felt uneasy in the green New York forest was because the monster inside her loved it.

Chapter 6

Kane liked the determined way Lilly strode through the woods. She reminded him of some warrior princess, her long legs eating up the ground with an athletic and graceful movement, her straight blond hair streaming behind her. He found her desire to walk interesting, as if she thought she could outpace whatever demons haunted her.

By the time she left Leaning Tree and him, he hoped she would have managed to completely vanquish them.

Ignoring the sharp pang he felt at the thought, he trod after her. As he inhaled the pine scent of the woods, he realized how much he'd missed his childhood home. He wondered if Lilly found it as beautiful as he did, wishing she felt comfortable enough with him to walk by his side.

Someday. His chest constricted. He needed to give her time. And also, he needed to remember that in the end, once all the loose ends had been tied up and Lilly was free to live her life, he'd have to let her go.

Finally, she appeared to have worked off her anger or whatever it was that drove her to push herself so hard. Stopping, she put her hands on her legs and bent over, trying to catch her breath. As he drew close to her, he made sure to stop several feet away, allowing her the distance she wanted.

"So." Straightening, she rocked back gracefully on her heels. "What's next?"

"Would you like to go into town this afternoon?" he asked, keeping his tone gentle. The stark misery in her gaze made him want to pull her close. Since he doubted she even knew he could see the emotions she so valiantly battled, he didn't.

"What for?"

A casual shrug. "I thought you might want to see a bit of the area. Plus, there's an Irish pub where the corned beef is a once-in-a-lifetime experience. I've been craving it every since I knew we were coming back here."

Even saying the words made his mouth water. Corned beef. His particular Achilles' heel. In fact, nearly every Shifter he knew couldn't resist the temptation of red meat perfectly prepared. Judging from the way Lilly had reacted to that hamburger while they'd been on the road, he figured she was just like all the rest of them.

"Do they have anything else?" she asked, scrunching up her face like a child tasting a lemon. "I'm not normally a big fan of beef."

Not a fan? He let that pass, pretty sure that she hadn't been out in the real world long enough to even know what she liked. "Sure they do. There's shepherd's pie, some lamb stew, all kinds of excellent dishes."

"Do they have fish?"

"Of course."

"I could eat that. I don't eat a lot of red meat. Even when I was younger, I knew it wasn't good for you."

He nearly rolled his eyes. Those were words he hadn't ever heard another Shifter say. "You ate a burger on the way here. And seemed to enjoy it, from what I could tell."

"I did." Expression abashed, she nodded. "I allow myself something like that every couple of months. Beef's really not healthy for you, you know."

This he couldn't let pass. "Maybe not for humans, but we're different. We need our red meat."

"I'll stick with fish."

He cracked another smile. "Okay."

Arms crossed, she continued to eye him, looking impossibly gorgeous, with her mane of blond hair and bright blue eyes. "I thought you wanted to keep me hidden?"

Now he let his smile become laughter. "First off, Leaning Tree is a small town. Everyone already knows you're here, I'm sure. They just don't know who you are or why you're with us, and we'll keep it that way. Second, I grew up here. Most everyone in town is Pack, and even if your true identity is somehow found out, I can promise you we look after our own."

From the way she looked at him, he could tell she didn't understand. The entire concept was foreign to her. Of course it was. From the time she was fifteen years old, she'd never had anyone else looking after her or even caring about her. Her twin brother had believed she was dead. Meanwhile, her own father had betrayed her, mistreated her and tortured her. He'd actually hired doctors to perform experiments on her while teaching her she was possessed by demons. Kane figured it couldn't get much worse than that.

"If it'll make you feel better," he told her, "you can put your hair in a ponytail and wear a baseball cap and dark glasses."

Expression solemn, she considered his words for a moment, and then nodded. "I think that'd be best."

So he found her a Yankees ball cap and borrowed one of his sister's many pairs of dark sunglasses that Kathy always left lying around. Handing them to Lilly, he waited while she took them into the bathroom so she could see how she looked once she'd donned her disguise. In that respect, he supposed she wasn't much different than any other woman.

When she emerged a minute or two later, he grinned. With her long hair in a jaunty ponytail, the ball cap pulled low, and the oversized dark glasses perched on the end of her delicate nose, she looked like some Hollywood starlet trying too hard to avoid the paparazzi.

"You know you'd look much less conspicuous if you ditched the hat and glasses," he pointed out.

"I like them."

Of course she did. Lilly didn't do well in one-on-one situations. She thought the hat and sunglasses would help her hide. Who knew, maybe she was right.

"Come on." He held out his hand without thinking. Peering at him over the sunglasses, her gaze traveled from his face to his outstretched arm and then back again. When she finally slipped her small fingers into his, warmth flooded him.

Maybe, she had begun to trust him. If so, this was sooner than he'd expected.

His Corvette navigated the familiar winding roads effortlessly. He pointed out the stream he and his brothers had often fished in during the summer as kids, the corner store where they'd all ridden their bikes to buy candy after school and then the elementary school itself. The two-story brick building looked as new as it had the year it'd been built, when he'd been in the third grade. Prior to that, he'd had a long bus ride to a school in the next town over.

Lilly listened to him ramble, her expression bemused as she craned her neck trying to see everything the instant he pointed it out. She seemed more at ease than he'd seen her, so he continued to share his hometown with her.

Finally, they turned another tree-lined corner and reached the outskirts of town. Here, old Victorian houses had been lovingly restored. These soon gave way to funky little art galleries, restaurants with sidewalk cafés, the old grocers with one of the best meat markets within fifty miles and various other shops and establishments, most of which looked exactly the same as they had when Kane was a child. Apparently, nothing ever changed in Leaning Tree.

"We have some great restaurants here, too," he told her. "Sue's Catfish Hut, Papa's Pasta, Joe's Coffee Shop, plus Dublin's."

She nodded. "I'm getting hungry."

The normally bustling downtown area looked sleepy in the midday sun.

"It's beautiful," Lilly breathed. "Like something out of one of those books Blythe reads."

Since Blythe was partial to reading romances, Kane took this as a compliment.

"Here it is." They pulled up in front of the storefront that had been made to look like an ancient Celtic church. "We're in between the lunch and dinner crowds," he said, pleased. "I'm sure there's still the odd tourist, but our timing is perfect. Dublin's won't be crowded."

"If you say so." Though she still sounded less than happy, she couldn't hide the interested excitement in her voice.

He parked in the small lot to the side of the pub. "Here we go."

The dimly lit interior felt familiar and welcoming. Despite her desire for independence, Lilly stayed close to him as he walked the creaky old wooden floors and headed for the long mahogany bar.

Shawn Ferguson looked up from the beer glass he was polishing, his shock of red hair looking as unruly as ever. His frown turned to a grin of delight. "Well, I'll be. If it's not Kane McGraw, finally deigning to show his face here in town."

The two men clasped arms, slapping each other's backs.

"Give me a break, Shawn. I just got home."

Shawn's bright green gaze had already slid past Kane, the laugh lines around his eyes deepening as he gazed at Lilly. "And you've already found the prettiest tourist in town, I see." Grabbing her hand, he made a show of bending as he kissed the back of it.

Kane fought the urge to growl low in his throat. "Lilly's no tourist. I brought her home with me. She and I are staying at Wolf Hollow. Together."

Immediately, the other man's entire demeanor changed. He released Lilly's hand as though it were a live coal. "I'm sorry, McGraw. I didn't know she was your—"

"It's okay." Kane cut him off before he could say *mate*. The last thing he needed was something else to frighten Lilly. She was as skittish as a newborn fawn that'd found itself alone in a wolf's den. "We came to eat. I've been craving your corned beef and cabbage ever since I got here."

At his words, Shawn's worried expression smoothed out. "It's your lucky day," he drawled. "I just happen to have a bit left over from the lunch rush. I'm still cooking the one for tonight's dinner crowd."

"I'll take it." Kane climbed onto one of the bar stools, indicating that Lilly should do the same. "And a pint of Guinness."

Shawn grinned. "Coming right up." He looked at Lilly,

this time the twinkle in his eyes a bit more constrained. "And what would you like, pretty lady?"

Swallowing, she squared her shoulders and lifted her gaze to meet his. "I'd like fish, if you have it. Rainbow Trout? And a glass of iced tea."

"You got it." Hurrying behind the bar, Shawn got Kane's Guinness and hurried into the kitchen to place their orders and fetch Lilly's tea.

Once he'd gone, Lilly turned and faced Kane, her blue gaze direct. "What was he about to call me?"

He pretended not to know what she meant. "When? I didn't hear him say anything."

Biting her lip, she shook her head. Shawn hurried back into the room, bearing her drink and a plate of something else.

"Fried pickles!" Shawn crowed, placing them on the bar. "On the house."

Lilly wrinkled her nose.

"Try one," Shawn urged. "I promise, they're good."

Lilly reached for the plate with the same tentative, two-fingered grip one might use for a bug. She snagged a fried pickle and brought it to her nose to check out the scent. Kane wondered if she realized this was a wolf thing since wolves used their sense of smell more than any other. He decided not to mention it. Instead, he watched as Lilly screwed up her courage and popped the fried pickle into her mouth.

Kane found himself captivated as she slowly chewed.

"It's good," she said, sounding shocked as a tentative smile hovered on the edge of her lush mouth.

"Told you!" Shawn grinned and high-fived Kane.

Lilly ate a couple more pickles before excusing herself to go to the bathroom.

The instant she disappeared around the corner, Shawn's

smile vanished. "Kane, you should know that Anabel Lee thinks you've come back for her."

"Anabel Lee?" Kane nearly groaned. "Why would she think that? I haven't seen or talked to her since before I left for college."

"That doesn't surprise me." Shawn grimaced. "Her husband was killed in Afghanistan six months ago. Ever since then, she's been lost. And now she seems to have fixated on you. She was in here just last night, talking about how you'd come back for her. She said now that you're in town, she expects to have an announcement soon."

Kane narrowed his eyes. "How'd she know I was back?"

"Probably the same way we all do. You know how it is. News travels fast in a small town. And Debi does like to talk."

Debi was his brother Kris's wife. She'd always enjoyed the gossip.

"Still, what the heck is the deal with Anabel?" Kane dragged his hand through his hair. "You mentioned a husband. Surely she's had some sort of life in the eighteen years since high school."

Shawn nodded. "From all appearances, she and David were happily married. They were together five years before his tank hit an IUD and killed him. They never had kids. She was pretty broken up about losing him. Folks say she never quite got right in the head."

"I'm sorry for her loss, but I don't understand what any of this has to do with me."

"Who knows?" Turning away, Shawn grabbed a bar glass and began polishing it. "But for whatever reason, she's apparently convinced herself that you're her true mate. Maybe it's her way of dealing with her grief, I don't know. I can tell you, though, she's not going to take too well to your showing up with another woman. This Lilly, she seems delicate."

Both men glanced toward the bathroom.

"What's your point?" Kane finally asked. "I don't really care what Anabel thinks. While I feel bad that she lost her husband, hell, I don't even know her anymore. But I do want to keep things as quiet as possible for Lilly."

"My advice—let Anabel down gently. But in order to keep her away from you, you're going to need to publicly claim Lilly as yours." Shawn leaned in, his expression earnest. "Not only so word gets back to Anabel, but to keep all the single guys in town from beating a path to your doorstep."

Stunned, Kane looked at his old friend. "I hardly think that's necessary."

"What's necessary?" Lilly asked, her unexpected appearance nearly making Kane jump.

"Nothing," Kane answered, shooting Shawn a quelling look. "What's keeping our food?"

Taking the hint, the other man hurried off to check with the kitchen. A moment later, he returned, carrying two steaming plates.

Grateful, Kane smiled his thanks before leaning forward to breathe in the aromatic smell.

"This looks wonderful." Lilly sounded appreciative as she did the same with her perfectly cooked rainbow trout.

Shawn flashed them a smile before discreetly stepping back to the other side of the bar so they could eat.

When they'd finished, Kane paid the check, telling Shawn he'd see him around. He then turned to Lilly, reached out and lightly touched her shoulder. "How about we take a stroll around the downtown square?"

Again, Lilly seemed to draw back inside herself. "Why?"

He helped her down from the bar stool. If he kept his

hand on her skin a little longer than necessary, he told himself he had a valid reason.

"First off, to show you the town." He slid his hand down her arm and took her hand. This time, she curled her fingers trustingly around his without hesitation. "Second, I want you to see other Shifters, so you can see how at home everyone is in their bodies."

When she turned to look at him, her gaze had gone flat. "Trying to undo my conditioning?"

Surprised, he frowned. He could have hemmed and hawed, but he believed in honesty whenever possible. "Yes. You never know. It might help you."

"Been there, done that. You forget, I was going to therapy while I was in Seattle. They took me to some church full of Shape-shifters." She shuddered. "It was creepy. Reminded me of Sanctuary, even though they could change into wolves."

Kane wanted to find that therapist and wring his or her neck for their stupidity. "I hope Lucas didn't waste a lot of money on that shrink," he said instead. "Sounds like an idiot."

This at least coaxed a reluctant smile. She nodded. "He was. And yes, Lucas realized it. He switched me to a woman after that. She was a little better."

They'd made it to the parking lot. He stopped, enjoying the feel of her hand in his and aware he should give her a choice. "Do you want to see the rest of downtown? Or would you rather go back to Wolf Hollow?"

She gave him a long considering look before slipping her sunglasses back over her eyes. "We can take a short walk."

The flush of happiness he felt seemed way out of place. Or did it? He'd been charged with protecting her. He'd always planned to help her become physically stronger. If he could do so for her internally, as well, so much the better. It was nothing more than that.

As they turned, he kept her hand tucked into his, unwilling to release her just yet. Hand in hand they strolled, and hounds help him but he took pleasure in the knowledge that they looked like any other couple, out for an afternoon walk around the town. He felt...content. Maybe even happy, at least the most he had in a long time. Intellectually, he knew he and Lilly would never have any sort of future together, and he wasn't deceiving himself about that. He was her bodyguard, soon to be teacher, and his goal was to make her a stronger, more centered woman who could finally accept her dual nature as something good. Once the Protectors caught up with the last stragglers from Sanctuary, he hoped Lilly could go forward with confidence and the knowledge she had a right to a long, happy life.

Other people glanced at them, but took no real notice. It had been so long since Kane had been to Leaning Tree, he wasn't surprised he didn't see anyone he knew. Truth be told, he was actually glad. He didn't want his afternoon with Lilly to be interrupted.

Lilly continued to look at everything with a sort of interested delight. She constantly studied various groups of people, a slight frown creasing her creamy skin. "So all of these people are Shifters?"

He grinned. "Most of them. Do you see the auras?"

Lowering her sunglasses, she turned in a slow three-hundred-and-sixty-degree turn. "Yes," she said, her voice rising in excitement. "I do."

"Good. And the ones who have no auras, those are most likely humans. Or—" he hesitated, and then decided he might as well go all in "—they might be vampires."

After a startled second, she laughed. "Good one."

"I'm serious."

She shook her head, a smile still playing around her mouth. "Even if vampires did exist, it's broad daylight. And sunny."

"That's a myth," he began.

"Like vampires aren't?"

Kane laughed out loud, enjoying the verbal sparring. "You have to think of it this way. If Shape-shifters—aka werewolves—are real, then why not vampires?"

Her expression stilled and grew serious. "You're not kidding, are you?"

"Nope."

Silence while she pondered this. He gave her time, aware how much broader her world had just become.

They continued walking, stopping in front of store windows, lingering a while at the stained-glass shop. Still holding hands, which astounded him. With anyone else, he would have considered this too long for the kind of relationship they had. They weren't lovers, after all.

Lovers. The second the thought occurred to him, he had a mental image of her under him, naked and welcoming.

Damn. The flash of instant desire nearly had him pulling his hand away from hers. Nearly. He glanced at her, to see if he'd somehow communicated his need. Apparently not. With her fingers still intertwined with his, she appeared to be gazing across the square at the little curio shop, lost in her own thoughts.

"Vampires," she mused. Relieved that she hadn't noticed his insanity, he nodded.

"Yep."

They reached the park with its paved walking trails and a freshly painted white gazebo, surrounded by vibrant blooming rose bushes.

"How pretty," she said, smiling up at him.

"Yeah, it's a popular spot for weddings and photographers."

She nodded. "I imagine." Then, as they started back the way they'd come, she took a deep breath and squeezed his hand once, causing him to look at her.

"What else is there?" she asked, sounding slightly breathless. "I mean how much of the stories are real? Werewolves, vampires... Are there fairies and elves and zombies, too?"

Somehow he managed to keep a straight face. "I've never seen or heard of such a thing as a zombie."

"Really?" Peeking at him over her large sunglasses, she said, "Though I noticed you didn't say anything about fairies or elves."

He shrugged. "What can I say? The world is much more diverse than most people know."

For whatever reason, learning this appeared to energize her rather than add to her fear. Amusement flickered in her eyes, her expression animated and more alive than he'd ever seen her.

"I think I'd like to investigate this further."

He smiled back at her, aching with the need to kiss her. To distract himself, he glanced at his watch. "We should probably head back. I think you've had enough excitement for one day."

Her smile faded, causing him a pang of regret. "Since you're interested in learning, I'll rustle up some books for you to read."

True to his word, when they reached Wolf Hollow, he made a quick stop at his parents' house, running inside and snagging a few of the many books on Shifter history. Handing them to her, he drove the rest of the way to their cabin, unable to keep from smiling at the way she excitedly started paging through them.

They spent the rest of the afternoon reading. Lilly curled up in the big armchair by the window, while Kane took the couch.

Though he tried, he couldn't get lost in his story like he usually did. Lilly's presence proved too distracting.

But Lilly didn't seem to have any problem tuning him out. She dove into the books, beaming with an almost childish delight. Fascinated, he watched her, careful to appear engrossed in his own book whenever she looked up.

Lilly couldn't believe the wealth of knowledge now at her fingertips. For the short time she'd been in high school fifteen years ago, she'd loved history. The fact that these books were an appealing combination of myth and truth made her that much more eager to read them.

Doing her best to ignore Kane's continual perusal, she even managed to forget about that as she got lost in the words.

Deep into reading about vampires, a sound from outside had her lifting her head. Two big men, boisterous and happy. Their deep voices had a similar lilt and cadence. Kyle and Kris, Kane's two brothers. She could hear them before they even reached the porch.

Lifting his head from the book he'd been reading, Kane cocked his head. He heard them, too. She hoped he'd intercept them outside. Instead, he carefully marked his page and closed the book, placing it on the coffee table.

"It's about time they came for a visit," he said, smiling broadly.

Though she nodded, she couldn't help but consider taking her books and retreating into the bedroom. Once again she wished she could be stronger, confident. Not worrying about meeting men who, if they were anything like Kane, were kindhearted and honest. Good men.

The instant their boots clomped on the porch, Kane yanked open the door, not even waiting for the knock. "Hey," he said, thumping one and then the other on the back. Since men seemed to do this all the time, she guessed it didn't bother them, which was good. She would have thought it would hurt.

"Hey, yourself." Kyle's gaze, a darker gray than Kane's, drifted to Lilly. "How are you?" he asked, politely holding out his hand for her to shake.

Swallowing, she squared her shoulders and stepped forward. There was nothing left for her to do but take it.

When she did, he pulled her in for a quick bear hug. "None of this handshaking stuff for me," he said, laughing. 'We're all family here."

The instant Kyle released her, Kris mimicked him. She couldn't help but notice they both smelled the same, like pine trees and the outdoors.

Greetings finished, they turned in unison to look at Kane. "We're going hunting after dark," Kyle said. "We thought you might want to join us."

For a second, Lilly thought she saw Kane's face morph into that of a wolf. She blinked, and it was gone. Which meant she must have imagined it, since he hadn't started shape-shifting or anything.

"I do," he said, and then glanced at Lilly. "I thought you could hang out with Sharon and Debi while we're gone."

"Kind of like a girls' night in." Kris beamed. "I have to tell you, our wives are so excited. They've rented some chick flick for you all to watch and Sharon's making some of her famous margaritas."

Put like that, there was no way she could refuse. Slowly she nodded, hoping her smile was enthusiastic enough.

"What about Tom?" Kane asked. Tom, Lilly remembered, was his sister Kathy's husband. "Is he going with us? I know Kathy loves those girls' nights."

"Nope. They drove up to Albany for the weekend. Going baby furniture shopping or something."

Kane nodded. "What about Dad?"

Kyle's smile faded. "He's not feeling well. Mom took him to the doctor this afternoon. They haven't gotten back yet."

"You sound worried." Kane glanced from one brother to the other. "What's wrong with him?"

"I don't know. You know how Dad is. He keeps saying he's fine. Mom said he was a bit dizzy." Kris waved his large hand. "I'm sure Doctor Miller will get him all fixed up."

Kane nodded, though he didn't seem convinced.

"So you're in?" Kris scratched his head.

"What time?"

"Debi will pick Lilly up at seven," Kyle said. "They'll be at my house. I figured us guys would hit the woods right at sundown."

Lilly's stomach clenched. She had to force herself to concentrate on breathing normally so she wouldn't hyperventilate. She had three hours. Plenty of time to get ready.

"Sounds good." After another round of back slapping, Kane's brothers left.

Neither Lilly or Kane spoke as they stood, side by side, listening as the sound of the two men's voices faded.

Finally, Kane cleared his throat. "Are you okay with this?"

Taking a deep breath, she nodded and tried again to smile. "It sounds like fun. As long as I don't do anything… wrong."

"You'll be fine." He cocked his head, his silver gaze

darkening. "Just don't let them play twenty questions with you."

"What do you mean?"

"Debi loves to gossip. I imagine she and Sharon will try to pry as much information out of you as they can. Don't feel you have to share anything you don't want to."

Again she nodded. "I've read about these kinds of get-togethers. I guess it's high time I actually experienced one, even if it scares me to death."

For a second, he looked puzzled. Then, as his handsome face cleared, he slung his arm around her shoulder and pulled her close for a hug. Just touching him, no matter how briefly, made her feel better.

"How long will you be gone?" she asked. Then, embarrassed, she shook her head. "What I meant to ask is how long will this girls' night last?"

"Probably three or four hours, I'd guess. You've got the movie, plus snacks and drinks. If I know Debi, there'll be lots of good food."

Again she swallowed, trying to ignore the flutter of panic in her belly. "What should I wear?"

At this, he chuckled. "Wear whatever you want. I imagine everyone will want to be comfortable. You can wear jeans or shorts with a T-shirt."

Though she felt as if her feet were rooted to the floor, she managed to walk a few steps away. "And you'll be in the woods with your brothers? Hunting?"

"Yep. Changing. Hunting as wolves." The way he flashed his teeth in a quick smile reminded her of a wild animal. "It's been way too long for me. I really need this."

At the thought, she shuddered. She couldn't help herself. Kane's gaze sharpened. He'd seen. Thankfully, he didn't comment. Heaven help her, but she thought he might really understand. She didn't know if she should feel warm and fuzzy about that, or afraid.

Chapter 7

For the next several hours, Lilly tried on different outfits from her limited wardrobe, paced in front of the full-length mirror, and tried to rehearse possible conversations inside her head. She'd probably speak as little as possible, but she also wanted to be prepared. She knew the other women were extremely curious about what her life had been like as a captive for fifteen years and needed to find a polite way to say "none of your business."

Other than that, she supposed she'd survive. That didn't prevent her stomach from twisting in a knot, though.

Exactly two hours and thirty-five minutes later, she stepped into the living room, as ready as she was ever going to be. Kane sat on the couch, reading. He looked up, his gaze traveling over her, the warm glow of his approval making her feel hot. "You look...perfect."

Attempting a smile, she finally gave up and settled for a nod. "I wish I wasn't so nervous."

Pushing himself up in a fluid motion, he crossed the room to her. She stood frozen as he loomed over her. Heart in her throat, she stared up at him, wondering. One side of his mouth curved in a smile as he reached out and casually fingered a tendril of her hair. She sucked in her breath, heat pooling in her lower body. Her heart pounded and she wondered if he would hug her or…something. Instead, he simply smoothed her hair away from her face. The gesture felt more intimate than a kiss, making her feel even more exposed and naked.

And more. She burned.

Shocked, she jerked away, hand to her throat, breathing fast. He didn't speak, or come after her. He just let her go.

Which was good. Wasn't it?

Rattled and confused, she pushed past him to the front door. As she stumbled outside, she inhaled fresh air, her mind whirling.

What exactly had just happened?

The sound of car tires on gravel interrupted her attempt to think things through. A bright red convertible, top down, pulled up. Debi, her mop of curly black hair secured by a colorful, paisley scarf, waved. "Are you ready?"

Glancing back at the cabin, Lilly nodded. She reached for the car handle and turned one more time. Relief flooded her as Kane appeared in the doorway, lifting his hand in a wave. She waved back and then got in the car.

Debi grinned at her and gunned the motor, making the tires spin and kick up dirt and rock. She cranked up the radio as they barreled down the narrow road, taking the turns as effortlessly as Kane's car had while Lilly gripped the door handle and tried not to look worried.

To her surprise, they'd barely turned from the gravel road onto the paved main one, before Debi hung a quick right. "We all live on part of the family land," she explained, correctly interpreting Lilly's silent question. "You could have actually walked here if you'd cut through the woods, but I was afraid you'd get lost since you're not familiar."

Debi's rapid-fire way of talking made Lilly's head ache, even though the other woman's tone was friendly.

They pulled up in front of a beautiful stone and wood A-frame house. Two other vehicles, a white minivan and a four-door sedan, were parked in the drive.

"Sharon's already here," Debi told her, killing the engine and jumping out of the car. She raced across the drive toward the house, moving gracefully despite her platform heels.

Lilly glanced at her own flip-flops and shrugged. She climbed from the car and hurried after the other woman, who'd already disappeared inside. The front door stood wide open and the sounds of music and laughter drifted out.

Hesitating, Lilly smoothed her shirt down and took a deep breath. She placed one foot after the other, making her way toward the kitchen.

The instant she went around the corner, Debi looked up, beaming, and motioned her forward. "You know Sharon. She makes the best margaritas."

On cue, Sharon reached for a pitcher and, her long, perfectly manicured nails gleaming, poured some into a blue-rimmed margarita glass. "Here you go."

Accepting the drink, Lilly took a sip. To her surprise, it tasted good. "I like this," she marveled, realizing too late she should have tried to keep the shock out of her voice.

Both Debi and Sharon laughed. "Of course you do!" Sharon's long, red curls bounced as she moved. The freckles that covered her pale skin looked as if they'd been painted on, a kind of natural adornment. Next to the two vibrant women, Lilly felt mousy, with her straight, dirty-blond hair and ordinary figure. But they took her in to their circle as if she was just like them, and made her feel welcome and at home.

The next couple of hours passed before Lilly realized it. They talked and joked and watched a long, mushy movie that she didn't entirely understand, but which made the other two women cry. She lost track of how many of the delicious margaritas she had, but it didn't seem to matter as she didn't feel any different.

At least, until she got up from the couch to go to the bathroom and the entire room tilted crazily. "Oh, gosh!" she said, and then giggled. Which so wasn't like her, but she didn't seem to care.

Debi and Sharon giggled with her. "Careful, honey. There's more tequila in that drink than you realize."

Lilly nodded, but that only made the spinning worse. She stumbled into the small powder room and closed the door. When she caught sight of herself in the mirror, she stared. Her pupils looked dark and unfocused and why on earth was she smiling that goofy smile?

She moved too quickly and the room spun. She began to feel queasy and had the uneasy feeling she might get sick.

Gripping the door frame to steady herself, she squared her shoulders and took a deep breath. When she made it back to the den where the movie credits were just now rolling, she went over to Debi and lightly touched her arm. "I need to go home."

Debi peered at her, squinting as if her eyesight had become impaired. "I thought you were staying the night?"

Pushing back the stab of panic, Lilly shook her head, which turned out to be a mistake. "No. I don't...feel well."

The other woman stared at her with a mixture of fascination and horror. "Are you about to get sick?"

"I don't know." Lilly concentrated on a single spot on

the wall, willing everything to stay still. "But it's likely. And if you don't mind, I'd rather do that in my own cabin."

Debi and Sharon exchanged glances. "Neither one of us is in any shape to drive."

"That's fine," Lilly hurried to say. "Earlier you said I could have walked here. If you'd just point me in the right direction, that's what I'll do."

"I don't think it's a good idea for you to go stumbling around in the woods," Sharon put in drily. "Why don't you stay a while longer, have some water or coffee, and see how you feel?"

But a sense of urgency had taken hold and wouldn't let go. Lilly had to fight the urge to run for the door and rush out of there. "Really, I'll be fine."

She must have sounded convincing or, more likely, the others were equally impaired because Debi finally shrugged. "Fine. I'll walk outside with you and show you which way to go. As long as you stay headed that direction, you'll end up back at your cabin."

Lilly thought she did a convincing job of walking a straight line as she followed Debi outside. Sharon hadn't protested, too occupied with mixing up one final batch of margaritas. Lilly imagined the two of them would pass out on the sofa before the night was over.

Once they reached the driveway, Debi marched around to the back of the house. She pointed to a star shining through the upper tree branches. "Follow that star and you'll be fine."

"Thanks."

"I'd go with you," Debi offered half-heartedly. "But these shoes weren't made for tromping around in the woods. At least you don't have to worry about wild animals. They tend to leave our kind alone."

Our kind? Lilly guessed she meant Shifters. She started

forward, keeping the star in her sight. One wave and Debi turned around and went back into the house, leaving Lilly alone.

She could do this. Slipping into the woods, Lilly breathed in the scents of pine and oak and earth and felt her head clearing. Moving carefully as her eyes adjusted to the darkness, she felt a thousand times better. Even better, the alcohol appeared to have put the monster inside her into some kind of stupor.

Since she didn't have a watch, she had no way of knowing how much time had passed, but after walking a while, always keeping that dang star in view, she thought she should have come across some part of Wolf Hollow. Instead she came to a small stream, managed to cross it and continued on, hoping she didn't end up lost.

A while later, she had to admit defeat. Stopping next to the massive trunk of an ancient oak, she pondered her next move. Should she stay put and wait for the sun to come up or continue on and hope for the best?

The sound of a wolf howl made her freeze. It was close. Really close.

Since Kane and his brothers were out here somewhere, hunting in their wolf shapes, she hoped it had come from one of them rather than a wild animal. But then she realized she didn't even know if they'd recognize her while they were wolves. She knew pathetically little about her own kind and what she'd managed to learn before being taken prisoner, she'd been forcibly made to forget. While she knew what she'd been taught––that they were demons out to take souls––was nonsense, she couldn't shake her terror.

Heart pounding, she felt around on the tree, wishing she could find a branch so she could pull herself up.

Something screamed––the shrill death cry of a small animal. Lilly froze, horrified.

At that instant, the thing inside her made a break for freedom.

Defenses down, Lilly reacted a second too late. Alcohol had dulled her senses. She slammed her mental barrier down, but the beast had already begun reshaping her body. Painfully.

As she fell to all fours, she let out a cry of pain, an awful cross between a howl and a snarl. Dimly, she realized her clothes were tearing as her bones elongated. With her last human thought, she hoped none of the others found her. She'd learned the last time how deadly her monster was to anyone or anything that dared approach it.

Kane. As she pushed herself off the leaf-strewn forest floor, noting the blood among the pieces of human clothing, she squashed the awful urge to use the last remnants of her human voice to call him to her.

But she couldn't. Not only did she know she couldn't bear him to see the horrible beast she was inside, but she would be dangerous to him. Not only to him, but to any male shifter.

Long ago, in the midst of the too-horrible-to-think-of experiments, the doctors of Sanctuary had performed on her, she'd listened and learned they wanted eventually to mate her and get her with child. A super-beast, they'd called it. They'd wanted to create an army of demons eventually.

At that moment she'd vowed to do whatever was necessary to prevent that from happening. Even as they'd injected her with hormones, used specially formulated pheromones to make her irresistible to Louis, the other poor soul they'd captured, planning to put them together and perpetuate the most unholy indignity of all.

And then he'd died. Poor Louis had been tortured and experimented on as much as she. They'd said too much testosterone and steroids had made his heart give out. Jacob

Gideon, the man who'd called himself her father, had not been pleased.

As she moved forward, keeping to the shadows to better hide her misshapen form, she realized with a start that her thoughts were still logical, clearly human. Not the mish-mash of furious rage she'd come to associate with her other self.

Strange. Emboldened by this, she moved forward, using her powerful nose to track the presence of Kane and his brothers. Though her beast's natural instinct was to seek them out, Lilly had enough self-control to push in the op-posite direction. She would hunt, for the first time in na-ture since she'd been fifteen, and then make her way back to the cabin so she could regain her human form.

Hopefully, no one would be any the wiser.

A small rabbit was foolish enough to cross her path. When it saw her, rather than running, it froze. She made short work of killing it, feasting on the fresh meat. Then, leaving only the fur and a few small bones, she lifted her snout and scented the wind, searching for the unique scent of mankind.

Wolf Kane skidded to a stop, causing his brother Kris to crash into him. He snarled a quick warning, but barely spared either of his siblings a glance. Below him lay the fresh remains of a recent kill. And the scent of something else, a Shifter perhaps, but no scent he recognized.

Kyle growled low in his throat, making the same con-nection. No one in town was foolish enough to hunt on the McGraw family land without an invitation. Since he and his brothers had made their plans way in advance for this night, he knew no one local would have come here.

Then who?

The scent, decidedly female, made his wolf self go into

high alert. His brothers, even though they'd already found their mates, whined. The scent made them uncomfortable rather than aroused. Which meant the scent only affected him.

A sneaking suspicion made him freeze. Lilly? He discounted the idea. She was with Sharon and Debi.

Another female Shifter. Remembering what Shawn had said about Anabel Lee, he snarled. Spinning on his paws, he took off for the place where they'd left their clothing. Once he'd changed back to human form, he'd get to the bottom of this.

His brothers were close on his heels as they raced for the protected clearing where they'd first shifted into their wolf shapes.

Not only was her sense of smell forty times better, but her animal self had eyes that could see much better in the dark. She managed to locate the cabin, even though not a single light was burning. Padding up as close as she dared, she lowered her belly to the ground and tried to force the beast to let her have her human shape again.

Of course, monster that it was, it resisted.

Keeping her breathing deep and even, Lilly employed the techniques she'd been taught. Despite having learned them at the hateful hands of the doctors of Sanctuary, they were effective. In a few moments, her body began to contort and twist. She found this part extremely painful, but eventually she was herself again. Naked, sore and aroused, which she always seemed to be for some reason.

At least no one was around to witness her humiliation. Not like the old days at Sanctuary.

Tiredly, she pushed to her feet and padded up on the porch, hoping Kane hadn't locked the door. Luck was actually on her side, and the knob turned easily.

Once inside, she headed straight for the shower. Under the hot water, she shampooed her hair and soaped every inch of her skin, and then repeated it all for good measure.

When she'd finished, she toweled off, found a clean T-shirt and panties, and climbed up on the bed, not even bothering to turn on the light. Closing her eyes, she let herself slide off to sleep.

Once he'd become human again, Kane grabbed his clothing and got dressed. Behind him, both of his brothers were doing the same.

"What the hell was that?" Kyle came up beside him, frowning. "I didn't recognize the scent."

Teeth clenched, Kane managed to shrug. "I don't know. Are you familiar with every local Shifter's scent?"

"Pretty much," Kris joined them. "At least any of the ones who'd be running on our land. This one wasn't local."

"A tourist?" Kyle scratched his head. "That'd be kind of weird. They'd know to check in with the town Pack, who'd give them directions to the safe common area for changing."

"I'm betting this wasn't a tourist," Kane said, already striding off toward Wolf Hollow. "I have a pretty good idea who it might have been."

As his brothers hurried after him, their sharp intake of breath told him they'd realized who he meant.

"Lilly?" Kyle jogged up next to Kane. "Do you think she's finally over her issues with shifting?"

"I don't know," Kane said.

"She's supposed to be with Sharon and Debi," Kris put in. "So I doubt that was her."

Cutting across the swath of forest that led to Kris and Debi's house, Kane slowed to a jog when the stone building came into view, halting before he reached the sidewalk.

Kyle did the same, but Kris strode past them, heading for the front door.

Exchanging a quick look, Kane and Kyle followed.

Once inside, the blaring television was the only sound. The half-empty tequila bottle, a glass pitcher and three matching margarita glasses bore testament to the party the women had enjoyed earlier.

None of the women was anywhere in sight. Of course, Kane glanced at the wall clock, it was nearly 1:00 a.m.

Kris reappeared. "Debi's asleep in our bed and Sharon has the guest room. I can't find Lilly, though."

"Wake Debi up," Kane demanded. "I need to know what happened to Lilly."

Though Kris didn't look too happy at the prospect, he went to get his wife.

A few minutes later, a bleary-eyed Debi appeared in the kitchen. Swaying, her eyes bloodshot, clearly still inebriated, she peered at Kane and Kyle with her brow furrowed in confusion. "What's going on?"

"Where's Lilly?"

Looking down, she shuffled her feet uneasily. Her unruly dark hair fell over her face. "She wasn't feeling well, so she went home."

"Did you drive her?" Kane asked, even though he suspected he already knew the answer.

Debi bit her lip as she met his gaze. "No. I think she drank too much. We all did. And by the time she decided she wanted to leave, there was no way I was going to risk driving her."

Furious, Kane glared at her. "She's not used to alcohol. Come on, Debi. You and Sharon were supposed to look after her. Instead, you let her go wandering around the woods drunk in the dark."

At his words, Debi paled, looking as if she was going to be violently ill. "She...she didn't make it home?"

"We haven't checked there yet," Kris hurried to reassure his wife, after shooting Kane a furious look. "I don't know why you're getting all worked up. For all we know, she could be in bed asleep."

"She'd better be," Kane snarled, spinning on his heel and heading for the door.

After the briefest hesitation, his brothers followed.

Cutting through the woods in the direction of the cabin, Kane cursed when he nearly stumbled over Lilly's torn and shredded clothing. He stopped, picking up the scraps of cloth, noting the blood.

Kyle winced. "Damn. That must have been some painful change."

Again Kane cursed. "She'd better not be hurt."

"I'm sure she's all right." Kris touched his arm. "You need to calm down."

Moving swiftly, barely keeping his violence contained, Kane knocked his brother's arm away. He gathered up the remainder of Lilly's clothes and took off running.

When he reached the cabin, the first thing he noticed was the complete absence of light. His heart stuttered in his chest as he took the porch steps all at once. He burst through the front door, belatedly realizing it was unlocked, and flicked on a lamp.

Ignoring Kyle's urging to slow down, he headed for Lilly's bedroom. The door was closed, but that meant nothing since she'd left it that way. Taking a deep breath, he turned the knob and pushed it open. And froze. Lilly slept, her head pillowed on her hand, long hair streaming out alongside her, oblivious to all the ruckus.

Kyle and Kris came up behind him, peering over his shoulder.

"Whew," Kris whispered, clearly relieved.

Kane moved them back, carefully shutting the door and motioning them back outside.

"See," Kris said, the instant they were back out under the stars. "You were worried for nothing."

"I'm still worried," Kane told him, his jaw clenched so tightly it hurt. He held up the torn and bloody clothing. "I have to find out what happened to her."

"Let her rest, bro." Kyle peered at him, his expression concerned. "You can talk to her in the morning."

Taking a deep gulp of air, Kane tried like hell to retrieve his earlier sense of well-being and calm. He couldn't shake the notion that he'd failed Lilly. By leaving her in the company of his brothers' wives, he'd left her unprotected. The fact that Debi had foolishly let Lilly go alone into the forest proved this.

"You can go home now," he said, aware he sounded brusque but beyond caring. "I'll see you guys in the morning."

Though Kyle still looked worried, he nodded. After a moment, Kris did, too.

"See ya," they chimed in unison, trying to sound normal and not entirely succeeding. Lifting his hand in a wave, Kane watched them until the darkness swallowed them up. They didn't know how to take his extreme behavior, but there was no way in hell that he could explain the entire reason to them. They understood the bare bones, but Lilly's story was hers to tell or not.

Returning to the house, he found himself back in the bedroom, as if compelled. Lilly still slept soundly, her chest rising and falling with each breath. He stood in the doorway and watched her, aching, still clutching her ruined things.

Then, gathering up every ounce of his willpower, he forced himself to back out of the room, and shut the door.

* * *

Lilly woke, her head aching. Heck, her entire body felt as if it had been stretched on some sort of medieval torture rack. Stretched. She sat up in bed, too quickly, making the room spin and nausea rise in her throat.

Last night, she'd let the beast inside her free. Her monster had, however briefly, won.

Stunned and sickened, she gagged. She'd drank too much, for starters. She should have known better, especially since she hadn't ever had alcohol. Sipping mixed drinks wasn't an activity the people of Sanctuary had been prone to. In fact, she remembered the kids in high school talking about getting drunk, as though it was fun. This had been before her father had put her under lock and key.

Though Debi and Sharon had seemed to enjoy it, Lilly knew it wasn't something she'd try again. Ever.

Pushing herself off the bed, she grabbed the edge of the door to steady herself, and took a deep breath. She staggered into the bathroom, her head pounding, wishing she could get rid of the awful taste in her mouth.

Turning on the shower, she peeled off her T-shirt and stepped under the hot spray.

When she emerged from the bathroom, not feeling a whole lot better, her heart sank as she realized Kane waited for her, his expression once again turned to stone.

Did he know? Had the scent she'd left behind in the woods alerted him to the fact that when she shape-shifted, she wasn't a wolf, but something else entirely? Something much, much worse?

Some of the panic that had flared inside her must have communicated itself to him. As she stared, waiting for him to speak, his expression softened.

"Come here," he said, his voice quiet as he held out his hand. "I want you to tell me about last night."

Still, she stood frozen, unable to make herself move. She'd learn to lie, and well, in her time at Sanctuary, but this was different. Kane didn't want to cut her up inside just to find out what made her tick. He asked out of concern rather than a desire to hurt.

She took a deep breath. Unable to shake the notion if she took his hand, he'd somehow be able to discern everything from her touch, she moved past him without touching him.

Taking a seat on the couch and demurely crossing her legs, her heartbeat skipping fast, she hoped like hell she appeared calm and composed. Slowly, she dragged her gaze up to meet his. "I had too much to drink last night. I wasn't feeling well, so I walked back here."

Truth, so far.

Kane didn't respond. Arms crossed, he waited. Though he still seemed remote, he didn't appear threatening. Of course, ever since she'd met him, Kane had been nothing but kind to her.

"And?" he finally prompted, letting her know he was aware she had more to tell.

"My...beast—" she struggled over finding the proper word to describe the thing inside her "—my beast fought me. It...won."

A gleam of interest made his silver eyes glow. He moved closer. "You changed?"

"Yes." As shame flooded her, her entire body grew hot. "I did. But as soon as I could regain control, I changed back."

"You should have hunted with us." His tone, while fierce, also sounded gentle. "My brothers and I would have welcomed your company."

Horrified, she could only stare at him, wondering if he'd lost his mind. "I thought you understood." Her voice broke. "Whatever those people at Sanctuary did to me..."

Unable to finish, she turned away, unwilling to let him see that her eyes had filled with tears.

Grateful when he didn't comment, she used the time to pull herself together. Of course he didn't understand. He hadn't been there. He hadn't seen. He didn't realize the thing inside her was a danger to him and any male it came into contact with.

As he lifted her head, the words hovered on the tip of her tongue, but the look on his face stopped her. Pity.

Pity from the last person she wanted it from. Pity from the only one she'd thought she could trust.

Chapter 8

Watching as Lilly tried not to weep, Kane had to clench his fists to keep from going to her and taking her in his arms.

At last he finally understood. Like an anorexic who, when looking in the mirror, always saw a heavy body, Lilly truly believed her wolf was deformed, some kind of monster. Part of her healing process would be confronting her wolf self and discovering that she was a wolf, nothing more. Nothing worse.

Looking at him, she gasped. "Don't." She shook her head so rapidly her long hair whipped around her. She sounded broken.

Damn propriety. In three strides he reached her and hauled her up against him. With her head tucked under his chin, he inhaled the shampoo scent in her hair. "I'm sorry," he murmured, meaning it.

"Don't be." Holding herself stiffly, her low voice vibrated with pain. "I'll be fine."

When she pulled out of his arms, he had no choice but to let her go. And ache as he watched her, back to him, struggle mightily to keep all of her emotions buried inside her.

He wished she'd simply get angry, beat on him with her fists, something. Anything would be better than pretending she didn't feel anything.

Maybe some exercise would help her. "Go and put on some loose-fitting clothes."

Clearly shocked, she swung around to face him. "What?"

"We're going to my sister's house. She and her husband have a state-of-the-art workout studio out back. It's time you start learning a few self-defense moves."

"Okay," she said, surprising him, before disappearing into her bedroom, closing the door after her.

While she changed, he located a pair of gym shorts and put those on. As he was lacing up a pair of sneakers, she emerged. She'd tied her hair back in a ponytail and wore what looked like expensive yoga clothes. He tried not to notice the way the workout shorts clung to her shapely bottom, or the way her fitted yoga top highlighted her new lush curves.

Despite himself, his body stirred. He turned away, disgusted with himself. Of all the times for his libido to start acting up.

Since Kathy lived right around the corner, they were there in under a minute. Kane had an open invitation to use the gym so he didn't have to phone ahead. He retrieved the key from its hiding place inside a fake rock and unlocked the door.

Once he flicked on the light switch, he stepped aside so that Lilly could enter.

"Wow, this is really nice." She stood just inside the doorway, surveying the large open space with one mirrored wall and all kinds of professional gym equipment. With the sunlight illuminating her dirty-blond hair, her aura had taken on a golden glow. It looked almost healthy.

"Kathy's husband must be serious about working out," she continued.

"He is. Tom used to be a professional bodybuilder," Kane told her.

Moving to the center of the room, he took out two mats and placed them on the floor.

Lilly followed, constantly turning to take in every aspect of the room. He didn't blame her. The entire family always joked that Tom could turn the place into a paying gym if he wanted to.

"So what now?" she asked.

"First, we warm up. Do what I do." Smiling at her, he began to move. "Do what I do." He ran through a serious of jumping jacks, push-ups, sit-ups, then stretching. Finally, he showed her a few basic kicks.

Her form looked good and she completed every exercise. By the time they'd finished the warm-up, a light sheen of perspiration covered her forehead, making her creamy skin appear to glow. This captivated him for a moment, before he shook it off. Still, he had to wonder what the hell was wrong with him. Focus. He needed to focus.

"What else?" Balancing on the balls of her feet, she appeared energized by the exercise. "I'm ready to learn how to fight."

He grinned. "Bloodthirsty, aren't we?"

Grinning right back, she gave an exaggerated shrug. "It feels good to be in control, even if it's only practice."

Again, he felt another flush of attraction, which he managed to ignore. "Good. Now remember an assailant isn't going to walk up to you and calmly ask you to go with him or her. Most likely, they'll be jumpy and jittery. You can turn that against them."

She nodded, appearing focused and comfortable.

"You look relaxed."

She flashed him a smile. "I am."

"Don't be. Adrenaline is important," he told her. "You can use it as a tool. We're going to run through some attack scenarios. Start by targeting your attacks to the body's most vulnerable points. The eyes, neck or throat, face, groin, ribs, knee, foot, fingers, etcetera. You hit them where they're most vulnerable. Your goal is to counterattack as quickly as possible."

"In other words, how to end it efficiently." Her tight lipped smile looked more like a grimace.

"Yes. In addition to that, you have to develop an awareness of your surroundings so you can escape if possible."

"I'm ready."

"Then let's go." First he walked her through a potential choking situation, showing her how to break the hold and also what not to do. He split each move into steps and they practiced one at a time. First a block, then a palm strike and ending with a quick knee to the groin.

Once it seemed she had all the moves down, the time had come to try it at full speed.

Surprisingly, she balked at this. "I don't want to hurt you."

He couldn't help himself; he laughed. After a startled second, she did, too. It felt good, releasing the lingering tightness in his chest.

"I'm sorry." Biting her lip, she peered up at him through her long lashes, looking not the least bit contrite. "But I sometimes don't even know my own strength."

"You need to learn."

She nodded. "All right. I'm ready."

The first time, he took care to be gentle, holding back a large portion of his might. She flipped him easily, partly because he anticipated it.

Frowning at him, she shook her head. "Don't hold back."

He gave her own words back to her. "I don't want to hurt you."

"It doesn't matter whether I'm hurt or not. I want to learn. If they come for me, the last thing they're going to care about is not hurting me."

Because she had a valid point, he pushed up from the floor and launched himself at her. At the instant before he connected, she twisted, ducked sideways, and took him down with a swift kick to the knee.

Stunned, he didn't have time to protect himself and fell, his right hip taking the full weight of his body.

"What the…"

She'd taken a step back, looking as shocked as he felt. In that second, he realized what the wrong response would do to her already fragile self-confidence.

"Excellent!" Steeling himself not to wince as pain stabbed through him, he pushed to his feet. "Again."

This time, he made his movements more deliberate. Still, she managed to elude him, shaking off his grip while at the same moment landing a powerful kick to his stomach.

Winded, he grinned at her while he tried to recapture his breath. "Good job."

Though she didn't appear entirely convinced, she flashed a quick smile and came closer, extending her hand. "Are you all right?"

"Fine," he huffed, even as he realized he wanted to grab her fingers and pull her down beside him so he could kiss her. Just the thought was enough to catapult him to his feet.

Careful not to look at her in case she read his desire in his eyes, he crossed to the small refrigerator and pulled out a couple of bottles of water. "Want one?" he offered.

"Please." When she reached for it, their hands connected. A jolt of pure lust ran through him, fingertip to arm, straight to his groin. He covered this by opening his water and draining the bottle.

After a moment, she did the same, though she only drank half of hers. "Are we done?"

Was that his imagination, or had her voice gone husky? Quickly, he decided he was hearing things thanks to his overheated libido.

"Not yet." He managed a casual smile. "We're going to do more push-ups, but this time I want you to jump up into a palm strike. Kind of like a burpee with a punch. This will prepare you in case you ever get knocked to the ground and have to fight for your life."

She nodded. "Now?"

Though his hip still ached from his fall, and his abs still felt the impact of her blow, he nodded. "Now."

A few rounds of this and he called it. "I think we've done enough for one day."

Though she was barely breathing hard, she agreed. "I'd like to go back to the cabin and shower. Then I want to spend the rest of the afternoon relaxing."

About to take her arm, he thought better of it. "You've earned it."

"So have you." The warm gratitude in her smile matched the glow in her blue eyes.

Raw need had his blood heating. The surge of desire again angered him at its inappropriateness. He was her Protector, not her seducer. Yet even that knowledge didn't stop him from desiring her.

"Let's go." Though he knew he sounded gruff, there was no help for that. He led the way out the door, stepping aside to allow her past, before locking up and replacing the key in its hiding place.

Lilly couldn't decide what she'd done. Kane had been the epitome of friendliness, grinning his devilish grin at her and helping her learn how to take an assailant down quickly.

But then, something had changed. Surely he wasn't angry that she'd knocked him to the floor? She'd only done what he'd taught her to do.

No, she believed she knew him well enough now to know that wasn't it. Then what?

Every time she thought about asking him, the words stuck in her throat. Truth be told, she wasn't entirely sure she wanted to know.

She wanted to kiss him. And maybe more. At fifteen, when she'd been imprisoned, she'd been a complete innocent. In the fifteen years since, that hadn't changed. Though she realized she might be the only thirty-year-old virgin around, she hadn't been free, or normal, long enough to change that. And she wasn't even certain she wanted to.

Until now. Kane made her want things she couldn't even articulate. She ached for his touch and dreamed about his kiss. This had to be a crush, much like the ones she'd had when she'd been fourteen, a kind of formless yearning. Kane would probably laugh if he knew.

They arrived back at the cabin only to find Kane's mother had left some sandwiches and chips on the table for them. They ate together, which felt both familiar and uncomfortable. Every time Kane's glance touched on her, Lilly burned.

When they'd finished, she murmured something about needing to rest, and promptly disappeared into her bedroom.

Instead, she showered again, as if by doing so she could wash off the strong pull of desire. Clean, she put on a pair of denim shorts and a T-shirt and blow-dried her hair.

As she debated checking out the latest fashion magazine Kathy or one of the others had left for her, Lilly heard the clear notes of Kane's guitar. Cocking her head, she stood still and listened, waiting for the music to quiet the ever-present struggle still roiling inside her.

Instead, he stopped playing. Disappointed, she opened her door, realizing he'd gone outside on the front porch. She stood still, waiting as she heard him pick out another note or two.

Again silence fell. Intrigued, she went outside.

He sat on the edge of the steps, with his guitar and a pad of paper.

"What are you doing?"

When he looked up, his mouth curved into an unconsciously seductive smile. "Trying to write a song. I used to do this for fun, but it's been too long." As if to demonstrate, he strummed a few more chords. "Listen to this." And he played the better part of a melody.

Something about it touched her deep inside. Though she wasn't vain enough to think he might have written it for her or about her, the melody felt personal.

He played it once more. "What do you think?"

"I like it." She smiled, tentative. "I actually feel as if I could be good at making up words to that particular tune."

"Do you?" He smiled back, encouraging. "Why don't you try then? Let me hear what you've got."

And he strummed the guitar and began to play once more.

Though she hadn't sung out loud since she'd been a child, Lilly couldn't help herself. She'd never had a reason to, not before. Music equaled contentment, happiness, joy and peace. And perhaps something more. All she knew, right now, was the time was right.

So she began singing, some of the words fragments that had been running through her head ever since she'd left Seattle. The others, she made up as she went along. She didn't know if she had a good voice or bad, she only knew with music, she felt free of her demons. The time had come to let her voice free.

And she sang.

After one, quick, startled look, Kane nodded and continued playing. As if they'd worked together before, he fell into the rhythm. Joining with her, as if they were inside each other's minds. Creating, making music.

Glorious.

She let her voice soar, abdicating rational thought or limitations, vaguely aware that this song connected the monster inside her with her true self, in ways that felt real and right. And maybe, not so evil after all.

Darkness swirled, lightening into something seductive, and she glanced at Kane. He watched her, expression savage, as though need and yearning and desire had transformed him into something else.

Something else... She didn't understand, but she realized it had something to do with her voice, with the song. Heart sinking, she understood the awful power she could wield over this man. Those damn experiments they'd done on her—she had no idea of all the changes those doctors at Sanctuary had made to her psyche. Had this been one of them?

Horrified, she closed her mouth, turning to run from him, not wanting to see what she'd done. Too late. He shoved aside his guitar, uncaring when the instrument hit the floor with a discordant clang. Even as she leaped forward, he was faster, and his fingers closed around her arm, the opposite of gentle.

Desire made his eyes molten silver. He yanked her toward him, letting her feel the strength of his arousal. She knew what he was about to do. Oh, she knew and some small part of her reveled in it. The power, the craving, the need, all tangled up together like some horrific spider's web, leaving nothing but chaos in its wake.

He slanted his mouth over hers, his lips hard and cruel and possessive. Not like him at all, she felt, then gave up any attempt to think. Heat flared, feeding her hunger. Angry, she wanted him to ravish her, even as she struggled to escape his hold.

Ecstasy flared, dark and bright and urgent, all at the same time.

This wasn't her, yet was. And Kane, he'd become a savage stranger, the blankness of his gaze telling her he knew not what he did.

She wanted him, but not like this. This wasn't real, wasn't about her at all. Something else, her siren's song, compelled him. It would be up to her to bring this to a crashing halt. If...she wanted to.

Her senses reeled, sending her equilibrium diving and crashing. Blood pounded through her body, searing her with a fire that craved only one release. Him. Buried deep inside her.

She gasped as his mouth seared a path down her throat. Her legs turned to putty, and she sagged against him, even as her hands moved of their own volition to the bulge in the front of his jeans.

No. What was she doing? From a distance, she heard herself protest, then heard herself scream. Somehow, she found the strength to push him away. Expression glazed with passion, he came at her again. He was strong, too strong for her to overcome, and she knew her only chance would be to try to reach inside to the man he truly was.

"Kane." Her voice, hesitant and frightened, didn't reach him. She tried again. "Kane. Stop. Right now."

Something flickered in the liquid silver of his gaze. Recognition? Sidestepping, she managed again to evade him, though every bone in her body ached to let him crush her against him once more.

"Kane." Louder. "You don't want to do this. Wake up. It's me, Lilly." Her voice rose. "Kane. You're supposed to be protecting me."

That reached him, she could tell. He froze, shook his head as forcefully as a wounded bear and growled. When he blinked, she saw him come back to himself. "Lilly?"

"It's okay," she soothed, aware of the bitter irony. "You're all right."

"What have I…" The instant his arousal registered, he flushed a dark red. "I don't understand. I…apologize." Turning away, he bowed his head. "You need to leave."

Though she didn't want to, she couldn't help but see the wisdom in that. Still, despite that, she stood her ground. "I need to explain."

"Not. Now." He ground the words out through what sounded like clenched teeth.

For the first time, she sensed that maybe his arousal hurt him. She who had zero experience with men or sex had no idea if that was possible or not. "Fine." Conceding, she spun around and headed into her bedroom. "Call me when you're ready to talk. I suspect I've got a lot of explaining to do."

Kane watched her go, his body throbbing. What the hell had just happened? He had no clear memory of it; the last thing he knew, he'd been strumming his guitar and then Lilly had come into the room and started singing. Even the memory of her seductive voice sent a thrum of desire through his blood.

Hell hounds. He'd played some chords, and she'd started to sing. They'd been writing music, he thought. What had happened after that, he couldn't remember.

Obviously, she knew what had happened and why. And

as soon as he got his overheated body under control, he meant to get some answers. For now, he gulped in air, wondering why he had to struggle even to breathe.

As soon as he could walk normally again, he made it into the kitchen, popped open a beer, and drank half the can in a few swallows. He wiped his mouth with the back of his hand. Again, he pictured Lilly. Her mouth had appeared bruised and swollen, matching the tingling in his. Had they kissed? He knew damn well he'd definitely remember if they had. Instead, he drew a complete blank. How on earth could he have no memory of something so momentous?

Stepping outside, he breathed deeply, hoping the pine-scented air would help clear his head.

He glanced at the chair, his guitar next to it, decided no, and kept on going. He needed to go, he needed to run. Yet, he realized he couldn't outrun her. Hell, he couldn't leave her. He was her Protector.

But who the hell was going to protect him from himself?

He wanted her. Of course he did. He'd felt that click of connection the first time he'd seen her, when he'd been part of the team who'd rescued her from the basement underneath Sanctuary. Then, he'd thought it was because he'd become friends with her twin brother. But later, during one of his many visits to her while she'd been hospitalized, he'd come to understand it was more. Deeper. Deeper than it should be, perhaps. But he'd believed he could handle it, aware of the strength of the barriers he'd erected around his self-control. He had not the slightest doubt he could keep them intact, no matter the provocation.

And now this. How the hell he could black out while playing music and then come to, fully aroused, was beyond him. Especially since he knew if he ever got together with Lilly, he'd sure as heck remember.

As he moved off the front porch, his cell phone rang. Not

his regular one, but the disposable phone he'd purchased to keep in touch with Lucas. Lucas had the exact same phone.

"What's up?" Kane asked.

"They burned my house," Lucas said, sounding furious. "Broke in while we were all out to dinner and torched the place."

Kane cursed. "No one was hurt?"

"That's the only good thing. The fire department came right away, but the place is a total loss."

"You're sure it was them?"

"Oh, yeah." Now the other man's voice rasped, positively savage. Previously, Kane had only heard his friend use that tone when planning the assault of Sanctuary to free Blythe and her daughter. "Even in my human form, I can smell the accelerant. Worse, the fire department's arson investigator wants me to come in for questioning. They think I set my own home on fire!"

"What are you going to do?"

"After I deal with the arson investigator and the police, who also want to talk to me, I'm taking Blythe and Hailey and disappearing for a while. We're heading to my cabin."

"Good idea." Kane had always envied Lucas his isolated retreat in the Colorado mountains. It would be the perfect place for him to shield his family from the madness engendered by the crazy followers of Jacob Gideon. "Even though their leader's in prison, they just don't give up, do they?"

"My guess is that whatever they did to my sister is extensive enough that they feel they've got to get her back. Has she told you any information about her time while in captivity?"

"Not yet." Even with her twin, Lilly had been extremely reluctant to share the horrors she'd endured.

"She alluded to experiments," Lucas continued. "But other than saying her inner wolf was no longer a wolf, she refused to elaborate. Which fits in with what they tried to do to Blythe while she was there. I imagine they perfected their methods on Lilly since they had fifteen years to implement them."

The anger that surged through Kane stunned him. He wanted to break something, punch someone, or rip something in half. "I need to change," he muttered.

Lucas's short bark of laughter told him the other man knew exactly what he meant. "I bet you do." His tone lowered, became serious. "Just be careful around Lilly. She freaked out the few times I mentioned it to her."

"Same here. But she's going to have to do it sometime," Kane mused. "Otherwise she's going to start having other problems."

"I think…" Lucas's hesitation completed his sentence. Kane knew Lucas thought that some of the problems experienced by shifters who went too long without changing had already manifested in his sister.

For all Kane knew, he might be right. "Do you know if such things are reversible?"

"That's a question for the Healer."

Kane agreed. "I've already started a list. I've been instructed to contact her, but not until I have a good handle on things."

"Keep me informed," Lucas said. "Listen, I'm going to go. I wanted to let you know where we're going to be. We've got to get out of Seattle before those idiots come back and decided to try for Blythe or Hailey."

"Make sure you're not followed."

"Of course. Talk to you later." Lucas ended the call.

"Who was that?"

Kane turned, finding Lilly eyeing him thoughtfully. He wondered how much of the conversation she'd heard, and then wondered why he hadn't heard her approach. At the very least, the sound of the dead leaves under her feet should have alerted him.

Quickly, he filled her in on what had happened to her brother.

"He loved that house," she said numbly. "He and Blythe were in the middle of renovating it. Why would someone do something like that?"

Though he hated to tell her, she needed to know the truth. "To get to you. They're trying to flush you out."

The stubborn tilt of her chin told him she wasn't buying it. "That makes no sense. I wasn't there. Lucas and his family weren't even there, thank goodness. It sounds like they're trying to prove a point."

Relieved, he nodded. "That's right. In a way, they are. They want to make sure we know they mean business."

"Even though their leader is in prison?" She frowned, her expression troubled. "Sanctuary has been disbanded. Their building is empty. What could they possibly hope to gain?"

"You."

Grim-faced, she nodded. "But why? What are they going to do once they have me?"

Though he didn't even like to consider the possibility, he managed to shrug. "Maybe since they apparently still regard Jacob Gideon as their prophet, they expect him to raise Sanctuary up from the ashes once he's freed."

"That's not going to be for a long time."

Unless he escaped. Briefly, Kane wondered if the Protectors had even considered this possibility. Of course they had. He decided not to mention it to Lilly.

"Who knows what whackos like that think? The important thing is that Lucas and his family are safe."

"True. Where are they going to go now that their home is gone?"

"He has another place, hidden away."

She nodded. "It's probably best that I don't know."

Another flash of misgiving. Was she aware of something that might happen, something he wasn't? He pushed away the supposition, well aware that in situations like this, he could only act on facts, not speculation.

"In case I'm captured," she elaborated, looking grim. "They're awfully good at torture, you know."

Then he understood. She could only face little pieces of her horrific past at a time.

His heart clenched. "Come on. We need to talk."

Looking down, she studied her hands. "I was afraid of that."

Chapter 9

Once they reached the cabin, Lilly hurried inside, heading straight for the kitchen. She looked up, flashing a sheepish smile. "I feel better if I can keep busy. I might as well get something started for dinner."

As she stood up on tiptoe to inspect the contents of the top shelf of the pantry, he couldn't help but admire her slender curves and the way her legs in her denim shorts seemed to go on forever. Instead of her earlier ponytail, she wore her hair lose, and the silky strands swirled around her shoulders. She moved like a dancer, completely unaware of either her beauty or her grace.

Kane swallowed hard, battling the urge to go to her and take her in his arms.

Instead, he crossed to the other side of the breakfast bar, keeping it between them, and climbed up on a stool.

"Do you want to tell me what happened earlier?"

She froze, turning slowly. "I don't know, exactly." Lowering her lashes, she flicked an imaginary insect off her arm.

"Try."

"I started singing and you…had a strange reaction."

Though he knew she had no idea how sensual he found her voice, desire once again stabbed him.

"I can assure you," she muttered hastily. "I won't let that happen again."

"Let *what* happen again," he pressed, keeping his tone calm and patient.

Expression miserable, she dropped her chin. "I'm not sure, but I think it has something to do with all the experiments the doctors were doing on me at Sanctuary."

The words, hung there, almost sounding like deluded ramblings, except for one thing. Kane had been in the laboratory at Sanctuary; he'd seen. And he recognized the possible ring of truth in what she said.

A shudder of foreboding passed through him. The Pack Protectors would have to be notified as soon as he had the full story.

Lilly had already been through more than most. More than enough. If the three missing members of Sanctuary were to recapture her, he could only imagine what they'd try to do. Their experiments would be accelerated since they would be aware they could be captured at any moment.

Lilly would once again be nothing more than a lab rat.

The thought of this made his gut twist. He couldn't let anything like that happen to her. Not only would he have to protect her from the Sanctuary fanatics who were searching for her, but from her own, inner psyche. Damn.

"Sit." Releasing her, he indicated the rocking chair. He waited until she was seated before lowering his bulk into the one next to her. "How much did they tell you?"

"About what they were doing to me?" Her full lower lip

trembled, giving him the urge to softly run his thumb over it. "They taunted me with it every day. But I don't have any idea what was truth and what was lies."

He saw agitation boiling up under her outward demeanor. While he desperately wanted to know, gut instinct told him that here, he needed to go slow.

"It's not your fault." Reaching over, he gave her shoulder an awkward pat, aware what he really wanted to do was pull her onto his lap and hold her. Kiss her. And more.

Dammit. He shut the thought down. "You can tell me more when you think you're up to it," he said, feeling the warmth of her grateful smile.

"There's not much more to tell. They barely spoke to me, except when they prayed for the demons to release their hold on my soul."

He shuddered. "You do know they are insane, right?"

As she stared at him, one corner of her mouth lifted in the beginning of a smile. "The longer I'm away from them, the more I've come to see this."

He refused to let himself smile back. Pushing up from the stool, he moved toward the bathroom. "Let me get cleaned up, and then I'll help you make something to eat."

Lilly refused to let Kane help with the cooking. She wanted to try out her extremely limited culinary skills. She made grilled cheese sandwiches and canned tomato soup for their dinner. Kane devoured his with as much pleasure as if she'd prepared a gourmet feast. She found herself watching him instead of eating, wishing she could take that much pleasure in something. She'd bet he dreamed in vivid color rather than the muted shades of gray that made up her own dreams.

"How about we pay a visit to my family?"

His voice, deliberately casual, startled her. She'd just

carried the plates to the sink and started cleaning up the kitchen after their meal.

"Your family?" Stalling, she couldn't come out and tell him how much his boisterous kinfolk frightened her. Anyway, she guessed he already knew.

"We can't avoid them the entire time we're here," he pointed out, still sounding calm and reasonable. "If we try, they're just going to show up here at our cabin. I'd rather keep what privacy we have and meet them on their own turf."

Put that way, she understood. "I don't mean to be so..."

"It's okay." He squeezed her shoulder, a friendly touch which reassured her. "I promise they don't bite."

Again, the image of a wolf, jaws open, sharp teeth gleaming, flashed into her mind. She couldn't help but shudder, wondering how they dealt with such a vicious animal inside them. She'd tried to talk to her brother about that, but Lucas hadn't understood and she'd given up. Since then, she'd known better than to try to explain her feelings to anyone, including the therapist she'd seen in Seattle several times.

She sure as heck wasn't mentioning it to Kane.

"All right," she finally said. "Let's go."

At least this time, they were headed up to the main house after the rest of the family was sure to have finished eating.

She liked that he also knew when to be quiet. They set out side-by-side from their cabin, each lost in their own thoughts. She could tell he also enjoyed the myriad of sounds that meant the wood creatures were awakening and felt no need to warn the animals of their presence with needless chatter.

The feeling of companionship, of kinship with this tall, muscular man—though it puzzled her if she thought too hard about it—was something to be savored and appreciated.

As they rounded the corner in the path, side-by-side, the front door opened and several of the older children spilled out. Laughing and jumping and wrestling, they chased each other on the small patch of lawn, weaving in and out of the trees.

The adults followed, moving more slowly, but talking and gesturing with as much animation. Kane's family lived with vibrancy and a love of life they were willing to share with anyone lucky enough to pass into their orbit. They'd certainly reached out and welcomed her time and time again, undeterred by her repeated efforts to distance herself. Sometimes she thought they somehow knew how badly she wanted to share in their world and how badly her fear held her back.

No one had noticed Kane and Lilly yet. They were moving toward a footpath that led through the trees up a hill to the east of the main house, talking and joking. The scent of pipe tobacco drifted back from Kane's father's pipe.

Kane watched his family with a sort of bemused envy. She guessed he badly wanted to go with them, whereever they were headed.

"What's going on?" Lilly asked, frowning. "It'll be twilight soon."

He glanced at her, the light in his eyes fading. "They're heading up to a part of the woods that adjoins the Catskill Forest Preserve. It's really isolated and not accessible by vehicle."

"Why? To hike? Do you want to join them?"

Slowly he shook his head, never taking his gaze off her. "No. I completely forgot that they told me they're going into the forest to change tonight. You know, shape-shift into wolves. They invited us to join them, but after your reaction last time, I said no."

She stared, ignoring the tiny flutter of panic. "I can't..." she said, expecting him to try to change her mind.

Instead, he nodded. "I know. It's okay. Everything will come with time."

Not this, she vowed silently. He and his family had no idea what kind of thing lived inside of her. Nor would they ever find out, at least as long as she drew breath.

Together they watched silently as his family trouped up the hill and vanished from sight. Lilly found herself wishing she had enough nerve to take his hand.

"Come on," he said, as the last person disappeared over the hill. "How about you and I do a bit of exploring on our own?"

Another frisson of fear. "Won't we get in their way? I'd hate to run into them."

A shadow crossed his face. Regret? She wasn't sure.

"We won't. They'll be far enough that we shouldn't, but just to make certain, we'll go the opposite direction. Don't worry, I'm familiar enough with these woods that we won't have a problem."

Aware he was making sacrifices for her, she shook her head. "Why don't you go and join them. I promise I'll go back to our cabin and wait for you."

"Absolutely not." He didn't even hesitate. "I'm not leaving you here alone." Glancing at the house, he flashed a smile. "I have an idea. We'll grab a few things from the house—I know my mother baked lots of treats—and we'll have a hike and a dessert picnic. Desserts and champagne. Would you like that?"

Her heart melted at his almost boyish eagerness. Still, she hesitated. "It's going to be dark soon."

"So? We've got flashlights and lanterns. Plus the moon's still close to full. It'll provide a lot of light."

Though she had her misgivings, she had to admit it sounded like fun. Or at least better than another night alone with him in the cabin, each of them trying too hard to be like friends. "Okay."

"Great!" Grabbing her hand, he tugged her toward the main house. "This is going to be awesome."

His enthusiasm appeared to be contagious. Heart skipping, she let him pull her. They hurried along, through the front door, toward the kitchen. Passing the main refrigerator, he headed toward the laundry room. "She keeps a second one in here," he said. Sure enough, there was another one nearly as big as the first.

He let go of her hand to open the stainless-steel door. "Jackpot!"

Inside were cakes, pies and assorted other sweets. She counted at least four kinds of cookies, chocolate-covered strawberries, which made her mouth water, and what looked like custards and puddings or flan.

"My goodness. There's enough here to feed a small army."

His grin widened. "Exactly."

"Are you sure she won't mind?"

"Are you kidding me?" He shook his head, continuing before she could even answer. "This is what my mom lives for. She loves to cook and bake, and feeding people is her vocation. So look around and pick out whatever you'd like."

While she deliberated, he grabbed a basket from a stack on a shelf. "She keeps these here in case any of her kids or grandkids want to take food home or have a picnic."

Inside, she saw a red-checked cloth, plastic cutlery, paper plates and napkins. "Ready-made picnic?"

"Yep."

She picked out a few things that looked appetizing, including the chocolate-covered strawberries, then backed away and let him choose the rest. He grabbed a bottle of champagne from the door of the fridge, two plastic glasses and a corkscrew, and closed the basket.

"All ready." He sounded so happy, she couldn't help but smile.

"I wouldn't peg you for someone with a sweet tooth," she commented.

His only response was a conspiratorial grin.

Once outside again, he led her in the opposite direction from that his family had gone in. This helped quell some of her nervousness. "How much land does your family own?"

"Forty acres. And beyond that is the Catskill Forest Preserve. So we're pretty isolated out here."

Which she supposed was good if one was a Shapeshifter.

"What about the people who live in town? Where do they go when they want to change into wolves?"

"The preserve, mostly. No one would trespass on our land without being invited."

Though she knew he'd added the last to reassure her, she couldn't help but glance out into the thick forest. They reached a clearing, a small glade really, with a couple of large boulders stacked on top of each other.

"Here we are." He set down the basket. "When I was a kid, I loved to use this rock as my own personal fort."

Helping her up, she marveled at the way her skin seemed to tingle where his hands touched. He passed her the basket, which was surprisingly heavy, before climbing up and joining her.

Once he'd gotten settled, he spread the checkered cloth on the flat part of the rock, placed a few paper plates, and then removed all the delicacies he'd packed in the basket.

Once they were all on display, in their delectable, tempting beauty, he popped the cork on the champagne.

"Only a small glass for me," she cautioned, as she popped a chocolate-covered strawberry into her mouth.

Ignoring her, he filled the plastic glass before handing it to her. "Here you go."

She watched as he sampled one of everything, finally settling on a large slice of cheesecake. He ate with relish, the way he did everything, and she enjoyed watching him.

After eating a couple more strawberries and taking a few more sips of champagne, she settled with her back against the large boulder, and looked around at the wilderness. "Will you be able to find our way back once it gets dark?"

For an answer, he reached inside the basket and brought out a flashlight. "Yep, with this to help us."

Before she could respond, a howl drifted on the breeze, otherworldly and eerie. The sound sent a shiver up her spine.

Kane noticed. "No worries. They're a good distance away."

Glancing at him, she nodded. Then she took a second look. His aura...for a moment the vague glow had coalesced, resembling one of the wolves that haunted her dreams.

"Are you..." Hesitant, she asked, "Are you okay?"

One dark brow rose. "Sure. Are you?"

His profile seemed to waver, flashing from human to wolf and back again. Suddenly nervous again, she couldn't help but wonder if he was about to change shape. She didn't know how she'd react to this, and she really didn't want to find out.

More howls, several together, the sound rising and falling and drifting into the air.

The monster inside her woke, stretching, reaching out with razor-sharp claws. Reacting.

She swallowed hard and slammed down her mental prison. "What's going on?" she asked, unable to keep the rising panic out of her voice. "Are you about to shift into a wolf? Is the sound of your family as wolves affecting you?"

"Maybe a little," he admitted. "But it's all right. I'll change later, after you go to sleep. Don't worry, I'm not going to go all lupine on you."

"Lupine?" And then she knew. The word meant *wolf*.

A veritable chorus of howls made talking difficult. "I don't know about you," she said, her breath catching. "But I think they're getting closer."

He cocked his head, listening. "Maybe you're right. Though that doesn't make sense. We never venture over this way unless…"

Twisting her hands in her lap, she waited for him to finish. When he didn't, she prodded him. "Unless what?"

Unfolding his long legs, he pushed up from the ground, holding out his hand and pulling her to her feet. "Unless they're following prey. They're hunting after all. Come on, I'd better get you back to the cabin."

Blind terror made it difficult to see. She hated this about herself. Despised the unreasonable panic, the character flaw that had taken away any backbone she might have once had. Intellectually, she knew this was due to years of conditioning and suffering as Jacob Gideon's captive, but emotionally the frustration could be overwhelming.

Worse, the instant she let down her guard, the thing inside her tried to fight its way free.

"No." Gripping Kane's hand, she leaned into him, taking strength from the warmth of his body.

"You don't want to go?" Sounding surprised, he squinted

at her. "I mean, I know they wouldn't hurt you, but I thought you..."

His words barely registered as she struggled internally. Heaven help them all if her monster managed to break free around anyone else. It had happened once, in the lab. Before they'd shot the tranquilizer dart into her, she'd killed two lab technicians and a doctor. Worse, she had absolutely no memory of doing it.

The numerous tortures that followed had ensured she'd been well and painfully punished for that.

She wouldn't change, couldn't allow the beast inside her to win. Not now, not ever. But was she strong enough to hold it back when it had become this determined?

"Help. Me." She pushed the words from her, reaching out blindly, hoping and praying she could somehow add his strength to her own.

More howls. The sound excited her beast, energizing it and encouraging it to double the attempt to force her to change.

She felt her bones begin to lengthen. "No," she cried, writhing in pain. "I can't let this happen."

At that, he pulled her close, wrapping his strong arms around her. Her inner animal didn't know how to react to this, and Lilly seized this advantage to force it back inside its mental cage.

As she struggled, Kane continued to hold her. Gradually, she became aware of the sound of his heartbeat under her ear.

"Shh." His large hand swept over her hair. "It's all right. I won't let anything happen to you, I swear."

Did he still think his family's wolf howls frightened her? The next second, she had her answer.

"Lilly, if you want to change, I'll help you. I can stay human if you'd like, or change right along with you."

Horrified, she pushed him away. "You have no idea what you're saying."

"I think I do. Your inner wolf responded to the sound of the howls. That's all right—mine did, too. I know it's been a while for you and Lucas also told me how those idiots at Sanctuary conditioned you to think shape-shifting was evil. I promise you, once you let yourself go, release your wolf, you'll feel better. You'll see. You'll feel like a different person."

"There is no wolf," she told him, her voice flat. "That's what you and my brother don't understand. The people of Sanctuary killed it. They destroyed my wolf and left something twisted and misshapen in its place. I've seen it and I promise you, it's truly hideous."

He stared at her. Was that *pity* she saw in his handsome face? She knew he thought she was crazy. She'd seen the exact same expression in her brother's eyes when she'd attempted to explain it to him.

Turning away, she shook her head, swiping at the lone tear that escaped from her eye. He didn't understand. How could he? He hadn't been there to see. All those that had been were now dead or in prison.

Except for the three that hunted her still.

A shudder wracked her. Once more, her monster snarled and tested the edge of its cage, which thankfully held. "I'd like to go back now," she said, ice in her voice and her spine. "If you want to stay out here and try to find your family, I'm sure I can make my way back alone."

"I'll go with you."

She glanced at him, and a growl split the air in the underbrush nearby them. Instinctively, they both turned.

Something—a black blur—launched itself out of the bushes at them.

Kane snarled as his human form wavered. Hands up,

he caught the thing, holding it away from him as it made rumble sounds and bared its tiny, sharp, white teeth.

"A wolf pup," he said, sounding relieved. "One of the youngsters must have wandered away from the pack."

He held the squirming creature up, revealing a small, furry thing whose fierce show of bravado changed to wiggling, tail wagging, submissive friendliness.

"My nephew Reggie." Shaking his head, he set the puppy on the ground. It sat, panting, tongue lolling.

"Your mother is going to be very upset with you," Kane admonished. "You may as well change back to a boy."

Head down, the pup slunk back into the bushes, apparently to do exactly that.

"I thought young children weren't able to shape-shift yet," Lilly said.

"That's right, they can't." Kane nodded. "But he's not that young. I don't know if you noticed, but the smaller kids didn't accompany everyone into the forest. One of the parents stayed back to watch them. Usually in order to change, one has to be at least a preteen. Reggie's twelve."

As she and Lucas had been the first time. Lilly had never forgotten the first time she'd changed. She and her twin brother had been amazed and excited. They'd spent the first few years learning what their wolf selves could do. Thinking back, she was surprised they'd been able to keep it secret for as long as they had. Especially given the depth of Jacob Gideon's hatred for what he called demons.

A fierce longing seized her. How she wished she could simply step away, shed her clothing, drop to the ground and change into a wolf. Like she and Lucas used to do when they were teenagers. Back then, she'd found joy in the other part of her.

No so much now. Because her wolf had been distorted, ruined, until the beast had become a monster of death and ugliness. Changing no longer brought happiness, just agony and rage.

The thing inside her snarled, feeling her hatred. She snarled right back. She wanted it gone and her wolf returned. Now. Being among Kane's family, this town, a group of other people who were like her, who *celebrated* what they were, made her long to be able to share in their joy.

Fists curled so tightly her fingernails dug into her palms, she tried to move, to break away from Kane so she could make a run for the cabin.

Instead, Kane grabbed her arm. Startled, she rounded on him, letting down her inner guard for just a fraction of a second. A crack but enough for her monster to try to slip through.

Again her bones began to lengthen and shift painfully. She screamed, a shrill cry of pain.

"Lilly." Hauling her against him, he put his face so close to hers that his breath tickled her cheek. "Sweetheart, it's all right. I won't let anything happen to you."

Barely conscious, she moaned. She couldn't let her beast hurt him. She wouldn't. With everything that she was, she hung on to this thought, clinging to him.

"Get me inside," she managed to croak.

Just like that, he scooped her up in his arms and, leaving the picnic basket behind, headed back the way they'd originally come.

Chapter 10

Once he reached the cabin, he stopped, breathing hard. Lilly had gone so still in his arms, he feared she'd lost consciousness.

Carefully, he set her down in the porch chair. Though she slumped a little to the side, her amazing blue eyes were open, though fixed on nothing.

"Lilly?" Keeping his movements slow and gentle, he stroked her cheek. "Are you okay?"

She blinked, stirring as though awakening after a deep sleep. "Hey, Kane." A tiny frown creased her brow. She gasped and sat up, remembering. "Did I…"

"No. You did not."

Heaving a sigh of relief, she stood, appearing shaky. "I'm sorry I ruined your picnic."

"You didn't." He managed a smile, aware he couldn't reveal how badly she'd worried him. "We got to eat, that's the important part."

"What about the champagne? And the basket?"

He shrugged. "I left it in the woods. I'll go back and get it later."

"Maybe you'd better get it now. You don't want a bunch of drunken wild animals roaming your land." Her tentative smile made him realize she was trying to joke with him.

"It's almost dark," he told her. "Why don't we get you inside."

"And then you'll go retrieve it?"

Holding the door open, he stood aside to let her pass. "I don't know if I should leave you here by yourself."

She waved away his concern. "The danger has passed. I'll be fine. In fact, if you want to join your family on their hunt, go ahead. I'm just going to clean up and read some before I go to bed."

"No," he said, more to dispel the instant flash of carnal images at the thought of her going to bed. "I'll run out and get the basket and the bottle and be right back. Shouldn't take me more than a couple of minutes."

One elegant shoulder lifted in a shrug. Even this, he found sensual.

"Suit yourself," she said, barely hiding a yawn. "I'm going to go change into something more comfortable."

The old, tired line took on new meaning when she said it in that silky, sensual voice of hers. For a second he forgot what he was about to do and simply stood, staring at her.

She took a step back, making him realize the raw desire had most likely shown in his face.

"I'll be right back," he said brusquely, and then turned and headed right back out the door before he did something he was going to regret.

He could only hope like hell he had himself under control by the time he got back. He'd pocketed the flashlight, so he used that to retrace their earlier steps.

Once he'd gone deeper into the woods, the tell-tale signs of his family's hunt revealed exactly how close they'd come to him and Lilly. They'd killed something large, a deer from the looks of it, and dragged the carcass away. The blood-stains and bits of bone testified to the fact that they'd already begun to feed.

He had no idea where they were now, but he couldn't smell or hear them. Oh, he could follow the scent of the deer, but right now he just wanted to get the damn basket and champagne and get back to Lilly.

He found everything where he'd dropped it, though the champagne had run out of the bottle into the ground. Gathering it all together, he hurried back to the cabin.

As he approached, the yellow light beaming from the windows appeared welcoming. His heart—*dammit*—started to pound as he pictured Lilly in whatever "get into something comfortable" meant to her. Though she'd probably been talking about a T-shirt and jeans, his imagination took him to some other interesting outfits.

More proof that he was acting like a fool.

Opening the front door, he stopped just inside. Curled up on the couch, Lilly appeared engrossed in one of the books on Shifter history he'd given her.

She looked up, her slow smile taking his breath away. "This is good stuff," she said, brandishing the book. "I had no idea. I wish I could share this with Lucas."

"I'm sure your brother has learned a little about his heritage," he said, smiling back. "But in case he hasn't, we can always let him borrow it."

This seemed to reassure her. "Thanks."

"Are you ready to call it a night and try and get some sleep?"

She stood, absently running her fingers thought her long, luxurious wealth of hair. Remaining motionless for a moment, she seemed to struggle with her own emotions. "I don't know what happened out there," she began.

"No worries," he reassured her, aware he had his own struggles to face. "And no pressure, either."

Finally, she nodded and looked up, a grateful smile curving lips that begged for his kiss. Again, he had to shut his thoughts down. He had to figure out how to stop wanting her, but that was his problem, not hers.

"There's more I want to teach you," he continued. "In addition to the basic self-defense moves we've practiced, I want to teach you how to feel comfortable with a gun."

She eyed him, not protesting, despite her uncertain expression. "I'm not sure I can—"

"You'll do fine," he assured her.

Still she seemed doubtful. "How do you know these things? I mean, you said you were a veterinarian by trade."

"And a Pack Protector. I'm in the reserves. Just like the U.S. military. And I received extensive training." He smiled. "Plus I occasionally teach a woman's self-defense course in Fort Worth."

Nodding, she appeared impressed, though he found her poker-faced expression difficult to read.

"Where do you go to shoot a gun? Are we driving to a shooting range or something?"

"Nope. The nearest shooting range is fifty miles away," he told her. "There's a meadow where I used to go at sunrise to do my tai chi. It's big and flat. We'll set up some targets and shoot there."

A worried frown creased her brow. "When?" she asked.

"We'll play it by ear. Maybe tomorrow morning. Pretty early, before the heat of the day sets in."

Lilly lay awake in her bed long after she'd turned out the light. An entire new world had opened up for her since

Kane had taken her away from Seattle. Remembering her performance in the self-defense training, she felt a flush of pride.

A gun was a different matter. She wasn't sure how she felt about Kane's desire that she learn to handle one. She decided to simply, as Kane had put it, play it by ear.

And thinking of Kane, with his large, capable hands on her body, she became aware of a low thrum of desire. She finally fell asleep aching with need.

That night, instead of pleasant dreams, the old night-mares returned. She found herself back in Sanctuary, strapped to the metal laboratory table as the doctors came at her with needles and knives.

Somewhere in the dark of the night she awoke gasping, drenched in perspiration. She knew they'd come for her in darkness. Lying in her bed, alone and aching for Kane, she felt a frisson of fear. Who knew how these acolytes of the church of Sanctuary would manage to find her and worse, what they wanted to do to her. Had she been slated for death, a decree given by the man who'd claimed to be her father, while he served time in prison?

He'd certainly been furious enough for that.

Grabbing her small flashlight, she got out of the bed and opened her door, taking care to move quietly so she wouldn't disturb Kane.

Straight through the living room she went, unlocking the front door and stepping outside on to the front porch. She dropped into the chair, breathing deeply of the fresh night air. The waning moon provided enough light that she was able to turn off her flashlight.

At first, the crickets had gone silent when she emerged. They started up again in full force, which made her smile. She felt the tension leach out of her, enjoying the energy of nature. For the first time since she'd arrived in Leaning

Tree, she didn't allow the monster inside her to ruin the moment. She'd suffered enough in the past and now, thanks to Kane, she'd begun to step outside of her shell. She liked the flush of confidence learning self-defense had given, liked even more the heady sensuality she experienced when she was around Kane.

As if thinking about him had summoned him, the front door creaked open and Kane emerged. He had a serious case of bed head, which somehow made him look edgy and even more sexy.

"Hey," he greeted her, taking the chair next to hers. "You couldn't sleep, either?"

She gave him a rueful smile. "Oh, I could sleep. It was the nightmares that got me up."

When he nodded rather than pressing her for details, she silently thanked him. Reliving the terrors of those dreams wasn't pleasant, whether awake or asleep.

"We need to talk," he said, his deep voice serious. "I'm coming to understand that there's a lot more to you than I, or anyone else, realizes."

"I warned you I was messed up." She tried to keep it light, and failed miserably. "Fifteen years of captivity will do that to a person."

He took her hand, stunning her into temporary silence. "It was more than just captivity, I know. You mentioned they experimented on you."

Her nod was the only answer she could manage.

"Do you know if they were…successful with any of the experiments?"

"Successful?" The concept was so foreign to her, the word might almost have been in another language. "I know what they wanted to do with me." And what they'd tried to turn her into. She thought of what the doctors had called the Siren, and realized, yes, they'd succeeded. At least in that.

As if she'd spoken out loud, he leaned closer. "Lilly, I need you to tell me what happened to me when you sang."

Once, she would have hung her head. In fact, the person she used to be would have stammered out an apology. But this was not her fault. None of it was. So she lifted her chin and looked Kane directly in the eyes.

"I don't know." She shrugged, refusing to allow herself to feel dejected. "It had to be because of what they did to me at Sanctuary. I don't understand all the technical aspects. I just know they tried to make modification after modification to me. To my DNA, my body, my spirit and my beast. If they could have figured out a way to get to my soul, I have no doubt they would have."

Still holding her hand, he nodded, waiting for her to continue.

She shrugged, refusing to give in to her embarrassment. "I don't know how or why, but apparently when I sing, my voice is like the mythical sirens', compelling men. As it did you."

Narrow-eyed, he stared. "Then why can't I remember? Even if you could make me do something, you shouldn't be able to make me forget."

Now she did look down, knowing how much this proud, strong man would hate what he'd momentarily become under her spell. "I don't know. But you kissed me." Her face heated, which meant she was most likely a fiery red. "And you wanted to do more, but I was able to stop you."

"Stop me? You say that like I tried to force myself on you or something."

She let her silence be her answer.

His lowered brows told her what he thought of that.

Watching him as he wrestled with this knowledge actually brought her physical pain, low under her breastbone. Because that sensation felt unbearably uncomfortable, she yanked her hand free, pushed herself up out of the chair and went back inside the cabin, leaving him alone on the porch.

Still trying to make sense of her words, Kane didn't react. He was too busy trying to figure out what the hell had happened when she sang. Nothing she'd said made any sense. Even if her singing could somehow intensify the desire that already simmered constantly in his veins, how could her voice make him lose all memory of what he'd done?

She'd hinted that he'd tried to force himself on her.

No, no way. He wasn't that kind of man. He didn't force women to do anything, not ever.

Too restless for sleep, he got up and followed her back into the cabin.

She stood in the kitchen, her back to him, the lights still off.

"You know, you're eventually going to have to change." As he spoke, he flicked on the light switch.

She spun around to face him. He didn't miss the spark of panic that flashed into her eyes.

"Why?" Crossing her arms, she lifted her chin. "Are you punishing me now for what happened when I sang?"

Shocked, he recoiled. "Of course not."

"Then why? I don't see the need."

"Lilly." He softened his voice, aware that what he had to say next might be news to her. "Every Shifter has to change periodically. If they don't, they'll go insane."

To his surprise, she greeted this statement with a short bark of humorless laughter. "Insane? I think that ship already sailed. It's too late for me, Kane."

"Don't say that." He couldn't help himself; even though she wasn't looking for sympathy, he pulled her into his arms. Once he had her, inhaling the sweet scent of her freshly shampooed hair, he wondered how he'd ever let her go.

Lilly decided that for him. Pushing him away, she fixed him with a glare. "I'm not joking."

"I didn't think you were. But still, you're a long way from the kind of insanity I'm talking about."

From the way she cocked her head, he could tell she didn't believe him.

"I've seen it," he continued quietly, aching now that he no longer had her in his arms. "People driven so mad they were reduced to rabid beasts, foaming at the mouth and tearing at their own skin with their fingernails. And not only were they a danger to themselves, but to others."

Something in his voice must have gotten through to her. Sorrow softened her expression as she relaxed her stance. "How is it possible that you've seen such things?"

"The Protectors," he told her, remembered horrors still clutching him. "Once, not too long ago, these Shifters were called Ferals. Those that lived outside society for whatever reason. Our task was to hunt them and bring them in."

"For what?" Now she watched him as though she expected another monster to emerge. "Please tell me you didn't experiment and torture them like the people of Sanctuary did."

"Of course not." He sighed. "This was a dark period in our organization's history. Corrupt and evil men had gained power, and they overstepped the bounds of decency. But Protectors revolted against them, because by our very name we knew we'd been charged with Protecting our own kind, nothing more, nothing less."

She still hadn't moved. "What did you do to them, these Ferals?"

"They were offered a chance to be rehabilitated." This

said, he prayed she didn't ask about the others, who refused this offer.

"Define rehabilitated."

"They were given medical and mental-health care and once healed, were trained to reassimilate themselves back into society."

Staring past her, he remembered the chaos, the unnecessary bloodshed, and the brave revolt. "Now our organization has been cleaned up. The corrupt officials were arrested and stood trial."

Though she nodded, her gaze still appeared troubled. "What about the ones that refused?"

Crap.

"Refused?" he asked carefully. "That was an extremely rare occurrence."

"Still, it happened, right?"

Reluctant, he nodded.

"So what did you do to them?"

He wanted to balk, wished he could lie. But the one thing above all others that Lilly deserved was honesty, whether she liked the answer or not.

"The directive given at the time was extermination."

"What?" Clearly shocked, she recoiled. "You...you killed them?"

"I didn't, not personally. I was one of the ones who refused. I was put on furlough while they considered whether or not to put me up for court-marshal."

To his disbelief, she came close and put her small hand on his arm. "Thank you," she said, confusing him.

"For what? I wrestled with my conscience back then. I respect the Society of Pack Protectors. I believe in them, always have, even then. You don't know how closely I came to blindly following orders."

"But you didn't." Her dulcet voice hummed with pleasure. "Because you're not that kind of man."

In the end, he hadn't been. He and many others had refused to brutally slaughter the Ferals. Some had been mentally ill and were able to get help. Others...they'd preferred to live in the wild, outside the radar. As long as they weren't a danger to others, the new directive had been to let them be.

"Thank you," she said, pressing a soft kiss against his throat.

At the gesture, desire flared, thickening his blood and his body. He half turned, aching to capture her mouth with his. But when he saw the tears trembling on the edge of her eyelashes, he managed to rein himself in.

"What's wrong?" Gruff voiced, he pulled her in for a platonic hug, angling his body so she wouldn't feel the strength of his need for her.

"I can't stop thinking of all the ones who lost their lives." Her voice caught. "I wonder if they suffered, the way we suffered at Sanctuary."

"We?" He watched her closely. One of the things he and her brother, Lucas, had wondered had been how much Lilly had known about the others. She hadn't been the only Shifter Jacob Gideon had captured for his barbaric practices. He'd been taking children, apparently believing their young spirits would be easy to bend to his will.

But she shook her head and wiped at her eyes with the back of her hand. "Enough of this talk," she declared.

"Agreed. We circled around what I originally wanted to talk to you about."

Her quick nod told him she was completely aware of that.

"You need to change."

She sighed. "You never give up, do you?"

"Not when it comes to keeping you safe and healthy."

Head down, she didn't immediately reply. When she lifted her head, the stark agony in her face made his breath catch in his throat.

"I'm a monster."

Once again he pulled her close, smoothing her hair and wishing he knew the best way to reassure her. "You're not. That's Jacob Gideon's brainwashing speaking. We're Shape-shifters. Humans and wolves. Not monsters."

"Maybe you are." Leaning back, she looked up into his eyes and shook her head. "But not me. I'm not normal."

He knew he had to try a different tack. "How do you know? Have you actually seen yourself, like in a mirror?"

"No." Briefly, she closed her eyes. "You don't understand, Kane. They had me change once, there in the lab. I must have blacked out because I don't remember anything about what happened. But when I changed into a human again, one of their doctors and two lab technicians were dead. The carnage was unbelievable."

"How do you know it was you who killed them?"

Mouth twisting, she waved his question away. "Who else? Those that survived, they saw. Somehow, they'd managed to get me chained up."

"So you took their word for it? How do you know they didn't stage this, to make you think it was you?"

An utterly flat and lifeless look came into her eyes. "Because, Kane. Because when I came to, chained and shackled to that damn laboratory table, I was covered in blood."

He didn't know what to say. He supposed, given time, he could come up with dozens of reasonable explanations, other arguments, but not now, not at this instant. Instead, he held her, aching and wishing he could discover a way to help her find herself.

Only then, could the healing begin.

"How about this?" He kept his voice level, as if what

he was about to ask was perfectly logical and reasonable. "How about I help you change?"

"Are you crazy?" Chest heaving, she shook her head. "There's no way. I couldn't risk it. What if I hurt you?"

"You won't. Your beast is fighting you. I've seen it several times. Wouldn't it be much better—and safer—to manage the time and place of the change, rather than simply let your wolf self wrest control?"

While she appeared unconvinced, at least she still listened.

"Plus, once you let your wolf out, allow him to hunt and run and just be, he'll be sated and quiet. You'll get a much needed rest from constantly battling him."

This appealed to her, he could tell. She swallowed, quietly considering. "Maybe," she finally conceded, making him feel as if he'd won a huge victory. "If there were safeguards in place to ensure no harm would come to others."

"When?" Now that she'd agreed, he knew he had to keep pushing, or she'd overthink things and refuse.

"I don't know." She shot him a cross look. "Not right now."

"Why not?" he persisted. "The timing couldn't be any more perfect. It's the middle of the night, no one else is around, and the weather is comfortable."

Her eyes widened. "Are you serious?"

"Yes. In fact, there are a couple of caves up on some cliffs about a half mile away. We can go there."

Biting her lip, she swallowed. "Do you have chains or rope?"

"What for?"

"Restraints." Her chin came up. "You've got to make sure I'm restrained, tied up. Otherwise, once I give that monster full rein, he could go after you or your family."

Though he felt 99 percent convinced that the monster

part was a product of the intensive conditioning she'd received and thus, all in her mind, he nodded. "I have rope. Though I'm not sure I like the idea of tying you up."

Her chin came up. "That's the only way I'll agree to this."

"Then rope it is. I have some in the trunk of my Vette." He took her arm. "You can come with me and get it."

Despite his gentle prodding, she still didn't move. When she looked up and met his gaze, the stark terror in her eyes made his heart ache. "It's going to be all right," he said. "I promise."

"I'm not sure I can do this." But this time, when he took a step toward the door, she moved with him.

Outside, he kept her close while he retrieved the rope from his trunk. Doing this made him feel vaguely criminal, and also vaguely kinky, like they were going into the woods for a bit of S and M.

Pushing away these thoughts, along with his own misgivings, he took her hand firmly in his and, using a small flashlight, led her unerringly along a path, past the small grove where he and his brothers often went to change, and up a rocky hill.

"Here we are," he said, trying to sound as normal as possible. "Check out these caves. Bats live there during the day, but they're out hunting right now."

She tugged her hand free. "Let me borrow your flashlight." Once he handed it to her, she turned a slow circle, shining the light into the mouth of the nearest cave. Next, she began walking, appearing to study the surrounding trees. "This one," she finally said, indicating a sturdy oak.

At first he wasn't sure what she meant. Then, glancing down at the rope in his hands, he understood. She wanted him to tie her to that tree.

Though he'd sort of promised, he still had to try to dis-
suade her. "Lilly, I really think—"

"No." Voice sharp, she cut him off. "That's a deal-
breaker. Either I'm tied up, or I don't change."

Again he looked down at the rope. "But how? If I tie
you up when you're human, when you're body becomes a
wolf, the ropes will simply fall off."

"Not if you tied it around my neck."

Horrified, he started to protest. This time, she held up
her hand to stop him, as if she already knew what he would
say.

"It's no worse than a dog on a leash." Though she tried
to sound nonchalant, the waver in her voice let him know
how she really felt. Still absolutely terrified.

He wanted to reassure her, but knew there were no words
capable of doing that, so he kept his silence.

"Give me that." Taking the rope out of his hands, she
looped it around her neck. He was relieved to see she didn't
make the type of collar that would choke her. Instead, she
tied off a circle, just loose enough to accommodate the
neck of a wolf, knotting it securely before handing the
rope back to him.

"Tie it to that tree, please," she said. "And make sure
you get a couple of good knots."

For some reason, seeing that rough rope around the
creamy skin of her delicate neck, he couldn't make his
feet move.

Then she tugged on the rope. "Kane? If you want to do
this, please get that rope tied up before I completely lose
my nerve. I think I'm pretty strong once I become—" she
swallowed hard "—the other thing."

This galvanized him into action. "It's called a wolf,
Lilly," he chided her with a teasing smile in the hopes of
reassuring her.

Taking the rope, he wrapped it around the tree and made sure to leave her enough room to move around before tying a secure knot. He hated the idea of confining her wolf but knew this was necessary this first time, until she could see there was nothing to be afraid of.

It did cross his mind to wonder, briefly, what would happen if she was right and the horrible experiments and torture she'd endured had somehow harmed her wolf self.

He'd deal with that if it happened. He'd consult the Pack Healer, Samantha. For right now, he didn't need any negative thoughts. He had to believe this would work. He didn't know what he'd do if it didn't.

After she'd inspected the rope and was satisfied, she wiped her hands on the front of her jean shorts and faced him. "What now?"

"With my family, we strip, drop to the ground and shapeshift."

"Strip?" Her question came out a nervous squeak. "I don't know if I can do that."

"If you don't, you'll rip your clothes." He tried to move past the searing image of her naked. "Would you rather I changed first? That way I'll be wolf before you have to undress."

Exhaling loudly, she nodded. "Yes, thank you. You change to wolf, and then...I will, too."

Though he could scarcely see her in the shadowed forest, he could hear the sincerity in her shaky voice.

"I won't let anything happen to you, Lilly," he promised. "Trust me on that."

Chapter 11

Though terror had Lilly shaking so hard she could hardly keep her teeth from chattering, she was still curious to see Kane shape-shift into a wolf.

She held her breath, trying not to stare as he removed first his T-shirt, then his khaki shorts. He showed no embarrassment as he stood before her clad in nothing but boxer shorts, but then why should he? The man had the kind of broad-shouldered, narrow-waisted body seen only in athletes and movie stars. His muscles rippled in the partial moonlight as he moved with a nonchalant grace a few feet away.

Slowly, as she watched, he stripped off his last scrap of clothing, making her mouth go dry. Then, while she unabashedly stared, he dropped to the ground on all four legs and began the change.

She held her breath. Not since she and her brother had shape-shifted as teens had she witnessed another person change into a wolf. Fascinated, she grimaced as his bones began to lengthen. A myriad of bright floating sparkles appeared around him, bathing him in a flickering glow.

She moved a tiny bit closer. Though the flickering lights were beautiful, she needed to see past them to Kane. But the swirl of colors was so thick, it was impossible to see. Still, she tried. As if her thoughts had become movement, the sparkles vanished. Lilly gasped out loud. A huge wolf stood where Kane had been.

The majestic black-coated beast padded toward her. Instinctively, she moved back. When she did, the wolf paused, lifting one large paw and cocking his head inquisitively.

Kane. This was Kane. She made herself move closer, her heart trip-hammering in her chest. Kane. Just Kane.

Finally, just a foot away, she stopped, reaching out with a tentative movement and tangling her fingers in the luxurious black fur. He allowed this, holding himself with a regal bearing that so much reminded her of the human Kane, she nearly laughed out loud.

Wolf Kane made a sound, a cross between a bark and a growl. Somehow she understood. He was merely reminding her that her turn had come to shape-shift.

Panic rose like bile in her throat, choking her so badly she almost clawed at the rope around her neck, wanting it off. No, that wasn't really her, it had to be the monster inside her, trying to trick her into doing something foolish and setting it loose.

At the thought, the knowledge of what she was about to attempt, her beast broke free. This time, the change easily overpowered her human will, though maybe this was because she had already anticipated this and permitted it to happen.

Battling to slow the change down for a few seconds, she ripped off her clothes and, imitating Kane, dropped to the ground. Just in time, for the instant she dug her nails into the damp forest dirt, the change initiated in earnest.

Ahh! It hurt. Was it supposed to hurt so much?

As her bones lengthened, she tried to look for the same sparkling light show as Kane's, but the pain became too intense for her to do anything but try to keep it from overwhelming her.

Gradually, the agony subsided and she rose up, wondering what kind of thing she'd become. Sniffing her furred leg, she smelled her own scent, which her brain told her was wolf, like Kane.

Even better, she felt like herself, in full possession of her facilities. Not crazy. Not full of a murderous rage. With pleasure, she sniffed the dead leaves and earth underneath her, amazed at the myriad of smells. Her lupine nose had her human one beat.

She sat. Glancing down at her belly, she believed she had become a wolf. Not distorted or twisted, but a true wolf, similar to Kane, though much less massive. Her soft gray fur glowed in the shadowy light. Pleased, she thought it kind of pretty.

Kane made a chuffing sound, drawing her attention. Full of joy, she looked up, caught sight of him, and then tried to rush toward him.

When she reached the end of her rope, the resulting tug jerked her off her feet. A yelp escaped her. Stunned, she staggered back to her feet, neck burning.

Kane shook his massive head and lay down. Again the firefly lights arrived, and then human Kane had returned. He padded over to her, his fingers working at the knots. A few minutes later, he'd managed to untie her.

As soon as he had, he went back to his spot, got down again on all fours and shape-shifted back into a wolf while she waited.

Barely able to contain her excitement, the instant he had regained his wolf shape, she rushed him, bowing playfully before nipping him on the hindquarters and running off.

They chased each other, rolling and play biting. He tore off through the woods and she followed.

When he slid to an abrupt stop, she plowed into him. Shaking her off, he nudged her, making her turn. The sliver of moon shone in a small pond, the still water peaceful.

He nudged her again, as though trying to make her understand. As she edged forward, she realized the pond made a pretty darn good mirror. Standing at the edge, if she leaned her neck out, she could see herself pretty clearly.

A wolf. Stunned, she looked again. She couldn't believe it. When she looked in the water, a pretty silver wolf looked back at her. She'd become a wolf. Exactly like she was supposed to. Nothing more, nothing less. No monster. No rage-filled killing machine. Which meant they'd either lied to her, or injected her with something to bring on hallucinations and madness.

Though either scenario was possible, she'd put money on the second.

But what about the deaths? She'd seen the blood and the bodies with her own two eyes. Had it all been staged? Or had someone else done the killing and made it appear as though it had been her?

Kane nudged her, his plumed tail high over his back. Then he took off running, appearing as if he was laughing over his shoulder at her.

For one frozen second, she stood, uncertain. Finally, her heart light, she took off after him, giving chase.

They ran and ran and then, tongues lolling, they rested. Finally, stealing into the nighttime forest, they hunted.

By the time they returned to the clearing, the sky had begun to lighten, signaling dawn would soon arrive. Sated and more relaxed than she'd felt...well, since she'd been fifteen, Lilly lay belly down on the damp forest floor. Next to her, the beautiful black wolf that was Kane watched her through golden wolf eyes.

This time, though she longed to remain a wolf a little longer, she initiated the change first. To her surprise, her wolf acquiesced readily. This time, the shift back to human wasn't painful. Instead, her body welcomed it.

Once she could see normally again, she blinked, automatically looking for Kane. While she was becoming human, he'd changed, too. Naked, he lay propped on one elbow and watched her.

"Welcome back." The sound of his husky voice sent a shudder of heat straight to her center. "Did you enjoy yourself?"

Mouth dry, she could only nod. Her entire body ached for his touch and she had to fight not to crawl over and climb on top of him.

"I...um." Licking her lips, she closed her eyes, hoping to blot out the temptation of his gorgeously naked body.

To her shock, he laughed. The masculine sound only served to make her want him more. Desire was foreign to her, something she'd never thought she'd feel since while at Sanctuary she'd not only been tortured and experimented on, but raped, as well.

This...feeling seemed about as far from that as her wolf did from the monster she'd pictured.

"I forgot to warn you," he said, as she kept her eyes screwed shut. "Most Shifters are used to it, but for whatever reason, changing back to human form makes us horny."

Horny? Great.

"This...didn't happen to me when I changed before."

"You were only fifteen. The desire part doesn't happen until you're fully grown."

Desire part. To her fogged and overheated brain, all she could think about was what part of him she wanted inside of her. She'd been brave enough to try what had been her greatest fear. Surely she could be bold enough to claim her reward.

Slowly, she opened her eyes, looking into his gaze. "I want you."

He swallowed, his gray eyes going dark. "I want you, too, but that's just the effects of changing. No worries. I'm used to it. I can control it."

Inhaling, she stood, letting him get a good look at her naked body, erect nipples and all. She crossed the distance between them, standing over him and speaking clearly and distinctly. "I don't want you to control it. I'm on fire, Kane. I need you."

His sharp inhalation of breath was the only sound he made as he stared up at her. With his gaze at first riveted on her face, he let it slowly roam over her, soft as a caress. The tingling in her nether regions made her melt inside.

He stood, his look a smoldering flame, and turned. He kept his back to her and slowly moved a few steps away, breaking her heart.

"You don't want me?" To her horror, she realized she was on the verge of tears. Even worse, his apparent rejection of her did nothing to lessen her craving for him.

"Lilly, I want you so badly I can hardly walk."

Though she wanted to, she didn't believe him. Her disbelief must have shown in her face. He shook his head.

"Look," he said simply, turning so she could see him, all of him, but most especially his massive erection.

She tried to throttle the explosive desire that consumed her, but her knees had gone weak. She could scarcely breathe, but somehow she took a step or two toward him, making a cry of desire low in her throat.

Pulse pounding, heart jolting, body aching and melting, she threw herself at him, trusting him to catch her, thrilling to the feel of the long, hard length of him pressing into her belly.

A ripple of excitement made her shiver as she felt him give what had to be an involuntary push against her.

"Lilly," he rasped. "Please stop."

Heady with power, buzzing with desire, she ignored him. Using her womanly instincts, she rubbed up against him, like a cat hungry for cream.

His reaction was swift, and violent. Grabbing her by both upper arms, he tried to hold her still. "Seriously. Stop."

"I don't want to," she purred, raw wanting making her dizzy. She inhaled sharply as he pulled her roughly against him.

"Don't start something you can't finish," he grated.

She had a second of misgiving as he let her feel the full weight of his arousal. Trembling, she clung to him as he moved against her. He no longer used his hands merely to hold her in place, but to caress her. Her skin tingled everywhere he touched her.

When he cupped her breast, her heart lurched. Body already throbbing, she gasped in delight, welcoming the strength and heat of his flesh as he surged against her.

A moan escaped her, the heat building inside of her rushed to every spot his hands caressed.

Belatedly, she began to hesitantly mimic the way he touched her, thrilling the muscles rippling under his firm flesh. He groaned as she slid her hand down his pecs, about to dare to go lower when his hand captured her, stopping her.

"Lilly, I—"

Raising on tiptoe, she pressed her mouth against his.

When he responded to her as though starving, sending spirals of ecstasy through her, she knew they both were lost.

She curled into his body, went with him as he lowered her to the ground. As he kissed her, their tongues mated, and she writhed against him, wanting more.

Savage, intense, his eyes glittered with heat as his body imprisoned her in a pulse of growing arousal. "Are you very, very sure?" he asked, as he kissed the hollow at the base of her throat, making her shiver.

She wasn't sure of anything, other than the fact that she wanted this man more than she'd ever wanted anything in her entire life. Caressing the tendons in his muscular shoulders, she let her body answer for her.

He entered her with one swift movement, the sheer size of him filling her completely, making her cry out. His hard body fit with hers, as if they'd been made for each other.

And when he moved...the heavens and the earth moved with him.

Tangled together, bodies slick with passion, he moved, and she moved with him, taking the full length of him, her body clenching with each powerful thrust.

Drowning, soaring, all at once. They danced, mated. Her blood pounded with passion, nearly shattering her. All at once, at the same time, she was on fire, she was on ice, as he made love to her.

And then...and then...gasping in sweet, perfect agony, she felt a shower of sparks explode as her body shuddered around him, tightening as if she wanted to wring every last ounce of passion out of him.

He cried out, a sound of triumph, of pleasure and of pain.

She held him while he emptied his essence into her, held him while their heartbeats slowed and their breathing quieted.

Savoring the scent of their lovemaking, she wanted to

capture this instant forever, to take out and look at in those dark, lonely times that were sure to come.

"This has been the absolutely, most perfect day," she told him, meaning it.

He groaned, though he didn't push her away. "I'm already having regrets."

"Regrets?" She refused to let his words hurt. "Don't you dare. You've given me the gift of my wolf self, and then this. We're both adults. There's nothing wrong with what we did and if you say there is, I just might have to smack you."

"You were vulnerable," he protested. "I shouldn't have taken advantage of you."

"Advantage?" Slowly she shook her head. "You've healed me. In more ways than you could ever imagine."

The bleak look in his eyes told her he refused to believe her. She knew that this time, she'd have to be strong, to keep him from beating himself up with guilt.

Gently, she slid out from under him and, brushing herself off, got to her feet. After a second, he did the same. Naked, they stood looking at each other. She drank in his male perfection with her gaze before taking a deep breath.

"Kane, all my body has known before today was abuse and pain. I've never…" She blushed as words momentarily failed her. Lifting her chin, she continued. "You showed me that two people can come together with pleasure and joy. Please don't try and take that away from me."

He made a strangled sound as he reached for her. This time, she evaded his grasp, wanting anything from him but his pity. "Come on." Turning her back to him, she snatched her clothes up from the ground. "Let's get dressed and go back to the cabin. If we're lucky, we might be able to get in a few hours of sleep."

Struck speechless, Kane wasn't sure what to make of this calmly assertive, and sexy, Lilly. He'd always known she'd eventually find an inner strength, but this sensual confident aspect of her wasn't something he'd anticipated so soon.

Though she'd assured him otherwise, he couldn't help but feel as though he'd taken advantage of her in a weakened state. He was supposed to be her Protector. He knew how the change back to human form made Shifters horny. Not only that, but he'd made love to her without protection. There could be a consequence. He stifled a groan. He should've taken precautions. Lilly had enough to deal with right now without having to handle an unexpected pregnancy.

Despite this possibility, she'd still claimed he'd given her a gift, when in fact it had been the other way around. He'd known lots of women in his lifetime and the sex had ranged from mediocre to fantastic. But this, this had been different. Not once with any of the others had he been even remotely tempted to call it *making love*.

Damn. Maybe he was the one in trouble, rather than Lilly.

Again he remembered her horrible imprisonment at Sanctuary. When he'd first seen her huddled in a metal bunk in a cold and damp basement, emaciated and filthy, he'd wanted to find the people who'd done this to her and make them pay. Only the fact that he was there as a professional law enforcement officer had kept him rational.

And now this. While he'd guessed she'd probably been raped while a prisoner at Sanctuary, hearing her confirm it in the same breath as she discussed the physical act they'd just shared, had been disconcerting, to say the least.

When they reached the cabin, she disappeared inside without a backward glance. He followed more slowly, wishing he could find the right words to straighten this mess out.

To his surprise, when he went in, Lilly waited for him in the kitchen.

"We need to talk," she said, getting two glasses of tap water and placing them on the countertop.

Instead of trepidation, he felt relief. "Yes, we do."

"I'm a wolf," she said. "An honest-to-heavens wolf. Not some sort of monster."

He nodded. "Yes, you are. And now you can shape-shift whenever you want."

"And I don't have to worry about anyone else getting hurt. What I don't understand is how the crazies at Sanctuary had me convinced I was some sort of monster."

Some of the tension eased from him. Taking a long swallow of water, he sighed. "I'm still not sure what they were trying to do. What could they hope to accomplish by making you think you'd change into some sort of fire-breathing dragon type thing?"

She bit her lip, looking surprisingly vulnerable. "Yeah, but apparently they succeeded with the singing thing."

"I'm going to have you do that again, but only when someone else, preferably female, is here to help you. I want it videotaped."

"Why female?"

"So they won't be susceptible." He smiled at her, trying for gentle, but knowing he probably looked grim. Just the thought of some other man being compelled by her song and putting his hands on her...made Kane feel violent.

She yawned, making him feel contrite. Glancing at the clock on the wall, he saw it was after 5:00 a.m. "I didn't realize it was so late—or early. We stayed out a long time. Maybe you should just go ahead and try and get some rest."

Her gaze, so intensely blue, seemed bemused. "Oddly enough, I'm not tired. I'm more energized than anything else. What about you?"

"I'm going to make a pot of coffee," he told her, grinning. "You're welcome to join me."

"Sure." She grinned right back. He was pleased at the absence of the shadows that usually haunted her. While he wasn't foolish enough to think they'd all been vanquished, the events of that night had evidently gone a long way toward healing her.

As he made the coffee, she sat silently and watched him. He liked that she didn't feel the need to fill the silence with chatter. Once the coffee had started brewing, he turned and let his gaze drink her in. Despite just having made love to her, he felt the same tug of attraction. Pushing that away, he took a deep breath, telling himself to focus.

"Uh, Kane? There's one more thing we need to discuss."

The tiny tremble in her voice alerted him. "What?"

"I need to make sure you understand…" Hesitating, she swallowed, and then raised her chin and met his gaze. "Despite the sex, there can never be anything between us."

He wasn't prepared for the emotions that slammed into him. Shock and surprise, of course, but more than anything he wanted to deny the truth of her words, and prove to her that she was wrong. Completely wrong.

Instead, he tried rationality. "If you think it's because you've got too many issues, I want you to know—"

"No." Her blue eyes had gone cold. "I know you're willing to work with me on those, and I thank you for that. It's not you at all, it's me."

The clichéd break up line seemed totally out of place coming from her, especially since they'd never been a couple. Had they?

"I've spent half my life in captivity," she continued. "I've never learned how to be strong enough to live on my own. You've shown me that it's possible, and I owe you for that."

She *owed him?*

"But I can't start any kind of relationship." Her earnest voice seemed at odds with her frozen expression. He had the sense she might be retreating again, hiding behind an inner wall for her own protection. To keep herself from being hurt.

Or that might have been just wishful thinking on his part.

"That's fine," he heard himself say, managing to sound relatively normal. "I wasn't looking for a relationship anyways."

Though he'd begun believing he spoke only the truth, the instant he'd said it he realized it was the first time he'd ever lied to her.

"Thank goodness," she said, sounding relieved. She cleared her throat, keeping her gaze averted. "So what's on the agenda for us today?"

Normalcy. Good. Better to get back on track and minimize the danger of saying something he didn't mean to say.

"I'd planned for us to practice shooting today, but I think we'll do that another day." He cleared his throat. "I want us both to be well-rested and sharp."

She nodded, still appearing skittish, which irritated him more than it should have. "We can always take a nap."

Again, the images that flashed into his mind made him lose the capacity for speech. Though he knew she'd meant actually resting, all he could picture was the two of them, curled into each other on the bed. There were a lot of things he'd like to do with her, and sleeping was the least of them.

He swallowed hard, reached into the cupboard and pulled out a couple of mugs. Keeping himself occupied would help him get his libido settled down. He didn't know what it was about her, but Lilly affected him, arousing him with a single look of her long-lashed baby blues.

She accepted her coffee with a lopsided smile, making

him see he'd added powdered creamer and one sugar without even asking.

"Just the way I like it," she said, taking a small sip.

Together they watched as the sky outside the kitchen window began to lighten. He felt a sense of peace, something he usually only felt occasionally, and then only when he was around his family.

"Thank you." Her silken voice yanked him out of his introspection.

Finishing his first cup, he grabbed her nearly empty one and made them each a second. He knew he was enjoying this more than he should have, but he decided to just go with it.

"It's hard to believe you grew up here," she said. "What was it like?"

"Not much different than it is now." He chuckled. "My two brothers and I ganged up on my sister. We had the entire woods as a playground. We had tree forts and spent most of the summer days outside. It was a great place to grow up. What about you?"

The instant the question left his mouth, he wanted to call it back. "Sorry. I'm guessing you grew up at Sanctuary."

She nodded. "For as long as I can remember. Still, Lucas and I did the best we could to have some sort of normal life."

"Did you go to public school?"

A shadow crossed her face. "Yes, at least until eighth grade. We were outcasts at school anyway, and then Jacob decided to homeschool us, which essentially cut off all of our contact with the outside world. At least I had my brother."

The sharp rap on the front door startled them both. Glancing at her, he tried to hide the way he automatically tensed. Especially since dawn had barely broken.

"Wait here," Kane told her. Since there was no peephole,

he tried looking out the front window, but couldn't get a good view of the front porch. Deciding he was being too paranoid, he cracked open the front door.

"Morning." His brother Kyle looked as if he hadn't slept much either.

"Barely," Kane responded. "It's 6:00 a.m. What's going on? Are Mom and Pop okay?"

"Yeah, everyone's fine. I came because Muriel Redstone just called. I don't know if you remember her, but she works the front desk at the Value Five Motel. Wanted to know if we had room for a party of three."

"Okay." Opening the door wider to allow Kyle entrance, Kane led the way into the kitchen. "Coffee?"

"That would be wonderful." Accepting the steaming mug gratefully, Kyle drank with appreciation.

Kane and Lilly exchanged looks. Finally, Kane shrugged.

"So you came over to tell me Muriel referred a party of three? Isn't that pretty standard since we are the only other lodging in town?"

Setting his mug down on the counter, Kyle's expression turned intense. "Three people—think about it." When Kane didn't respond, Kyle rolled his eyes. "They're asking about a woman from Texas. Even showed Muriel a photo. From what she described, they're looking for Lilly."

Chapter 12

Kyle barely finished speaking when Kane exploded into action. Locating his cell phone, he dialed the emergency number for the Protectors and punched in the prearranged code. The instant that was done, he started to call Lilly's brother, then remembered it would only be 4:00 a.m. in Colorado.

When he looked up, both Kyle and Lilly were looking at him as if he'd lost his mind.

"Are you okay?" Kyle asked.

"Never been better." He flashed them both a savage grin. Adrenaline felt a thousand times superior to simply waiting for something to happen, as they'd been doing. Now that it had, he could deal with it and eliminate the threat. Exactly as he'd been trained.

"What did you just do?" Lilly asked, the tiny wrinkle between her eyes attesting to her worry.

Though he wanted to go to her, wrap her tightly in his

arms and assure her she'd be safe, he knew if he did, his brother would read too much into the reassuring gesture. He settled for what he hoped was a reassuring look.

"I activated the Protectors. I dialed a number and punched in a code. They'll send a team, incognito." Kane inclined his head at his brother. "There should be six and they'll be here before sunset. Can we make room for them?"

"I've got one cabin available." Looking bemused, Kyle scratched his chin. "Though I told Muriel we had no vacancies. I knew there was no way we wanted those three on our premises."

"So we don't know where they'll be staying?"

Kyle shrugged. "Who knows? Maybe, since there's no room at the inn, they'll just move on and leave us alone."

"I wouldn't count on that." Truth be told, Kane hoped they wouldn't. Once his colleagues swept in, they'd take care of everything, removing the threat that had hung over Lilly's pretty head ever since she'd been freed.

"Kane's right." Standing, Lilly walked to the front window and peeked through the blinds as if she expected to see them strolling up the path at any moment. "Not these people," she said, her tone flat and emotionless. "They don't give up so easily."

From her tone, he could tell she was remembering the unspeakable horrors the followers of Sanctuary had already visited up her.

His brother's opinion be damned. Kane crossed the room, went up behind her and wrapped her in his arms, holding her close. "Don't worry, I won't let them get anywhere near you."

"I'm not worried," she said, her stiff posture contradicting her words. Her heart beat a frantic tattoo under his palm.

Behind them, Kyle made a sound, low in his throat.

Kane turned to find his brother eyeing him, a concerned expression on his face.

"What?" Kane asked, even though he knew.

Kyle shook his head. "Never mind." Picking up his coffee, he drained the mug and set it back on the counter. "Thanks for the java. I'm heading back to the main house to enlist help getting that last cabin ready for our guests."

"Thanks, man." Though he didn't want to let Lilly go, Kane released her, taking a step back. She didn't turn from the window so, after a moment, Kane crossed to his brother, and walked with him out the door and onto the porch.

"I really appreciate this," Kane began.

"Yeah. You got a minute?" Kyle asked, his tone still pitched low. Serious. "There's something else I need to talk to you about."

Kane looked up, and the worried expression in his brother's gray eyes caused his gut to clench. "There's more, isn't there?"

"Not about the three strangers. I told you everything I know about them. This has nothing to do with them."

"Then what's wrong? Kathy's all right, isn't she?" Their sister and her husband had tried for a baby for a very long time. If something happened to mess this up, Kane wasn't sure how Kathy would take it.

"Kathy's fine, as far as I know." Kyle waved his concern away. "Calm down. Let's go for a walk."

Glancing back at the cabin, Kane shook his head. "Not right now. I really don't want to go too far from Lilly. She's freaking out."

"I understand." Kyle glanced at the still closed door and grimaced. "But I don't think you want her to hear what I have to say. How about we go to the edge of the yard?"

"Okay." Perplexed, Kane fell into step beside his brother.

"Are you sure this couldn't wait? We've got enough going on right now as it is."

With a shrug, Kyle conceded the point. "It probably could. But I can't think of a better time for us to discuss it."

Kane nodded. "Fine. Though I can't imagine what it could be, I'm game. Go ahead."

"Just a minute." When they reached the spot where the circular drive went into the main path, Kyle stopped. "I wanted to talk to you about Lilly," he said, his expression tight. He held up his hand before Kane could speak. "Now you might tell me to go to hell, or that it's none of my business, but I feel I have to speak my piece."

Though Kane nodded, he had no idea what his brother could possibly have to say about Lilly. "Go ahead."

"From what you told me, you promised Lilly's brother you'd be her bodyguard, right? That you'd protect her from whatever people are searching for her?"

"True." As they continued walking, taking the trail up to the high ridge where as boys they'd often played, Kane thought he knew where Kyle was going. "Look, until now no one has surfaced looking for her, but believe me, if these three who just showed up are who I think they are, they're extremely dangerous. The Protectors have been actively searching for them. We need to bring those nut jobs from Sanctuary in—dead or alive. But I promise you, Lilly will never be in any danger."

"I don't doubt that." Kyle shot a sideways glance toward him, his gray eyes troubled. "This isn't about you keeping Lilly safe from them."

"Okay." More puzzled than ever, Kane eyed his brother. "Then what?"

"This is about keeping her safe from you."

"From me?" Stunned, Kane stared. "I'm not sure what you mean." But he knew. Deep down inside, the sinking in his gut added weight to the possibility Kyle was right. He'd already taken advantage once. Still, he felt he had to protest. Kyle didn't know about that. He couldn't. "You're not making sense."

"Bear with me and let me finish. You also told me you wanted to train her how to be self-sufficient, how to take care of herself once she is on her own."

Again stumped, Kane nodded. "And I am. She's had a self-defense lesson, and I'm planning to teach her how to feel comfortable with a pistol. We've only just gotten started, but by the time she leaves here, I'm confident Lilly will be able to handle herself in any situation."

"Will she?" Kyle stopped, lightly squeezing Kane's shoulder. "I have eyes, Kane. I see how you are together. Don't you think she's becoming a little too dependent on you?"

Dependent on him? How could his brother not see it was the other way around?

Kane couldn't help it—he laughed out loud. "Come on, Kyle." He shook his head. "Enough playing around. What did you really want to talk to me about?"

A muscle worked in his brother's jaw. "Dude, I'm serious. I know you're trying to help Lilly, but she relies on you for everything. I think once you bow out of her life, she'll be lost."

About to argue, Kane swallowed back the words. Kyle's particular phrasing had given him pause. Once he *bowed out* of Lilly's life. As he'd always planned to, as he'd known he'd have to eventually.

Then why did the thought make him feel so hollow and empty?

His churning emotions must have shown on his face.

"Hellhounds," his brother said, incredulous. "You're in love with her."

"No." Kane denied it without hesitation. "I care about her, but…"

"You should have seen your expression," Kyle persisted. "You love her. I recognize love when I see it. I've been there, brother. You can't stomach the idea of life without her."

Kane opened his mouth, and then closed it. "I…"

"Damn." Kyle clapped him on the back, suddenly gleeful. "Forget I said anything. Turns out I was worried for nothing. If you're not going to bail on the girl, then it's all good."

"What do you mean?" Kane narrowed his eyes. "Of course I'm not going to bail on her. I'm simply going to return her to her family once the danger is eliminated."

"Sure you are." Grinning from ear to ear, Kyle rolled his shoulder, shaking himself out as if he was in wolf form rather than human. As he moved away, he lifted his hand in a wave. "My work is done here. I'm heading back now." He quickened his steps, glancing back over his shoulder, still grinning. "I can't wait to tell Kris."

"Wait a minute." Kane hurried to catch up. "Tell him what? The way you're talking is crazy."

Increasing his speed, Kyle kept going. "Is it? I'm married, remember? I recognize the symptoms."

When his brother sprinted away, Kane let him go. Though he'd been away awhile, he should be used to his brother's teasing. Yet something about this cut too close to home.

Was Kyle right?

No. Not just no, but hell no. Kane had never been in love, nor did he intend to start now. What he felt for Lilly was protective, wasn't it?

An image flashed into his mind of her naked, writhing beneath him. Maybe more. Maybe just a little bit more.

He cursed. He didn't need this muddling up his thought processes right now. He had other, more important things to worry about.

Lilly wished she'd been able to catch some shut-eye, because with the tension so high, taking a nap would be damn near impossible. She drank a third cup of coffee and then regretted it. She really didn't need the caffeine. Her nerves were thrumming, and the constant adrenaline made her constantly battle the instinct to run away. She wanted to put as much distance between the sadistic doctors from Sanctuary and herself as possible. Even the possibility of seeing them again terrified her, making her want to retreat back inside her shell. A long time ago, she'd learned how to hide without going anywhere. She might not have been able to entirely keep her body safe, but at least she could throw up some kind of protection for her mind.

Now, even though Kane had done his best to show her how to be self-sufficient, and she'd made some real progress, she felt as if she'd lost significant ground.

Pretty much in combat mode, Kane ignored her, making her feel even more lost. He spent a lot of time on his phone, talking to his agency. When he finally called her brother, waking Lucas and Blythe despite his attempt to wait until a decent hour, he didn't even offer to let Lilly talk to her family.

Which was okay, she supposed. She wasn't exactly sure what she would have said anyway. She certainly didn't want her brother to decide she needed to leave here. Despite the threat, she trusted Kane implicitly to protect her.

Finally, he put his phone down. When he raised his head to find her watching him, the fierceness blazing from his eyes made her want to go over to him and let him wrap her in his arms and kiss her fears away. She longed to hang on

to him, grab him by the shirt, and demand he promise her
that she'd be safe.

With difficulty, she stifled the notion. She didn't want
him to know how quickly her newfound self-assurance
had disappeared. "Are you okay?" she asked instead, hating that her voice came out quavering.

He blinked. "Shouldn't I be asking you that?"

"How was my brother?" she asked instead of answering.

"Alarmed." Standing, he held out his hand. "I didn't let
you talk to him because I didn't want him to get you all
worried, even worse than you probably are."

"I'm not." Blurting out the false words, she slipped her
fingers through his, wondering if he'd notice how badly
she trembled. To distract him, she gave in to temptation
and placed her lips in a soft kiss on his neck, inhaling the
masculine scent of him. "I trust you to take care of me."

He shuddered, every muscle going tight, making her
pull back in surprise. When she looked at him, he smiled
at her, a tight smile that did nothing to soften the flat expression in his eyes. Gently, he unwound her arms from
around him, taking a stiff step back.

"Me and six others," he said, the harshness of his voice at
odds with his pleasant yet remote, expression. "Remember,
the Protectors are coming in. They'll round up those three
Sanctuary crazies. I won't have very much to do with it."

"And then I'll be safe?" Wrapping her arms around herself as if by doing so, she could find comfort, she leaned
her head back. She held his gaze, feeling almost belliger-
ent. She didn't understand exactly why it felt as if he withdrew more with every second that passed.

"Yes. Then you'll be safe."

She wanted to ask what would happen after that, but
didn't. She wasn't sure she wanted to know. Ideally, he'd
keep her around until he'd finished her training, but she

had a feeling that once the threat had been eliminated, he'd return her to the care of her brother and disappear forever out of her life.

Why this made her feel like her heart were hollow, she didn't even want to know.

"Let's go get some breakfast," he said, abruptly breaking into her thoughts.

She nodded. "Okay. Where?"

Again he flashed that generic smile. "The main house. Where else?"

This time, they drove instead of walking. Judging by the number of vehicles parked out front, everyone else had had the same idea.

Though nerves had her stomach churning, Lilly squared her shoulders and lifted her chin. She walked in to the crowded room trying to make herself feel as if she belonged.

The entire family had gathered around a restaurant-quality buffet. Chatter briefly ceased when she and Kane walked in, but picked up almost immediately. Lilly was glad to see there were no outsiders there. Evidently any guests had already been fed.

"What's the plan, son?" the senior McGraw asked eagerly, smoothing a lined hand over his shiny bald head. He wore his customary button-down short-sleeve shirt and jeans.

"No plan, Dad." Kane smiled, a cold tight smile that told Lilly he was back in what she thought of as his Protector mode. "The rest of the Protectors will be here soon. They'll take care of this."

"We want to help," Kyle said firmly. Kris and his father echoed the sentiment.

"I appreciate that, but…" Though Kane smiled, his silver gaze had turned to steel. "They're a team, specially trained to handle this kind of thing. The rest of you will need to stay out of their way."

His father and brothers looked as if they wanted to argue, but after Kane eyed them one at a time, his stare unflinching, no one else commented. Even the Senior McGraw finally grimaced and continued munching on his bacon.

After the brief moment of tension dissipated, everyone went back to piling food on their plates and eating. As Kane moved away, Lilly stared at the buffet, not only amazed at the sheer amount of food, but the variety. There were scrambled eggs, pancakes, French toast, hash browns, sausage, bacon and ham, as well as two kinds of toast—white and wheat. On a table near the food, she spied a coffee urn, and pitchers of what appeared to be orange juice and tomato juice.

Glancing at Kane's mother, Lilly wondered if the poor woman had cooked all this herself, or if she'd had help.

Kathy came up beside Lilly, touching her arm and making her jump. "Hey, you. Are you all right?"

Heart in her throat, Lilly nodded. She couldn't help but wonder what Kane's sister would do if she told her the truth: no, she wasn't all right. She was scared and lost and on the verge of becoming a total mess. "I'm fine," she said, choosing to continue to lie. "But I'm so glad to have all of you around me. It helps, a lot more than you know."

Apparently, she'd said the right thing. Kathy beamed. "Go ahead and get something to eat." She pointed at the buffet. "You've got to keep your strength up."

Despite the beautiful array of beautifully cooked choices, the idea of food, any food, made Lilly's stomach roil. "I will," she lied again. "I just need to wake up first." This despite all the coffee she'd already consumed.

As Kathy moved away, Lilly watched as Kane strode over to the buffet and loaded up his plate with scrambled eggs, pancakes, sausage, bacon and hash browns. When he turned, he met her gaze and came over, holding out the plate. "Here."

She made no move to take it. "What's this?"

"Breakfast. For you," he said. "You haven't had anything to eat since we hunted last night."

"I couldn't—"

"Please. At least try." Now, he seemed relatively normal, as if the old Kane had returned. He leaned in close, nuzzling her ear, making her shiver and sigh. "Unless you want me to tell everyone how you shape-shifted last night," he murmured. "And what we did after."

The contradiction of the delicious delight brought on by his closeness and his actual words had her briefly speechless. "You're blackmailing me?" she asked, uncertain whether he was serious or not.

She glanced up. His teasing smile still seemed at odds with his flinty eyes, which had not yet begun to thaw.

"Yep." He nodded. "For your own good."

She gave in and accepted the plate, which felt surprisingly heavy. "Thanks," she said.

"Thank you," he replied. "Why don't you take a seat and let me get my own and we'll eat together."

Though the scent of the food wafting up to her made her think she might be sick, she only nodded.

There were two empty chairs next to each other at the end of the long table. The instant Lilly took one, Kris's wife Debi dropped into the empty seat next to her. Today she'd wrestled her wild dark hair into a ponytail, though curly strands had escaped to frame her olive-skinned face.

"Hello there."

"Hi." Lilly gave her a weak smile, unable to keep from looking to see what was keeping Kane.

"No worries," Debi said, her brightly painted lips still

curving in a smile. "I just need a second. I wanted to apologize to you for what happened when we had girls' night."

Lilly had just opened her mouth to try a forkful of scrambled egg. She nearly choked. Chewing, she managed to swallow. "You didn't do anything wrong," she protested, as soon as she could speak. "I drank too much and wanted to walk home."

"Sharon and I shouldn't have let you."

The small bite of eggs sat like a rock in her stomach. "Let me?" Lilly asked, mildly. "Last time I checked, I was an adult. Neither of you is responsible for me."

Her firm declaration apparently startled the other woman. Debi started to speak, and then winced as Kane came up next to her. "I think I'm in your seat," she said, jumping to her feet.

She wouldn't meet Lilly's eyes as she hurried off.

"What was that all about?" Kane picked up a piece of crispy bacon and began eating it with obvious relish.

Lilly told him, trying another forkful of eggs when she'd finished. This time, she managed to swallow without gagging. Progress.

"Did you accept her apology?" Kane asked, his own fork poised over his towering stack of pancakes.

"I told her she had nothing to apologize for." Lilly shook her head. "You'd better eat up, or your food might get cold."

As delaying tactics went, that worked. Kane flashed a grin and then turned his attention to his meal. He dug in. After a moment, she tried to do the same. She managed to get down most of her eggs, one piece of toast, and the bacon. Eating the rest of the still-heaping plate was beyond her capabilities.

When all the women started clearing the dishes and breaking down the buffet, Lilly jumped up to help them. Staying busy would keep her from worrying.

After the meal, everyone drifted into the living room, where some sort of sports game played on the big-screen TV. The volume had been turned low, but all the men had their attention riveted on the game.

"Preseason football," Debi said, shaking her head and sending her long earrings flying. "Come on, we're starting a card game in the kitchen."

Lilly followed Debi and saw Sharon and Kane's mother were already seated at the dinette table.

"Do you know how to play gin rummy?" Sharon asked, her smile friendly. She, too, had put up her wavy red hair, though she'd made hers into a sock bun on top of her head.

"No." Lilly didn't know how to play any card games. "Maybe I'd better just watch."

"It's easy." Sharon patted the chair next to her. "Sit. We'll teach you."

Lilly won the first round. "Beginner's luck," Debi told her. "But we go to 500 points, so we've got plenty of time to catch up."

They played hand after hand. When the score finally topped 500, Kane's mother won by a landside. Lilly glanced at the clock, surprised to learn several hours had passed.

The football game was still on, but the men appeared to have lost interest. Kyle was glued to his phone, either checking email or playing a game. Kris and Kane were engaged in some sort of discussion, while their father alternated between watching the game and wearing a path from the couch to the front window. His wife watched him with an indulgent expression. "We get so little excitement around here," she told Lilly. "He's beside himself."

"I'd rather have the boring peace and quiet," Lilly confided.

"Me, too." Kane's mom slipped a friendly arm around Lilly's shoulders and gave her a quick hug.

Surprised, Lilly smiled her thanks, enjoying the glow of warmth the friendly gesture brought.

The Protectors arrived exactly as Kane had said they would. Lilly and he were still at the main house. Kane's father, who was at the front window, notified everyone of their arrival.

The quiet hum of conversation ceased as everyone went still.

"Wait inside," Kane told everyone. "At least until I make sure this is them."

Just then, his phone chimed, signaling a text message. "'We're here,'" he read out loud. "It's them."

Everyone started talking at once.

Lilly crossed the room to stand in front of Kane.

"So they're finally here."

He nodded.

"I want to go with you to meet them."

He studied her, and then nodded. "Only you," he said, raising his voice for the benefit of the others. "The rest of you, please wait inside."

The grumble of protest which followed seemed mainly masculine. Ignoring this, Kane headed to the front door.

As Lilly followed Kane out, she studied the nondescript black SUV that had pulled up and parked. As she did, six men emerged from the vehicle. The first thing Lilly noticed was they looked like ordinary men, except for the fact that they were all dressed in black from head to toe. She did a double take. Scratch that. One of them was a woman.

They greeted Kane with the ease of long familiarity. Lilly noticed how everyone, including the lone female, treated Kane with respect.

"Let me show you where you'll be staying," Kane told them. "Once you're settled in, we can go over strategy."

"Strategy?" A large man with a bulbous nose laughed.

"As far as I'm concerned, it's simple. We find these sons of bitches, arrest them and haul their asses off to jail."

The rest of his companions laughed.

"If only it's that easy, Sly," Kane said, clapping him on the back. "Grab your gear and follow me."

The cabin that had been allotted to the Protectors was the next one down from Kane and Lilly's. Though the building itself couldn't be seen from their front porch, a quick jog down the road and around a turn would put them there.

Lilly wished this knowledge made her feel safe. Instead, her gut instinct screamed at her to flee. Only the knowledge that she could now change into her wolf self and outrun any human was able to comfort her.

"We're just around the bend," Kane told the crew, pointing.

"Do you need a few minutes to decompress?"

This time the woman glared at him. "What do you think we are, trainees? What we need is to plot a quick strategy, change into civilian clothes, and head into town to do some recon work."

Kane smiled his approval. "Good deal. First check with Muriel, she's the front desk clerk at the Value Five Motel. It's an old place, back in the pines along Main Street."

"Got it." The large man with a silver flattop haircut tapped his phone. "All the info has already been relayed to us."

"Well, then. I'll leave you to it."

This clearly surprised them. They all glanced at each other in obvious confusion. "You're not coming with us?"

"Nope." Kane put a friendly arm around Lilly's stiff shoulders. "I have to stay here and protect the asset."

The Asset?

Though they all nodded and then went on about their business, Lilly kept herself absolutely still, seething. The asset? As if she was no longer a person, but an item. Worse, Kane had been the one to use it.

She eased out from under his arm, jaw tight, chest aching.

"What are you two going to do?" This from the female agent, standing a few feet away, the sympathy in her clear green eyes letting Lilly know she'd not only noticed, but understood.

"I'm thinking we might practice shooting after all," Kane answered, even though the other woman had been looking at Lilly when she spoke. Then, when Lilly made a soft sound that might have been a protest, he faced her.

His granite expression softened. "I want to make sure you can defend yourself if something happens to me."

Her anger evaporated. "Happens to you? What do you mean?"

"Yeah." The female Protector crossed her arms, her expression mocking. "Since you're staying here, what could possibly happen to you?"

Before he could answer, the rest of her team joined her.

"Yeah, McGraw," one of them said. "Is there something you know that you're not telling us?"

Once again Kane's expression turned to stone. "Nope. Just taking precautions for any possibility. You know that. It's part of our basic training."

Just like that, they all got busy doing something. Except Lilly. She wasn't part of any team, including the one she'd believed she and Kane had begun to form. For the first time since she'd been rescued from Sanctuary, she felt utterly and completely alone.

Chapter 13

"Come on." This time, when Kane reached for her, Lilly neatly evaded him. She marched to the door herself and stepped outside, not bothering to see if he followed her.

"Anger is good," he said, from right behind her. "You can use it to your advantage and channel that fierceness when working with the firearm. You'll be much more accurate."

She stared in disbelief. How was it possible for him to be that clueless? She climbed into his car without responding. She'd been ambivalent about the entire teach-Lilly-to-shoot thing before. Now she was pretty damn sure she didn't want to do it.

They drove the short distance down the road and stopped at their cabin. Kane asked Lilly to wait in the car while he went inside to retrieve a spare pistol and some ammunition. He didn't seem to notice her black mood or if he did, apparently assumed it had nothing to do with him.

When he returned to the car a few moments later, the happy tune he was whistling set her teeth on edge.

"All is apparently right with your world." She couldn't keep the furious hurt from her voice.

Clearly surprised, he cocked his head and looked at her, one hand on the ignition button he'd been about to press. "If everything goes as planned, everything will be perfect for you, too. Now that the Protectors are here, it won't be long until you're safe. Once those three nut jobs from Sanctuary are securely in custody, you won't need to worry anymore."

"True."

He made no move to start the car. "Yet you don't sound happy."

"Oh, this *asset* is perfectly fine." Though she fairly spat the words, the instant they were said she wished she could call them back. She knew learning to express her feelings had to be a good thing, but she wasn't sure she actually enjoyed doing so.

"That's what this is about? You're upset because I—"

"Referred to me as an object?" Crossing her arms, she glared at him.

"No, Lilly." Expression bemused, he dragged his left hand across his chin. "That's just Protector talk. The asset refers to whatever we must protect above all else. And that would be you."

His explanation didn't make her feel any better. "You're telling me you dehumanize people? That makes no sense."

"It's perfectly logical." Voice now fierce, his silver eyes flashed as he faced her. "In order to act efficiently as Protectors, we absolutely cannot allow emotion to get in the way. I won't risk you for anything, do you understand?"

Slowly, she nodded, even though she wasn't entirely clear on whether or not he'd managed to insult her again or given her the highest compliment.

When she didn't say anything else, he started the car and put it in gear. They drove out onto the main road, and then hung a quick right. "Are we going to your brother's place?" she asked.

"Nope. A little beyond there."

They pulled off the gravel and dirt road and he killed the engine. "Come on," he said.

Her head began to ache as she followed him. When they reached a large, grassy meadow, sheltered on all sides by dense underbrush and trees, her stomach had started hurting, too. Though part of her wanted to go along with his plan since he clearly only wanted to help her, even the idea of handling a firearm made her want to retch.

"Here you go."

She recoiled when he tried to hand her a shiny silver pistol. Instead of taking it, she stared, wondering what he'd say if she told him it reminded her of a poisonous snake. Dangerous and deadly. "What's this?"

"My favorite revolver. It shoots .38, which won't have too much recoil for you to handle."

Gathering up her courage, she made no move to take it. "I actually don't like guns."

He gave her a reassuring smile. "As long as they're handled properly, there's no need to be afraid of them. Respect them, always, but I want to get you armed so you can defend yourself if need be."

He wanted. Though she knew he was right, the aversion she felt to handling the pistol ran deep, unshakable. In the time she'd spent with Kane, she'd grown strong and more confident. She realized if she didn't take a stand on this, she would be taking a giant leap backward.

"No," she told him, meeting his gaze without flinching. "I know you mean well, and your wanting me to know how to handle a weapon makes sense."

Watching her, he waited. "But?"

"But I don't want to." She took a deep breath, gathering her resolve. "Honestly, I couldn't do it. Even if I knew how to shoot a gun, at that moment when I found myself pointing it at another human being, I'd freeze. I wouldn't be able to shoot."

His mouth twisted. "Even if you knew you'd die if you didn't?"

"Even then."

Despite her words, he continued to hold the pistol as if he thought she'd change her mind. "You're telling me you'd rather be recaptured by those religious fanatics, held prisoner and tortured than defend yourself."

"No." Glaring at him, she shook her head. "Put the gun away. Please."

Finally he did, making her exhale with relief.

Still, the black look he gave her told of his unhappiness. "I need to know, Lilly. What would you do if you found yourself alone and surrounded, with the Sanctuary doctors about to take you prisoner?"

She opened her mouth to speak, but he forestalled her. "And don't say you'll have me to defend you, because I might not always be there."

Though the thought stung, his assumption also angered her. "I wasn't going to say that. You've made it quite clear that I need to learn to rely on myself."

"Good." But his harsh tone conveyed a different message. "Then tell me what you'd do in that situation."

"I'd change into a wolf and attack them," she answered. "Or run. Something. But I wouldn't shoot them. I couldn't."

"I'm only trying to keep you safe." Though he still looked fierce, the tight line of his mouth had softened somewhat. "And in all actuality, I'd prefer to see them all dead."

She couldn't resist. "Can't let them near *the asset,* now can you?"

He laughed and finally reholstered the gun. "You win.

I'm not happy about it, but you've made your feelings quite clear."

Something about the way he acquiesced, the way he gave what she wanted precedence over his own wants and needs, touched her deeply. "Thank you."

His gaze felt like a caress. "I'm proud of you, you know."

The smoldering flame in his eyes lit a bonfire deep inside her. She took a step toward him, her heart pounding an erratic beat. A bolt of raw wanting ran through her.

He met her halfway, slanting his mouth over hers as if the touch of her lips was necessary for his survival.

Her entire body throbbed and she gave herself up to his kiss.

Then, as if someone had just dumped a bucket of ice water on him, he moved away, head and shoulders bent as though in some kind of pain.

"We shouldn't do this," he said, his rusty voice harsh. The obvious sign of his arousal gave lie to his words.

Aching, yet aware he was probably right, Lilly nodded.

"Come on, let's get you back to the cabin." Kane moved off without waiting to see if she followed. "We've got a lot more preparations to do if we want to keep you safe."

Though the hot ache inside her spread to her eyes, making her blink back unexpected tears, she nodded. Following his lead, she climbed into his car, buckled in and stared out the window as he drove them back to the cabin.

Kane had never been one for self-delusion. Calling Lilly the asset had been his last desperate attempt to return to the perfectly trained operative he'd always been.

Not only had it pissed her off, but it clearly hadn't worked.

And then she'd refused to learn how to handle a firearm. Not only had he not seen that coming, but he'd been ashamed at the relief that had flooded through him. He'd known that attempting to teach her to shoot would have become another exercise in torture. After all, he would have had to put his hands on her, to help show her the proper stance and way to hold the pistol and aim.

Even standing a few feet away from her, the scent of her made him dizzy as hell. Once he'd touched her, all bets would have been off.

The kiss had come out of nowhere, sending him dangerously close to losing all control. Though he'd fought it, he'd become so aroused he'd had to step back and clear his head or he'd have taken her right there in the meadow.

When they arrived back at the cabin, a shadow detached itself from the wall and moved to greet his car. Bronwyn, the female part of this particular Protector team.

"Wait here," he told Lilly, killing the ignition and reaching for the door handle.

"Like hell," she muttered, making him grin as she did the same.

"Where have the two of you been?" Bronwyn sounded pleasant enough, but the tightness in her expression belied her attempt to appear casual.

"Why?" Crossing his arms, Kane gave Bronwyn a look that he hoped would communicate that he wanted her to cut to the chase.

Though the tiny jerk of her chin told him she got the message, the way she cut her eyes toward Lilly let him know she wasn't comfortable speaking in front of the asset.

Even thinking of Lilly that way felt wrong. He completely understood why she'd gotten so upset.

"It's okay, Bronwyn." He clapped his hand on her shoulder. "Lilly can hear whatever you have to say."

Her shrug effectively removed his hand. "It's your funeral. Anyway, we've been all over this town. No one has seen or heard from those three. The only person who has seen them is the woman who works in the motel."

"Muriel."

"Yes." Bronwyn glanced again at Lilly. "How reliable is she?"

"I've known her since I was a little kid. She'd never make something like that up. And furthermore, we've been pretty quiet about how many from Sanctuary are still running loose. She has no way of knowing there are three."

"True, but we can't figure out why the perps would arrive and ask exactly one single person about their quarry, and then disappear."

"Perps?" Lilly asked.

Kane smiled at her. "Short for perpetrator." He glanced at Bronwyn, who watched him with an odd expression on her face.

"That's right," she said. "And they're not acting like they should, especially if they think you're here."

"Which doesn't make sense," Kane put in. "Why else would they travel to Leaning Tree? We're a small town in the Catskills, not even a major tourist destination like Woodstock."

Lilly cleared her throat, drawing both of their attention. "They won't do things the way normal people would. My guess is they know more than you realize. They've found someplace where they can hole up and watch and wait."

"How would you know?" Bronwyn didn't bother to disguise her dismissal, as if she was delivering an unspoken message that Lilly should leave things to the professionals.

As Kane watched, his little Lilly lifted her chin. "How would I know?" she asked, her voice silk and steel. "I think I'd know better than anyone else what kind of crazy those people are. Especially since I was their prisoner for fifteen freaking years."

To Kane's amusement, Bronwyn's stiff, military demeanor vanished. She inclined her head, conceding the point to Lilly. "I apologize," she said quietly.

"Apology accepted." And Lilly smiled, making her appear radiantly beautiful. Again Kane had to battle with the urge to pull her against him and publically claim her as his. Which of course she wasn't. And could never be.

To his horror, Bronwyn appeared to pick up on this. She studied him intently. "Are you two…mates?"

Mates. The word he'd managed to avoid even thinking.

"No," he answered quietly, the ache in his chest making him feel like a liar. "We're not."

Bronwyn and Lilly exchanged a glance, the kind two women do when they're having a private conversation. Except this one didn't even have any words.

"What else?" he barked. "Surely you have more to tell me than the sad fact that six trained Protectors can't locate three crazy cultists?"

His sharp tone didn't appear to faze her. Slowly, she shook her head. "Nope."

"What's the plan?"

"We're going to stay awhile. I need you to clear this with your parents. A few of us are going to try and get jobs in town, and see if we can blend in. We're betting the perps will surface eventually."

Behind him, Lilly made a sound low in her throat. "This is going to take a while, then?"

Both Kane and Bronwyn turned to look at her.

"It would appear so," Bronwyn said, her sharp gaze missing nothing. "I know you're probably ready to get out of the boonies, aren't you?"

"Yes," Lilly answered, way too fast. The pink flush on her cheeks told Kane she was lying, though he couldn't understand why.

"Hey, you're not insulting me," he told her softly. "I get stir-crazy if I spend too much time here. I don't blame you for wanting to get out."

Bronwyn cleared her throat, making him realize he and Lilly had locked gazes.

"I've filled you in, so I'll be going." Bronwyn's amused smile told him she'd noticed. With a casual flip of her hand, she took off.

As they watched her go, Lilly's pensive expression made him wonder.

"Sorry." He went past and held the cabin door open for her. "There's nothing I can do about your being stuck here with me, at least not until all of this is over with."

Pushing on past him, she didn't respond. Once inside, she headed directly to the kitchen, where she began rummaging in the cabinets as though looking for something to cook. The small frown line between her perfectly arched brows told him she still wasn't happy.

"Lighten up," he told her, fed up and surprisingly hurt, too. "For all you know, it might only be a couple more days."

Her head snapped up. "Do you think?"

"No." Passing deliberately close to her, he retrieved a soft drink from the fridge and popped the top. He took a long drink, set the can down on the counter and looked at her. "What's wrong, Lilly?"

"Nothing." But she wouldn't meet his gaze.

"It's only natural to be afraid."

"I'm not." Defiance blazed from her eyes. "I'm angry. I don't understand why they won't leave me alone. Why me? Haven't I suffered enough? Why can't they just go away and let me live my life?"

"I don't know." Though he wanted to gather her close, he resisted, sensing she wouldn't welcome his embrace, at least not right now. "But you're getting stronger, every single day. I think it's been good for you, being here."

Briefly, she lowered her lashes. "It has. I'm just feeling restless, that's all."

He thought he understood. "Ever since you learned the three Sanctuary doctors were in the area."

"I guess. I can't help thinking it's safer to go on the run."

"And then what?" Taking another drink of his cola, he sighed. "You can't spend the rest of your life fleeing."

Though she nodded, he could tell she wasn't entirely convinced.

Kane's cell rang. Caller ID showed his brother Kris's number. "What's up?" he asked.

Kris's voice rang with amusement. "You'd better come up to the main house. There's someone here to see you."

Kane sighed. "I don't have time for games."

"Games?" Kris sounded indignant. "This isn't a game, I promise. You really do have a visitor. Someone you haven't seen in a long time."

"Just spit it out. Who is it?"

"Anabel Lee."

"What?" Kane groaned, remembering Shawn Ferguson's claim that Anabel was on the prowl for him. He glanced at Lilly, also remembering that Shawn had said Kane would have to publicly claim her.

"Yeah," Kris continued. "She's in the kitchen, chatting it up with Mom. She acts exactly the way she did back in high school, when she used to come over and wait for you to get home from football practice."

"Just send her away." Kane didn't bother to keep the annoyance from his voice. "I don't have time for this."

"I'll try." Still chuckling, Kris ended the call.

"What's wrong?" Lilly asked softly.

"My old high school girlfriend is here." He sighed. "I have no desire to reconnect with her."

Her blue gaze roamed over his features. "Why not? Are you still in love with her?"

He couldn't help laughing at that. "Not hardly. But she's what they call a drama queen. I can only imagine she's here to make trouble."

"If you say so." She didn't appear convinced. "How long has it been since you've seen her?"

Trying to remember, he shrugged. "I don't know exactly, but it's been years."

"Listen." A shrill, feminine squeal came from outside.

Kane grimaced. "Hellhounds. I know that sound."

He went to the window and cursed. "I was afraid of that," he said, as Lilly joined him. "Somehow, she talked Mom into telling her where I was staying."

Anabel wore a long black dress and a huge purple hat, the brim completely shadowing her face. She'd always favored an eclectic style of dress, but from what Kane could tell, she looked downright…old-fashioned and frumpy.

"But why is she circling your car?" Lilly asked. "And making sounds like that?"

"Apparently she likes red corvettes. As to the pig-squealing sound, she's always done that. It used to drive me insane."

Lilly grimaced. "Is she a witch? I don't mean the Wiccan kind, but the other, dark type. Assuming there are such things."

"Hey, there are vampires, werewolves and fairies," he said. "So I'm pretty sure there are a few of our kind who practice the darker arts."

"Scary." She shuddered. He couldn't tell if she was joking. "Though I don't think they have anything on the torture artists at Sanctuary."

Again he wanted to hold her. And once more, he understood he could not. "What the hell am I going to do? I want to send her away, but we need to be careful not to make any enemies in Leaning Tree."

She shot him a rueful look. "I guess you've got no choice but to go out and greet her."

He muttered a curse word. "Only if you come with me."

Smile broadening into an all-out grin, Lilly shook her head. "I will. That's what best friends do."

Best friends? Though Lilly claimed she couldn't handle a relationship, he wasn't sure he liked the idea of her thinking of him as a friend, best or not. Yet one more thing he'd have to get over.

"Come on then," he growled, holding out his arm before he changed his mind.

Taking it, she laughed again, apparently amused at his gruff expression. "Do you want me to pretend to be your girlfriend?"

Though her tone suggested she was kidding, he decided to take her seriously. "Yes. More than that, actually." Hesitating, he bit the bullet. "I need you to pretend to be my mate. Shawn tried to warn me that night we ate at his place. She's pushy, but even a woman like Anabel Lee won't try to come between mates."

Though Lilly had readily agreed, hearing Kane use the word *mate* did strange things to her equilibrium. The term seemed fraught with meaning, more intense than a mere *fiancée, wife* or *spouse,* suggesting a lifelong commitment that had been predetermined at birth.

Worse, hearing it applied to her and Kane…the word *mate* fit somehow. Which was not only a foolish thought, but a dangerous one, as well. A man like Kane could never be saddled with a woman like her. He'd pity her if he knew how badly she wanted him.

As Kane yanked the front door open and pulled her outside, she had to admit she was curious about what kind of woman Kane had dated in the past.

Her first up-close glimpse of Anabel Lee made her think someone had taken being named after a character in an Edgar Allen Poe story a bit too seriously. Her raven colored hair was long, almost to her waist, and straight. Anabel also wore a floppy purple hat and flowing black dress that might have been patterned after one from an earlier era.

She turned with a flounce as Kane and Lilly approached, removing her hat and flipping her hair back over her shoulder in a gesture as antiquated as her appearance. Her heavily mascara'd brown-eyed gaze devoured Kane. She ignored Lilly completely.

"Kane!" She uttered a shrill squeal before throwing herself into Kane's arms.

Luckily for her, he managed to catch her. Holding her at arm's length, he shot Lilly a look so pleading she almost laughed.

Instead, she sidled up to the two of them and cocked her head. "Hello," she said, looking Anabel up and down and hoping her expression appeared friendly enough. What Kane had said made sense. They didn't want to risk alienating anyone who might come into contact with the Protectors or the doctors from Sanctuary.

Anabel straightened her spine and collected herself as Kane released her. Dusting off her arms where he'd held her, she gave Lilly a narrow-eyed, appraising look. "Who are you?" she demanded.

"I'm Lilly Gid— Er, Green," Lilly said, relieved she hadn't inadvertently blurted out her real name. She considered holding out her hand and then thought better of it, inclining her chin instead. "And you must be Anabel Lee."

"I am." Anabel glared at her. "What are you doing here?"

"Lilly's my fiancée," Kane put in, ever helpful, though Lilly couldn't help but notice how he kept his distance from both of them.

"Fiancée?" Anabel went completely still. The way she'd outlined both her eyes in heavy black eyeliner gave her a racoonish appearance. Kane's words appeared to stun her. Pain flashed across her face. She looked from Kane to Lilly. "That's not possible. Kane, you can't marry her. You're my mate. You belong with me."

For one stunned moment, her words seemed to hang there, bald and unbelievable. Anabel winced, apparently aware that now she'd just exposed her inner emotions without warning, she'd also set herself up for the possibility of being hurt.

Lilly felt a stab of sympathy for her.

"Anabel." Kane lowered his voice, sounding oddly gentle. "I haven't seen you since high school. We only dated casually in our senior year. You know we aren't mates. We never were."

"Liar." Anabel's eyes filled with tears, smudging her mascara and eyeliner. "I've waited for you all these years. Ask anyone." Her voice rose. "I gave Kathy letters once a week to send to you."

"Letters?" Now Kane blinked with bafflement.

Anabel narrowed her gaze. "Don't tell me your sister didn't give them to you."

"Of course she did," Kane responded quickly. Since even Lilly could tell he wasn't telling the truth, she had no doubt Anabel could, as well.

"Why didn't you ever write back?" The plaintive note

in her voice was both disturbing and, for whatever reason, tugged at Lilly's heart.

Kane shook his head. "Enough, Anabel. I really think it's time for you to go."

"I just got here," Anabel screeched. "I wait years for you to return to me and you finally come home, but you bring this…" Swallowing back a sob, she gestured at Lilly, her hurt and angry expression letting them know whatever term she eventually chose, it wouldn't be pretty.

Yet despite all this, the raw wretchedness in her face made Lilly want to comfort her. Crazy? Maybe. Or just confused. Whatever she might be, her raw sense of loss appeared palpable, as if she honestly believed every word she'd said.

As Lilly stared at her, at a complete loss for words, Anabel's wolf became visible, like a projector image superimposed over her face. It snarled and lunged at her. Lilly took a step back, right into Kane's arms.

She would have moved away, but he held her in place with a steel grip, shielding her in case the other woman did something crazy.

Meanwhile, Anabel covered her face with trembling hands and sobbed, giving voice to her sense of loss. "First my David goes and leaves me, and now you."

"Anabel, I'm sorry for your loss. But I really think you need to leave."

At Kane's sharp tone, Anabel appeared to physically pull herself together. She wiped at her tears, swallowing back a sob. As she stared at Kane, a mocking smile hovered over her hot-pink painted lips. "I know what you're doing here," she said, her cool tone containing a subtle threat. "And while I don't understand how you can break my heart just to protect her, I want you to know that I'll continue waiting. For as long as it takes."

After delivering that pronouncement, Anabel spun around and marched away.

Lilly watched her go in stunned silence. "What was that?" she asked, finally having the presence of mind to move out of Kane's arms.

"I don't know." His grim tone contained a note of worry. "Shawn told me she lost her husband six months ago in Afghanistan. Evidently the grief got to her and she's gone slightly nuts."

"I feel bad for her."

"I'm more concerned with the way she claims to know who you are."

"She didn't say that. She said she knew what I was doing here."

"Same difference." He dragged his hand through his hair. "I need to fill the team in. Just in case Anabel turns out to be a threat."

"Don't you think she's too obvious?" Lilly sighed. "I saw genuine hurt in her eyes. If it weren't for that, I would have thought the entire performance was an act."

"Hurt?" He shook his head. "She has no reason to feel hurt. None at all. She has to have some ulterior motive behind acting that way."

"She's grieving. Sorrow can do awful things to some people."

"Maybe. But I still need to talk to the team. I also need to get with my brothers and some of my old friends in town. Maybe they can shed some light on to what's going on with her."

"What about the letters she says she sent?"

"Kathy will know if that part's true or not."

Lilly cleared her throat. "From what I understand, if Anabel truly believes you're her mate, there's a very real possibility that you might be."

"No." He didn't even hesitate. "Anabel is most definitely *not* my mate."

Though the idea of him with anyone else made her entire body hurt, more than anything Lilly wanted Kane to find happiness. If Anabel might be his future, she had to give him a chance to find out. "I think you should go talk to her, just the two of you."

His eyes darkened dangerously. "Have you lost your mind? Why would I do that?"

Since she needed a good reason, she said the first thing that came to mind. "Because Anabel might just be the one person the 'perps,' as you call them, need to get to me. I think it's better if you don't make any enemies."

He cursed under his breath, but she could tell from his expression he knew she was right.

"I'll think about it," he finally told her.

"When?" she pushed. Then, because she couldn't help herself, she took a deep breath. "I'd hate to be keeping you from your destiny."

At her words, he went absolutely still. "I don't believe in destiny," he snarled, then strode into the bathroom and closed the door.

A moment later she heard the shower start up.

Staring after him, Lilly knew he had to give Anabel a chance. Even if in the end, he wasn't the man for her, the poor woman didn't deserve to live with such sorrow and regret. During her time in captivity, Lilly had become intimately familiar with grief and an overwhelming sense of loss. She'd spent fifteen years mourning the loss of her brother, only to learn Lucas not only lived, but had believed her dead also. They'd found each other and in the process, Lucas had found Blythe, his mate. Lilly had been delighted at the happiness radiating from them. This sort of joy was exactly what Kane needed.

And if Anabel might be able to give it to him, so much the better. If not, Lilly wanted to find a way to help the other woman move on, because there had to be something else over the next horizon.

Now she sounded maudlin. Kane would order her to take off her rose-colored glasses and face reality. Lilly had spent most of her life staring a mean and painful reality in the eye. She was ready for a little happily-ever-after.

Fine, Lilly decided. If Kane didn't want to befriend Anabel, then she'd have to do it.

Chapter 14

That night, the raw sorrow Lilly had seen in Anabel's brown eyes kept haunting her. Though she knew she shouldn't take it personally, she couldn't help but identify with the other woman. Maybe it was the simple fact that she, having suffered so much at the hands of others, simply could relate to pain.

While she wanted Anabel on their side, she wanted to help her even more. And if by doing so, she could help Kane, then all the better.

Yet, the gamut of emotions that flooded her at the thought of Kane with Anabel tore Lilly up inside. Wanting him made her selfish, especially since she knew he deserved so much more than someone like her, broken inside. Maybe if she found him true happiness, leaving him wouldn't be so damn difficult.

Lilly tried to come up with a plan, but couldn't. Since Kane insisted on staying near her 24/7, meeting up with

Anabel by herself would be difficult. She'd need help. Though she liked Kane's brothers' wives well enough, neither Debi nor Sharon seemed like the type to keep a secret. That left Kane's sister, Kathy. Who apparently had remained in touch with Anabel, at least accepting the letters for Kane. Lilly had to wonder why she hadn't forwarded them on.

"I haven't seen Kathy around lately," Lilly mentioned casually the next morning. She'd just poured them each a fragrant cup of coffee and Kane had promised to make them scrambled eggs. She loved the way he looked first thing in the morning, with his short dark hair all spiky and his silver eyes still molten liquid from sleep.

"That's because we haven't been up to the house around dinnertime," he said. "But I do need to talk to her. I want to ask her about those letters Anabel supposedly gave to her."

Opening the egg carton, he swore. "We only have two eggs."

Which gave her the perfect opening. Maybe, just maybe, if they had breakfast at the main house, Kathy would be there and Lilly could have a word with her separately from Kane.

"How about we have breakfast with your folks?" she said, acting as if she didn't care one way or another. "Maybe Kathy will be there and you can talk to her." She felt a flash of guilt as pleasure replaced the surprise in Kane's expression.

"I'd love that," he said quietly. "Let's go."

Outside, the breeze felt chilly despite the sun. They drove the short distance instead of walking, as Kane said he was too hungry to wait too long. When they entered the house through the back door which led directly into the kitchen, Lilly was disappointed to see no sign of Kathy.

Kane's mother beamed. "Welcome, you two. You're just

in time for my famous cinnamon French toast. Kathy and Tom are on the way, too."

"Great." After kissing his mother's cheek, Kane squeezed his father's shoulder and then pulled out a chair for Lilly. Once she'd taken her seat, he dropped down next to her. "Where are Kris and Kane and the bunch?"

"They went into town to help with the planning committee for this year's Labor Day Parade. Preparations have been in full swing for a couple of weeks. They're already building the floats."

Kane shook his head. "It's hard to believe summer is almost over."

"Labor Day is tomorrow." Mr. McGraw smiled at Lilly. "They need all the hands they can get. Maybe the two of you should volunteer to help. I think Lilly would enjoy it."

Lilly couldn't resist glancing at Kane. He knew her well enough to know how much she'd hate something like that. One corner of his mouth twitched in the beginning of a smile. "We'll keep that in mind, Dad."

Kathy and Tom blew in. Kathy's glorious mass of wavy hair had been pulled back into an untidy ponytail and she appeared radiant with happiness. "Look!" With a dramatic flourish, she pointed to her stomach. "I finally have a baby bump!"

Mama McGraw rushed over and enveloped her daughter in a hug. "I hope you're hungry. Sit, and let me get started cooking. You need to eat lots—remember, you're eating for two!"

Grinning at his wife, Tom pulled out a chair next to Lilly, fussing over Kathy as she settled herself in her seat.

"Good morning, Lilly," Kathy fairly sang the words. "Do you want to feel my belly?"

Taken aback, Lilly wasn't sure how to react. Finally,

she held her breath and placed her hand on Kathy's newly rounded abdomen. "Will I feel it kick?" she asked.

Kathy smiled. "Not yet. I can't wait for that. If you're still here, I promise to let you feel once the baby does."

If you're still here. Funny, how the casual words wounded her. Lilly managed to smile and nod, gently moving her hand away.

Luckily, Kane's mother returned with a huge platter of French toast. "Here you go," she said, setting it down. "I've warmed maple syrup. I just need to fetch it from the kitchen. There's butter in the bowl in the center of the table."

Mrs. McGraw returned with the syrup as everyone helped themselves. Silence fell, while they dug in.

Lilly nearly moaned out loud as the first bite melted in her mouth. "This is wonderful," she said, meaning it. Around her, everyone smiled and nodded and just kept right on eating.

When the platter had been emptied, Mrs. McGraw stood and began gathering the plates.

"Let me help you, Mom," Kathy said, pushing to her feet and reaching for the silverware.

Lilly saw her perfect opportunity. "I'll help, too."

"Let me assist you lovely ladies," Kane put in.

"Sit," Lilly ordered, before she had time to think. "I need a break from you." Everyone stared at her, looking amused. She thought about trying to explain, and then decided against it.

Surprisingly, Kane looked stung. But he remained where he was and Lilly continued to help clear the table.

Once everything had been gathered up, she followed Kathy and her mother into the kitchen.

"Dishwasher's broken, ladies," Mrs. McGraw told them. "We'll have to wash this batch by hand."

"Mama, go relax." Placing her plates on the counter near the sink, Kathy shooed her back towards the dining room. "You've done enough, cooking all this. Lilly and I can take care of the dishes."

Laughing, the older woman wasted no time returning to the rest of her family.

"I'll wash and you dry." Kathy handed her a towel. "Is that all right with you?"

Lilly nodded. "I've helped my brother's wife, Blythe, do this a lot back home."

After rinsing off the dishes and filling the sink with soapy water, Kathy began scrubbing. "Where's home to you?"

For some reason Lilly thought of Kane. Which confused the heck out of her. "I grew up in Texas," she managed to say without wincing. "And before here, I lived with my brother and his wife in Seattle."

"I love that city." Kathy handed her the first plate. Lilly carefully dried it before placing it in the dish rack on the counter.

They chatted a bit, working through the dishes, while Lilly tried to figure out how to ask her question. Finally, she simply inhaled and plunged into a gap in the conversation.

"Kane and I had a strange visitor yesterday," she said. "A woman named Anabel."

Though Kathy continued working on cleaning the silverware, Lilly noticed a kind of watchful stillness in the other woman.

"Really?" Kathy's brows rose. "I'm surprised I haven't heard about that yet. How'd it go?"

"She claimed Kane is her mate. And she also said she's been giving you letters to give to Kane."

"Letters?" Now Kathy turned to face Lilly, frowning. "That doesn't make sense. She has his email. Everyone does. His veterinary practice has a website." She paused, then reached for another handful of silverware. "I wonder if she's confusing him with her husband, David. She used to send him care packages along with handwritten letters. I know because I helped her box them up a couple of times."

Lilly pondered this. "Is she mentally ill?"

"Probably." Kathy didn't hesitate. "She stopped going to grief counseling after she fell apart in one of the sessions. I feel bad for her, but she won't let anyone help her. She's become a recluse these past few months. Rarely leaves her home and when she does, she dresses in an outfit that looks like a Halloween witch costume."

It was a pretty accurate description.

"And now she's fixated on Kane."

Kathy made a sound. "Poor him. How'd he deal with that?"

"He was kind," Lilly said, feeling compelled to defend him. "And firm. He told her they were never mates and asked her to leave."

"He's right about that. They aren't mates." Tone firm and no-nonsense, Kathy just looked at Lilly. "You do realize that, don't you?"

Lilly shrugged. "I don't know how to tell."

The strangled sound coming from Kathy might have been laughter, or something else entirely. "You honestly don't know?"

Slowly, Lilly shook her head.

"Kane and Anabel aren't mates, because you and he are. Anyone with eyes in their head can see that." Handing Lilly the last of the silverware, Kathy pulled the drain plug and began draining the sink.

Meanwhile, Lilly stood frozen, clutching a bunch of wet forks and knives before belatedly placing them on her dish towel. "No," she said faintly. "He and I aren't mates. We can't be."

"Why's that, hon?" Grabbing the dish towel from her, Kathy gently removed the pieces from Lilly's hands and dried them. "Why can't you and my brother be together?"

"We just can't." Oddly enough, Lilly felt like she might be about to weep. "Please, just leave it at that."

Kathy stared at her for a moment in silence, and finally nodded. "Have it your way," she said. "Come on, let's go rejoin the others."

"Wait." Lilly grabbed her arm. "I need your help." She glanced at the still-closed door. "I want to talk to Anabel without Kane."

Kathy studied her through narrowed eyes. Just now, the dove-gray color appeared more silver, like Kane's. "Why?"

"I think I can help her."

"You'd better talk to Kane about that." Kathy sighed. "I can't help you do anything that might not be safe. And with Anabel's fragile state of mind..."

"Please." Lilly continued to hold Kathy's arm. "It can be in a public place, and you can be there, too. I just need a few minutes with her. That's all."

Kathy's hand crept up to rest on her slightly rounded belly. "I still don't understand what exactly you're trying to do."

"Just talk. Nothing more."

"We need to run it by Kane." The firm set of Kathy's jaw told Lilly she wasn't budging on this.

Which meant Lilly wouldn't be meeting with Anabel. "How about giving me her phone number?" Lilly tried to keep her voice casual. "That'd be nearly as good. I can speak to her on the phone instead."

"I don't know..." Kathy glanced at Kane before looking back at Lilly. "All right," she finally said. "I can give you her number. I can't guarantee that she'll even talk to you, and I want your word you won't try to sneak off and meet with her."

"You have it." Lilly smiled as Kathy scribbled the number on a paper napkin. Pocketing it, she thanked her.

"What I don't understand is why you want to get involved in this," Kathy mused. "You have enough crazy stuff to deal with as it is. Why add more?"

"Because I truly believe I can help her. Since I was rescued, I've done nothing but accept assistance from others. It's time I give back."

Kathy smiled. "That's really nice. Good luck with it." They went back in the room and sat. For a while, everyone sipped coffee, sated and relaxed.

After they'd socialized for another half hour, Kane got up. "Come on, Lilly. We need to stop at the cabin before our drive."

Drive? Lilly knew better than to ask in front of Kane's family. Pushing to her feet, Lilly thanked Kane's mother for a wonderful meal. The older woman beamed at the praise.

Outside, the morning air still carried a bit of a chill, hinting that fall was just around the corner.

Once they were in the Corvette, Kane started the engine.

"I understand you want to talk to Anabel," he said, the instant they pulled away from the main house.

Her stomach clenched. "Kathy told you."

"Of course she did. I'm trying to keep you safe. I can't do that if you go around contacting people like Anabel. You don't even know her. Why would you want to do that anyway?"

She swallowed. "Because she's hurting and I know how that is. I identify with her. And I think she's just fixated on you as a way to cope with the loss of her husband." She lowered her voice. "I want to try and help her. Because if there'd just been one person during all my years as a prisoner, a simple kindness like a conversation would have meant the world to me."

His expression changed. "Just don't be hurt if she rebuffs you."

"I won't." She gave him a smile. "And don't be surprised if she doesn't."

One hand on the steering wheel, he handed her a cell phone. "Here. You can keep this. It's a spare prepaid one I bought before we came out here. Have at it."

Despite her brave assurances, Lilly's heart was in her throat as she dialed the number Kathy had written.

It went straight to voice mail. Lilly sighed, debated hanging up, and left a message instead. "This is Lilly Green. I met you yesterday, out at Wolf Hollow. I was hoping to talk to you. We have quite a bit in common. Please call me back at this number."

After disconnecting the call, she sighed. "Now I just need to wait and see what happens."

Kane shook his head as they pulled up to their cabin. "I doubt she'll call you back."

"Well, until she does, since you mentioned we were going for a drive, I'd like to go into town. I need to buy a few things."

"You can't," he said, grimacing. "Too risky until we find out where the cultists are. If you'll give me a list, I'll have Kathy or Debi or Sharon pick up whatever you need."

Her cheeks warmed. "How about we go to the next town over? It's been ages since I went shopping. Shopping is one of the things I really enjoy."

"What woman doesn't?" He chuckled. "All right. We'll stop in Kingston while we're over that way."

"Where are we going?" Fairly bouncing in the seat, she couldn't hide her anticipation.

"I thought I'd take you over to Woodstock. It's a touristy sort of place and at this time of the year it should be crawling with people. I figure it'll be safer that way."

"Safer." Though she nodded, a sudden realization struck her. "You know, since coming here, I've been almost as much of a prisoner as I was before."

His smile disappeared. "Ouch. I'm sorry you feel like that. Everything we do is only to protect you."

"I know that." Without thinking, she lightly touched his arm. He tensed under her fingers. "It's just that I've been feeling a bit like a butterfly, emerging from a cocoon. No." She waved away any potential comments. "Let me rephrase that. Like a bear waking up after hibernating all winter." She laughed, amused at her admittedly rough analogy. "I'm eager to discover and learn and fierce to protect my right to explore."

After a startled second, he laughed with her. He took a deep breath. "You've been doing so well with your self-confidence. I've seen a side of you I didn't expect to see, at least not so soon."

She smiled at the compliment.

They parked in front of the cabin. "You can wait here if you want. I just need to grab my backpack."

"I need to freshen up." She got out, closing her door quietly and hurrying in ahead of him. She felt like a kid, getting a day off from school to do something fun. Just because she was getting to do an ordinary thing, something other people didn't even think about before doing.

The instant Lilly disappeared into the bathroom, Kane sent a text to Sly, the leader of the Protector team on-site. He requested backup, needing someone to shadow them while they took in the sights. The most important aspect was that

Lilly not notice. Her newfound independence might be fragile. He didn't want to upset it.

After receiving the text response assuring him that Sly would have the situation handled, Kane relaxed. He grabbed his backpack, checking to make sure his camera battery was fully charged, and sat down on the couch to wait for Lilly.

When she emerged, his heart turned over. She'd put on a brightly patterned sundress, which showcased her long, creamy legs. Her soft, ivory shoulders and slender body made her look dainty and graceful. The low-cut bodice highlighted her shapely figure. She was a pleasing contrast of wholesome yet seductive.

Just like that, he burned for her.

Stunned speechless, he tried to find the right words to compliment her without betraying the way she affected him.

He knew he was staring, but he couldn't help it. Slowly, he rose to his feet, holding his backpack in front of him like a shield. "You look great," he rasped. He kept his gaze riveted on her face, but then, unable to help himself, let it travel over her once again slowly. As if he were photographing her with his eyes.

"Thanks." Her porcelain complexion turned pink. "Are you ready to go?"

Inside, his wolf roared. Looking at her, he swore he could see the faint suggestion of hers, doing the same.

Shaking it off, he turned and held the door for her. The light, floral scent she wore drifted to him as she passed, making him ache.

"It's a bit of a drive," he told Lilly. "But scenic. So relax and enjoy. On the way home, there's a great fruit-and-vegetable stand I want to stop at. Mom always likes for me to pick up stuff for her there."

She smiled back. "Sounds lovely."

The winding road meandered through the occasional older neighborhoods, large two-story houses set way back off the road. Traveling to the highway was easier if he drove directly through town, but he wanted to keep Lilly away from Leaning Tree, so he took the long way. This involved making a circle around town, cutting around the reservoir, and finally reaching the main road.

"I love this." Cheeks still flushed, eyes bright with excitement, Lilly seemed enthralled with their surroundings. "I bet it's really beautiful once the leaves start turning."

"It is."

As he hit the interstate, his cell phone rang. His brother Kris.

"Hey, Kane." Kris's voice sounded strange, completely unlike his usual jubilant self. "I'm just leaving town, but Mom called. She says there's a guy up at the main house with some sort of law enforcement credentials. He's asking a lot of questions about a missing woman who he claims has been abducted."

Kane swore. "Why didn't she call me?"

"She says I'm closer. She knew you were taking Lilly over to Woodstock today."

"Do you know if he has a picture of the woman he's looking for?"

"She said if he does, he hasn't gotten around to showing her yet." Kris sounded agitated. "I'm driving as fast as I can, but we're still a few minutes out. I have a bad feeling about this."

"I do, too. Why'd Mom let him in?"

"No idea. You know how she is. Too damn trusting. Why don't you call your Protectors and see if there's one still on the premises. If so, have them get over to her."

"Will do. And I'm on my way also."

"Kane," Kris cut in swiftly. "Absolutely not. Think, man. You need to take Lilly and disappear into the woods. Change if you need to, but get her the hell away from here."

He was right. But also wrong. "I'm not leaving Mom and Dad unprotected."

"I doubt it will come to that." But Kris didn't sound certain. "They're not here for her or us."

"Let me notify them. I'll call you right back." Kane ended the call and immediately dialed Sly's number. He passed on what his brother had told him.

"Hellhounds." Sly sounded furious. "No one's there. I'm the closest. I can be there in under ten minutes."

"Good. Get there as quickly as you can." Kane pressed End and called Kris back. "Sly is on his way. Who's all at the house with Mom?" Kane prayed Kathy and her husband had gone home.

"Just Mom. I think Dad went into town."

"Good." Kane took a deep breath. "Is Kyle heading back with you?"

"Yes. He's right here. We had Debi take Sharon and the kiddos home."

"Excellent. Do you and Kyle have access to weapons?"

"Weapons?" Kris sounded grim. "Of course we do, but do you really think—"

"The fact that you called me tells me you do, too. In situations like this, go with your gut. Do not let any harm come to Mom. Swear to me you'll do your best to protect her."

"Of course I will. But Kane—"

"Just go. Don't call me back until you know she's safe."

He savagely punched off, then tossed his phone onto the console. Damn. Kane glanced at Lilly. Blue eyes wide, she stared.

"What's going on?" she asked, fear vibrating in her voice.

"No time to explain." Pulling over to the side of the road,

he grabbed her hand. "Lilly, I want you to listen to me and do exactly as I tell you. Do you understand?"

Terror darkening her gaze, she nodded.

"Good. You're going to run into the woods and change. I want you to put as much distance between yourself and here as possible."

"What about you? Aren't you going with me?"

"I can't leave my family undefended. You'll be fine, as long as you follow instructions. Remember those caves, I showed you?"

When she nodded again, he exhaled. "Go there as a wolf, and hide. I'll come for you when it's safe."

"Why as a wolf?"

"Because all your senses are sharper. You'll be able to hear them coming from much farther away. And you can use your snout, too." Getting out, he yanked open the door and grabbed her. "Take off. Now."

Again she hesitated. Chest tight, he gave her a small tug. "Hurry, Lilly. Go."

Finally, she went, crashing into the woods and heading away from Wolf Hollow. He watched until he could no longer see her, feeling as if he was sending away his heart. Then he stiffened his spine, grabbed both his pistols and, after checking to make sure they were loaded, stuffed them into his hidden holsters. Jumping back into his car, he turned around and stomped on the accelerator, headed back home.

Heart pounding, Lilly took off running, exactly as Kane had ordered. She made it to the first clearing, stripped off her clothing, carefully folding her new dress, and initiated the change to wolf. Even in her animal form, she couldn't stop thinking about Kane's parents and the fact that they were in danger. Because of her.

And she was about to run and hide in a cave like a coward. She might have been able to do such a thing once, but not now. She was no longer the terrified victim she'd been.

As a wolf, she circled around, heading back to the main house, keeping her ears open for any out-of-the-ordinary sounds.

While she ran, she periodically scented the air, just in case. She didn't expect them, if in fact, this stranger was part of Sanctuary, to be out beating the brush for her. Not yet.

But she owed it to Kane and his family to make sure no one got hurt. They wanted her, not them. Well, she'd damn sure make certain they got exactly what they wanted.

Chapter 15

Though journeying on foot, even as a wolf, would be much slower than Kane traveling by car, Lilly kept moving. As a human, she had absolutely no sense of direction. As a wolf, she knew exactly which way to go.

She paced herself, keeping to a lope rather than a run, aware she had quite a few miles to go. When she reached the first road, one of the winding ones she and Kane had taken to reach the interstate, she looked both ways and waited until there were no cars in sight before crossing.

Since she had no watch, she wasn't sure how much time passed. Judging from the position of the sun, it took her close to an hour before she reached the boundaries of Wolf Hollow's land. She only hoped she wasn't too late.

Keeping to the ridge above, she remained in the shadows of the giant oaks when she finally reached the main house. Below, the place appeared quiet, like an ordinary morning at Wolf Hollow Motor Court. Kane's Corvette was parked in front, as was Kris's minivan and the elder McGraws' sedan. There were no other vehicles, nothing to indicate the stranger might still be there.

A slight rustle of sound caught her attention. She spotted two of the Protectors, weapons drawn, creeping up on the house from the back. They passed directly below her, not seeing her.

She watched as they reached the back door and tried the handle. Apparently they found it unlocked. Glancing at each other, guns still drawn, they opened it and slipped inside. All was quiet once more.

Now what? She wanted to do something, anything, to help, but didn't want to be in the way. If she was too late and the intruder had gone, at least she'd tried. If not, she'd be waiting while he made his escape.

Creeping closer, Lilly waited for several minutes. Holding herself absolutely still, she listened for any sounds of a scuffle or, heaven forbid, a gunshot. She heard nothing but the ordinary sounds of the forest. Birdsong and small creatures rummaging through the underbrush. The sounds of peace.

Should she try to enter the house? Remain wolf, or change back into a human? Since she had no clothing, she elected to stay wolf.

She cocked her head, listening. She heard the low thrum of voices, but detected no alarm or tension. Still, she knew she needed to be careful.

Cautiously, she circled around, heading toward the east side where the sliding glass door should provide a decent view of the inside. She kept low to the ground as she moved closer, every sense on full alert.

Reaching a decision, she rushed the same back door the two Protectors had just entered. Gripping the knob with her teeth, she managed to turn it enough so she could push the door open with her body. Moving silently, in full-out hunting mode, she entered the house.

It took a few minutes for Kane's heart to stop pounding. Adrenaline still flowed as he faced his parents, who were flanked by his two brothers. Sly and one of his team stood on the other side of the room, as though they'd formed sides and faced off. Everyone had turned and stared at him when he rushed into the room, weapon drawn.

"Put the gun away," Kris said. "He's gone."

Slowly, Kane thumbed the safety back on and holstered his pistol. Too late. Still, a quick survey of the room told him no one had been harmed.

His mother stood, head up, arms crossed, unharmed and unshaken. His father stood next to her, glowering at Sly as if the next move the Protector made would be his last.

"Mom." Kane moved forward, cutting off Sly and enveloping his mother in a hug. "Are you all right?"

"Of course I am," she said, her voice as unflappable as always. "I've already told your father and both your brothers, and now this man—" she glared at Sly "—has made me repeat it yet again. I don't know what the big deal is. The man who was here asking questions is gone. And I didn't give anything away."

"Of course you didn't," Kane soothed, shooting Sly a look that plainly told him to back off. "What did the stranger want?"

"He was on a fishing expedition," she continued, lifting her chin, pale blue eyes glinting. "Plain and simple. He was here trying to find out if Lilly is staying with us."

"What did you tell him?"

Her frustrated sigh reminded him of when he'd been a child and she'd caught him and his brothers doing something they weren't supposed to. "Absolutely nothing that could harm anyone. Sure, he asked about Lilly. I told him I hadn't seen her. But Kane, he seemed way more interested in you."

Kane exchanged a look with Sly. Without exchanging a word, they both knew what this meant. Somehow, the cultists knew Lilly was with Kane. They'd come here because they'd learned this was where his family lived. In other words, he'd led them right to her.

"Are you even sure this man was the one you're looking for?" his mother continued. "He might have just been an old friend of yours or maybe someone from college, trying to track you down. I swear he looked perfectly normal to me."

"Normal?" Kane gestured at Sly. One of the team members handed over a computer tablet. "Tell me mom, was it one of these men?"

He pulled up the file and opened it. When he passed it over to his mother, pictures of the two remaining male Sanctuary members showed.

Her eyebrows rose. "Well, I'll be darned. Yes, it was this man right here." She stabbed her index finger at the one on the left, who had an afro and large aviator glasses. "He sure doesn't look like a member of a religious cult. Where's the third? I thought you said there were three?"

"There are." Sly answered for him. "The third one is a female."

A sound from the kitchen made everyone freeze. Kane and the Protectors all withdrew their weapons, motioning at everyone else to move away and take cover.

As soon as everyone was safely around the wall and in the hallway, Kane opened his mouth to ask who was there. Before he could, a beautiful gray wolf padded into the room.

"Lilly?"

At her name, the wolf turned toward him, staring at him with Lilly's stunning blue eyes.

"Stand down," Kane ordered, even though Sly should have been the one to give the command. "It's only Lilly." He put away his gun.

Instantly, the other men did the same.

"Lilly?" Kane's mother breathed. Kane hadn't even heard her reenter the room. "Oh, you're so beautiful, sweetheart."

Then, with everyone looking on in amazement, the older woman dropped to her knees and held out her arms. "Come here, Lilly, and let me have a look at you."

Casting Kane one more swift look, wolf Lilly did as his mother asked. The two women—one wolf, one human—touched noses, a sign of respect. Lilly allowed the older woman to coo over her, stroke her fur, and she even lifted her paw in a gesture of friendship.

When his mother had finished admiring Lilly, Kane showed her the way to the spare bedroom, borrowed a T-shirt and shorts from his mother, and left her alone to change back to her human form. Though the clothes would hang loosely on her, they'd have to do until he could take her back to the caves and retrieve her own clothing. Briefly he remembered her brightly colored sundress and wondered if it had been ruined.

Most of all, he couldn't believe Lilly had put herself at risk and come back to Wolf Hollow.

Anger had replaced the adrenaline now. When Lilly emerged, looking like a street person from the alleys of New York City, he grabbed her arm and led her outside.

"What are you doing here?" he demanded. "You promised me you'd stay safe at the caves."

"I did no such thing." When she lifted her face to his, her enlarged pupils took his breath away. Since she'd just changed back into human form, he knew she was fighting her own arousal.

The thought, and the sight of her swaying before him, was enough to set his body on fire. Using every ounce of willpower he possessed, he fought his own sharp stab of desire. He even jammed his hands into his pockets to make sure he didn't reach for her.

"At first, I did as you wanted," she told him softly, the sensual thrum in her voice tantalizing his already over-heated body. "And while I was running, I realized I could no longer cower in the shadows, hiding from danger."

The cost of this bravery, the amount of courage it had to have taken for Lilly to decide to face her demons head on, wasn't lost in him. Wasn't this what he'd been trying to teach her all along?

Then why the fury? While he wanted her to have more confidence, there was a difference between being self-assured and acting foolishly. He just couldn't get past the idea that she'd willingly placed herself in danger for no good reason. Imagining what could have happened to her made him break out in a cold sweat. Yet since she'd come so far, he knew he had to choose his words carefully.

"Lilly, it's fantastic that you want to stand up to a threat." Unable to help himself, he leaned forward and placed a chaste kiss on her forward. As he did, she moved closer to him, apparently aware he was already rock hard.

In desperation, he took a step back, forgetting what he'd been about to say.

"Thank you," she said, her husky voice nearly a purr. "I can honestly say my progress in that area is entirely due to you."

Her voice caressed his nerve endings. He swallowed, realizing he was perilously close to losing all control. "I know you just changed back."

Purposely making his tone as harsh and cold as he could, he turned his back to her, breathing rapidly and fighting for self-control. "We need to go find that pretty little dress you were wearing earlier. After that, I need to meet with Sly and his crew. We'll need to develop a plan of action now that they've made their presence known."

"Okay." Her voice was right behind him. Close. Too close.

He wondered if she knew how he had to struggle to keep from taking her in his arms. Hell, taking her period, right there on the front lawn of his parents' house. As if he had no self-control left. Like the night she'd sung to him and he'd blacked out. Yet one more aspect of Lilly he needed to investigate.

She was dangerous to him. Even without her singing. He'd always been known for his unshakable self-control. And now part of him ached to forget his training, the situation, and reach for her, so he could luxuriate in the pleasure they gave each other.

This would be wrong, in more ways than one.

Luckily, the other part of him, the rational side, still had the upper hand. As of right this moment, at least.

Clearing his throat, he tried to find words. Any words, as long as they weren't *come to me*.

"So, do you want to go get my dress now?" Even with his back turned, he could hear the sensual smile in her voice. No doubt she had visions of the two of them, alone in the woods, desire pulsing like a living thing between them.

Dangerous. And he couldn't allow himself to be distracted, especially not now, when things might be coming to a head.

Without turning, he nodded. "I'm going to send you up there with Kris or Kyle. I've got to get with Sly right away."

She protested, as he'd thought she would. "I want to be in on the meeting with Sly and the team."

"Why?" He didn't want to hurt her, but every aching moment he spent near her only increased his arousal.

"I want an update."

"I'll make sure that you get one, as soon as I can."

"But—"

"Lilly." He cut her off. "We don't have time for this right now. Wait here, I'll send my brother out, and he'll go with you to retrieve your dress."

Unbelievably, she still argued. "I know the way. I can go myself."

Though he realized it was out of proportion, infuriated, he turned. First mistake. He saw her expression the instant she caught sight of the bulge in the front of his jeans. Desire, raw and primitive, blazed from her amazing blue eyes.

"Oh, Kane…" She took a step toward him.

He took a step back. "Yes, I want you. No, we can't. Not right now." He spoke through clenched teeth. "Now please. Go inside the house and get one of my brothers. Kyle or Kris, I don't care. Tell him what I need him to do."

Finally, she lowered her head, giving in. "Fine. Where are you going?"

Feeling savage, he had to bite back a snarl. "I'm taking a quick walk. Alone. Once I have myself under control, I need to go talk to Sly and his crew."

"We can walk up to the caves together," she offered.

"Lilly." His tone carried a wealth of warning.

Without another word, she turned and went back inside, her back ramrod straight.

Despite it all, he couldn't help but grin. Any other time, in any other situation, he would have loved to explore her emerging feistiness.

He took off in the opposite direction from the caves. He

hadn't gone far when he heard the sound of his brother's minivan starting. Good. Walking calmed his overheated body. Lilly's absence helped even more. By the time he reached the cabin where the Protectors were staying, he had himself back under control.

Sly and Bronwyn were waiting on the front porch. "I've already sent two teams of two out to try to sniff out that guy," Sly said by way of greeting.

"Good." Kane sighed. "I'm trying to decide if I should just take Lilly and get the hell out of here."

Both Sly and Bronwyn protested. "You can't. Not when we're so close. They took a huge risk today, sending one of their people out here. Sounds to me like they're getting desperate."

"Desperate?" Kane's short bark of laughter contained not one iota of humor. "You've been here a while. What's the status? Have any of your team even been able to locate where they're staying?"

Sly shook his head. "No. I'm not sure what's going on, but no one has seen those three since the desk clerk told them she had no room at her motel. They haven't shown up in town at all."

"Except today."

"Yeah." Grimacing, Sly and Bronwyn exchanged a glance. "If they hadn't made that move today, we were about to believe they might have moved on."

"Moved on?" This time, Kane didn't bother to hide his disdain. "Not likely. I don't think they'd give up so easily."

"I agree." Bronwyn cast a sidelong look at Sly. "We're thinking since they sent that one to question your mother, they know she's with you."

Crossing his arms, he waited her out.

After a second or two, she continued. "We're hoping they'll eventually start canvassing the town. They've got to. They're here for a reason. For them to just go under-ground like this makes no sense."

"Unless they know you're on to them." Kane kicked at a rock with the toe of his boot. "We need to find out what brought them to Leaning Tree in the first place. They have no reason to suspect Lilly would be here. Lucas and Blythe, her brother and his wife, have no ties to this place. I'm thinking someone must have tipped them off."

This time Sly responded. "Maybe. It's possible. But who?"

Jamming his hands in his pockets, Kane paced. "I don't know. My family are the only ones who know Lilly's true identity, and they wouldn't betray my trust. As far as the missing Sanctuary people know, she could be anywhere in the U.S. So why have they come here? What brought them to our small town here in the Catskills?"

Again Sly and Bronwyn exchanged a look.

"What?" Kane stopped, glancing from one to the other. "What are you not telling me?"

Sly stepped forward. "I'm going to venture a guess, even though I know you're not going to like it."

"Go ahead."

Sly nodded. "I figure you've probably already thought this through, so it won't come as a total surprise. We're thinking they tracked you."

Kane blinked. "Dammit."

"We're checking in to that now."

"It's possible since I worked undercover at Sanctuary," Kane said.

"And were instrumental at bringing down Jacob Gideon," Sly reminded him. "It could be you're high on their list of targets."

"If they even have one, which I doubt." Staring off into the distance, Kane tried to think. "I swear, if I find out that I'm responsible for leading them to her..." He didn't finish the sentence. He didn't have to. Sly and Bronwyn completely understood.

"Look." Sly clapped him on the shoulder. "They aren't professionals. They've got to make a mistake. When they do, we'll be there to grab them."

Lilly went silent as Kyle drove her to the same general area where Kane had let her out of the car earlier. He was talkative, full of questions, but after receiving several monosyllabic responses, he stopped asking.

"You can walk to the caves from here." He pointed. "I'll wait. It should only take you a minute."

Though she knew Kane would have wanted Kyle to stay with her for safety reasons, glad of the chance for solitude, she simply nodded and got out of the car.

She couldn't remember how far she'd gone before she'd disrobed and changed. Either way, tromping through the woods would help her mood. She needed to purge her body of this insane desire for a man who clearly didn't want her.

Kane. She didn't want to need him, especially since she'd decided she had to be strong and learn how to make it on her own. When this was over, she had no plans to go back to live with her brother and his wife. She wanted to find a job, doing what, she didn't know exactly, and she wanted to experience the joys and the terrors of a self-sufficient life.

She thought. She wasn't sure she had it entirely right, assuming it would be a weakness to need or rely on anyone else.

Either way, she owed Kane an apology. She might not have much experience at life, but even she knew it was wrong to use someone physically.

The sad thing was, if Kane would let it, she knew their relationship had the potential of being so much more.

But she didn't want his pity. Not that, never that. She wished she could have met him as his equal, someone to be admired rather than one who evoked sympathy.

Sighing, she spotted the bright patterned material of her dress and hurried toward it. Once she had it in hand, she hurried back to where Kyle waited and climbed in his car.

"Good job," he said, smiling at her. He was handsome, too, she noted dispassionately, but without the touch of rugged masculinity that made Kane so attractive.

"Thanks." She smiled back. "I'm glad nothing happened to this dress. Today was the first time I've worn it."

He nodded. "Where to?"

The question surprised her. "I guess I'll go back to the cabin. I need to talk to Kane when he returns."

Again the nod. Shifting into Drive, he turned them around and they headed back to Wolf Hollow.

When they reached the cabin, Kyle parked. This time, he got out of the car.

"No need," she said, waving him back.

"I want to make sure Kane's here before I go. He'd have a fit if I left you here unattended."

She began to wish she'd taken a bit longer in the woods. Solitude had become a rare commodity in her life these days.

As they stepped on to the porch, the front door opened and Kane came out. Her stomach did its usual dip and swoop at the sight of him.

"You found it?" he asked, his shuttered gaze going to the dress. When Lilly nodded, he strode to his brother and gripped his shoulder in a man hug. "I appreciate it," he said.

"No problem." Dipping his head in a nod, Kyle took off.

Lilly stood outside until the sight and sound of his vehicle had completely disappeared. Finally, aware she could put it off no longer, she squared her shoulders and faced Kane.

"I'm sorry," she began.

"Don't worry," he said at the same time. One corner of his mouth quirked in a smile. "Go ahead."

"You first." Moving past him into the house, she took a seat on the couch.

"I met with Sly and Bronwyn," he told her. "Four men are out looking for the guy who was here today."

"Do you really think they'll find him?" She didn't mean to sound skeptical.

"I hope so. Especially since it's Sly's opinion that I'm the way they tracked here."

"Because you helped take down Sanctuary."

"Yes. And because your brother and I became good friends."

She made a sound of dismay.

"It's okay. We're prepared," he reassured her. "The Protectors are going to be staying here awhile. At least until they've caught those three."

Awhile. She tried not to show her dismay. More time while she felt increasingly like a lightning bug, trapped inside a jar. "And then what?"

"And then you can go on with your life."

She winced, then immediately tried to hide it. She didn't want him to realize how his words brought her pain. While she pretended to consider, she attempted to keep from staring at the way his muscles rippled when he moved his arm.

When his gaze met hers again, the intensity blazing from his made her inhale sharply. "That is what you want, isn't it?"

With him near, she no longer knew what she wanted. With one exception. Him. She wanted him.

All the logic she'd worked out while in the woods disappeared. She'd planned to apologize, to make promises she couldn't keep. In the end, she'd let him choose. She craved him, the same way she craved air to breathe. She'd let him know and allow him to make the choice. When... *if* she found enough courage to do so.

"Lilly?" His tone sounded savage. "Are you going to answer me?"

Pushing to her feet, she crossed to him and wrapped her arms around his neck, curling her body into his. Her mouth found his and this one touch was all it took.

Passion instantly blazed between them. Familiar and exhilarating. And welcome. When they were together, she didn't have to think about anything other than how good he felt.

Another way of running from reality? Maybe. But she truly didn't care.

Suddenly, the words Kane had said once came back to haunt her. She lifted her mouth from his, breathing hard. "I don't want to spend the rest of my life running from them."

"You won't," he hastened to reassure her. "We'll apprehend them soon."

"Will you?" Restless again, she twisted out of his arms. "What if you don't?"

"We'll deal with that if it happens." He reached for her. She sidestepped, biting back her frustration, pushing away her desire.

"No." The fierceness in her voice finally reached him. Crossing his arms, he waited.

"I want to go after them," she said. "I've put a lot of thought into it, and that's the only way we can catch them."

"What do you mean, exactly?" He spoke carefully, making her aware he already knew what she was going to say.

"They want me. We want them. It's pointless for those

Protectors to hang around waiting for them to put in an appearance and you know it."

He took a deep breath, bringing his breathing down to match hers. "True, but we have no other options."

She smiled sadly. "But we do. We can make it look as if they're going to get me. I've got you and six well-trained Protectors to keep me safe. Put me out there for them to try and grab. Instead, we'll set a trap."

"Bait." A warning settled over his rugged face. He reached out to her, gripping her upper arms. "You want me to allow you to be used as bait."

Allow?

"Yes." Gently, she pried his fingers loose, so he could see the faint red marks on her pale skin. "It's the only way. I want this over with."

She thought he'd refuse, expected the next words out of his mouth to be "absolutely not." Instead, he cocked his head, staring off into the distance, as though giving her suggestion careful consideration. Meanwhile, the scent and power of their mutual desire lingered, swirling around them like a potent smoke.

Her body wanted him. Only her body. This wasn't what mattered right now, she told herself fiercely. He had to see the logic in her words.

"You know, you might be on to something," Kane finally said, studying her with a critical, narrow gaze. "As long as the proper safeguards are in place so you're not at risk. I'll take it up with the others."

"When?" she pressed. "I'll go with you." She wasn't going to give him a chance to stall. "Let's talk to them now."

Again he surprised her. "Okay. But let me lay the ground rules."

He held out his hand and she took it, without hesitation. Each day she grew stronger and more self-confident. Rather than holding her back, Kane appeared to have stepped back, giving her the necessary room to spread her newfound wings. A firefly, about to escape from the jar.

She almost grinned at the corny analogy.

Chapter 16

Watching Lilly, so full of newfound bravado, Kane felt a flush of pride combined with a grim sort of panic. It took every instinct he had not to sit her down and caution her about the reality of life. Though she'd emerged alive from fifteen years in hell, she hadn't been unscathed. Damned if he'd stand by and let her take a chance of getting hurt again.

Yet as she stared at him with that self-assured smile, her blue eyes bright with confidence, he hadn't the heart.

"Well?" She all but tapped her foot. "Let's put this thing in motion."

"Someone's been watching too many TV movies." Somehow he managed to tease her. He'd wanted to swear when she came up with her plan, wanted to grab her and hold her close and tell her absolutely not, no way in hell.

"Nope. I've been reading a lot of thrillers and romantic suspense books," she said. "Come on, tell me. What do you think?"

"Give me a minute." He looked down, holding his tongue while he pretended to consider her idea, which he hated. There was no real choice and she probably knew it. He'd realized she was right. They had to use her as bait. It was the only way. Simple and exactly the opposite of what the cultists would expect them to do. After all, they were Protectors. Their job was to protect, to keep Lilly safe.

Not to put her up for target practice.

If he believed they wanted her dead, he never would have agreed to her plan. But since they both knew the remaining doctors from Sanctuary wanted to capture her alive, so they could continue their horrible experiments, that was one risk they didn't have to worry about.

"We can try it," he said, keeping his tone cautious.

She met his gaze and dipped her chin. "Thank you."

They decided to walk over to the Protectors' cabin. Sly, Bronwyn and two other members of his team were gathered around the kitchen table having a quick meal.

"Come on in." Sly stepped aside, motioning them past. "I reheated some barbecued beef we picked up in town and we're having sandwiches. You're welcome to eat with us."

Though the aroma wafting from the table made Kane's stomach rumble, he shook his head. "No, thank you. I wanted to run something by you. Lilly's come up with a plan and, as much as I hate it, I think it might work."

Briefly, he outlined Lilly's suggestion that they use her as a lure to trap the cultists.

After a moment of silence, Bronwyn jumped to her feet. "I like it," she said. "And I really think it has a viable chance."

Sly and the others seconded her comment.

"Great." Lilly greeted their acceptance with a shy smile. "Now all we need to do is work out the details."

"We will." Sly gave her a high five.

The way the Protectors greeted the idea disturbed the hell out of Kane. He'd expected some reservations at the very least, not this outright enthusiastic response.

He glanced at Sly, trying to catch the other man's eye, but the team leader was busy giving Lilly a quick bear hug. "Quite the little she-wolf you've turned out to be."

Kane barely suppressed an instinctive growl. While Lilly had no way of knowing this was the highest compliment a male Shifter could give a female, Kane did. As his wolf self tried to protest, he realized he also didn't appreciate the way the other man was eyeing Lilly. Every instinct within Kane had him wanting to grab Sly and inform him in no uncertain terms that Lilly was his. *His.*

Except she wasn't. Never would be. And Protectors never lied to their teams.

"We've got to plan this carefully," Sly said, indicating Kane and Lilly should both take a seat. "I'm expecting the two remaining team members any minute, so we'll wait for them before we get started. Several of us have started working in town, so we're making contacts there. Still no sign of the cultists, though."

"That's what Kane was telling me," Lilly murmured, dropping into an empty seat next to Bronwyn.

As Sly made his way back to his chair at the head of the table, Kane remained standing. Seeing this, Sly stood also.

A sound outside had Kane's hand going instinctively to his weapon. Sly strode over to the window and peered out. "Stand down, man. It's just Drake and Stu."

He'd barely finished his statement when the last two Protectors stomped inside. "I can smell that barbeque outside," one of them said. "We're starving."

Sly jerked his thumb toward Kane. "We've got company."

"They can eat," Kane put in. "Hell, everyone go ahead

and have your sandwiches. Everyone thinks better on a full stomach anyway."

No one needed a second urging. Even Sly resumed his interrupted meal. "You might as well grab a bite," Sly told him.

About to shake his head, Kane's stomach chose that moment to protest. Loudly. Grimacing, he snagged a seat on Lilly's other side and loaded up one of the paper plates.

Silence fell while they all ate. Lilly made quick work of polishing off her single sandwich and then she watched quietly while the rest of them had seconds and even thirds.

Once everyone had pushed their paper plate away, Sly leaned forward. "Here's what I'm thinking. We've got to orchestrate this carefully. We'll figure out a way to put the word out that you're going to be in town. First up, we need to create a 'leak' as to who you actually are."

Kane glanced at Lilly. From her weak nod and queasy expression, he could tell she didn't like this, even though it had been her idea. Neither did he, but they'd both already committed.

"You can always change your mind and back out," Kane murmured.

"But you won't, because it's necessary," Sly said, apparently also correctly interpreting her expression.

Glancing from Kane to Sly and then back again, Lilly slowly nodded. "I won't back out. Your plan makes sense."

"How will we keep them from coming to Wolf Hollow to try and get her?" Kane asked, his tone a bit more savage than he'd intended. "I do not want to put my family at risk in any way, shape or form."

"Timing, my man." Clearly unfazed by Kane's tone, Sly continued. "We leak the info in the morning, and then have Lilly go into town in the afternoon. I'm going to arrange to make this a big deal. I have contacts at the local news station from Albany. I'll arrange for a live interview. We'll get newspaper coverage, and put the word out on social media."

Lilly blinked. "But why? Why would any of that even happen?"

Sly grinned. "Your book deal."

"My what?"

Kane understood immediately. He had to admit it was a damn good plan. "He's going to put the word out that you've signed a major book deal to tell your story. This will infuriate the Sanctuary people and might make them act less rationally."

"As if they were ever rational." Lilly lifted her chin, her blue eyes blazing. "I like it. When do you want to do this?"

"How about now?" Sly asked.

"No. Tomorrow is the big Labor Day celebration and parade," Kane put in. "There'll be too many people in town, which will not only make it difficult to keep on top of things, but will put too many civilians in danger of getting hurt."

Though he looked as if he wanted to argue, eventually, Sly capitulated. "Two days after the parade," Sly said.

Kane agreed. The remainder of the team watched the debate in silence, apparently willing to go along with whatever Kane and Sly decided.

"What do I do until then?" Lilly asked.

"For one thing, we're going to continue your self-defense classes," Kane told her, hating how she looked like a wild animal caught in a trap. "And I really wish you'd reconsider learning to handle a firearm."

"No." Lilly had begun shaking her head before Kane even finished. "No guns. I can fight with my hands or change into a wolf and fight with teeth and claws."

Looking from her to Kane and back again, Sly frowned.

"But what if they have guns?" he pointed out. "You'd stand a much better chance if you were armed."

"That's what I have you for." Lilly's icy tone made the other man cock his head. "I want you and your team to make sure it doesn't come to that."

The hell with it. Kane pushed back his chair. Crouching in front of her, he placed his hands on her shoulders and looked her right in the eye. "You have my word, Lilly. There's no way I'm letting those nuts get their hands on you ever again."

Gaze locked on his, slowly she nodded.

Sly's eyes gleamed as he looked from one to the other. "In the meantime, we'll continue to work the town. Since this parade is such a big deal, we'll fan out and keep searching the crowd. Maybe we'll get lucky and grab those cult members before we have to resort to our other plan."

The morning of the parade dawned with an overcast sky, the dark gray clouds threatening rain. Despite that, Kane seemed cheerful.

"It won't dare rain," he promised. "As far as I know, our Labor Day parade has never been rained out."

Though Lilly was skeptical, she decided to go with the flow. "I've never been to a parade before."

From the shocked expression on Kane's handsome face, she might as well have confessed to never having eaten ice cream, or something equally unbelievable.

"I thought you and Lucas were allowed to occasionally go into town. Surely even small Texas towns have the occasional parade."

She shrugged. "I imagine they do, but we were never there when they had one. I remember watching the big Macy's one at Thanksgiving, but I've never seen one in real life."

"That's a crime," he said, his silver eyes going briefly gray. "Well, that's about to change today."

Since attending the parade would mean going into town, Lilly's heart fluttered. "Did you change your mind then? Is today when we're going to implement our plan to use me as bait?"

"No." He shook his head. "Sly kept pressing for that, even after our meeting, but I overruled them. The town is too crowded. There'll be hundreds of civilians there. Kids and elderly people. Families. I don't want to take a chance on someone getting hurt."

Relieved, she nodded. "Then how are you going to disguise me so I can watch the parade? If I go into town, even with a ball cap and dark glasses, people will know who I am."

Now he grinned, a wicked, wolfish light coming into his eyes. "Kathy helped me put together a costume." He brandished a shopping bag. "Once we get you decked out in this, there's no way anyone is going to recognize you."

Wary and also resigned, she looked at the bag. "Hand it over. I might as well see what you two have in store for me."

Amusement still shone in his face as he passed her the bag. "You might need some help with part of that. If you do, just yell."

"I will." More curious than anything else, she carried the bag into the bathroom. When she pulled out the getup Kane and his sister had assembled, she couldn't help but laugh. A curly red wig, maternity dress and sensible shoes were the first things she saw. Lastly, there was some sort of stuffed pillow with straps. As she puzzled over that, she realized it was a pretend baby bump.

Kane was right. No one would recognize her, not even his family.

She got dressed with mirth bubbling up inside of her.

She'd always heard pregnant women glowed. Maybe, just maybe, she could actually pull this disguise off. It would be absolutely heavenly to go out in public and not have to worry about some crazy from Sanctuary snatching her.

The maternity dress Kathy had chosen for her was a matronly navy color, with an empire waist. The sensible flats were also dark blue and they made up in comfort for their ugliness.

After putting on the red frizzy wig, Lilly almost took it right back off. But after she adjusted it, picking at the curls, she realized she looked like an adult—and pregnant—version of Little Orphan Annie.

When she emerged, waddling slightly, Kane took one look at her and cracked up. She loved the way he laughed, all husky and rich and, oh, so masculine. The sound made her want to hug him…and she might have if her enormous belly hadn't been in the way.

"So now that I'm a pregnant lady, who are you going to be?" she asked, fluttering her long eyelashes.

His smile faded as he gave her a long, serious look. "I'm escorting you and Kathy, since Tom is working the parade. You're Kathy's pregnant girlfriend from the city."

"Perfect!" She clapped. "I'm ready, let's go."

All the way into town, Kane kept shooting sideways glances at her. At first, she thought he was still marveling over the costume. Then she wondered if her wig had slipped, or she'd misapplied her makeup. Finally, she couldn't take it anymore.

"What?" she asked. "Why do you keep looking at me?"

"I'm wondering if that disguise will even fool anyone. Especially if the cultists are watching me."

She gave him her most gentle smile. "If it doesn't, then we'll have to implement our plan early. You're still going to have me surrounded, just in case, right?"

"Yes." He still sounded glum. "The entire team is in plain clothes and in place. No one will be able to get within a few feet of you."

"Perfect. Then if someone makes an attempt…"

"We'll grab them. The only problem is there's three of them. I don't want to take a chance on any of them getting away."

"We'll be fine." She wished she could lend him some of her newfound confidence. For whatever reason, the fear and trepidation that had dogged her most of her life had disappeared. "I want those creeps caught."

"I do, too." His fervent reply made her smile.

"And if they are going to make some sort of move today, then I really, really hope they wait until after I've seen the parade."

Though the town had already begun to fill up and parking was at a premium, Kane's brother had saved him a spot in the grassy field behind the high school. He'd actually removed a lawn chair from his van and parked himself in the spot, so no one else could park there.

"Here we are," Kane said, grinning at his brother.

Lilly couldn't help but laugh. "That's nice of him."

Kris laughed when he caught sight of Lilly in her disguise. "Nice," he said. "You and Kathy look like two of a kind."

"We ought to," Lilly replied. "This is her dress, after all."

Once Kane had parked his Corvette and Kris had stowed his chair back in his van, the three of them headed toward Main Street. In the distance, they could hear the sound of the high school band playing. And the closer they got, the stronger the scent of burgers and hot dogs cooking became.

"This is the biggest crowd yet," Kris said, glancing to his left.

Kane nodded, though he didn't respond. Lilly eyed them.

He and Kris were busy casting furtive glances around them, clearly trying not to be noticeable. The way they were acting made her wonder if they expected someone to jump out from behind every parked car.

Once they crossed from the alley onto Main Street, the crowded sidewalk made walking slow. They moved through throngs of people, sidestepping babies in strollers and the occasional dog on a leash. Her fake baby bump made walking a bit difficult, and she soon found herself out of breath.

"Will you two please wait up?" she chided. "Being pregnant forces me to move much more slowly."

The two men slowed their steps for her. Lilly found herself wondering what it was like to really be pregnant. She couldn't imagine how it must feel to know a little life was growing inside you. For the first time, she wondered if she'd ever experience such a miracle.

All along the sidewalk, vendors had set up little booths with brightly colored awnings. All kinds of goods were for sale, from homemade jewelry and baked goods to artwork made by local artists. In between these were booths selling freshly made burgers or hot dogs, turkey legs and funnel cake.

People were everywhere, dressed in shorts and T-shirts. There were strollers and toddlers and children running and playing, laughing as they dodged in and out of the crowd. The noise and the scent were overwhelming. But delicious, too. Lilly wanted to stop and take it all in.

But Kane and Kyle continued to plow determinedly through the throngs of people. Lilly finally had to take hold of Kane's back belt loop to keep from being left behind. He turned and smiled at her, the brightness of that smile nearly making her lean in for a quick, unthinking kiss. Luckily, she caught herself in time.

"Where are we going?" she finally asked, huffing a little.

"Where the family is waiting for us," Kane answered.

"Everyone's staked out our usual spot in front of the shoe store," Kris elaborated. He glanced at Lilly, his gray eyes a paler imitation of Kane's, and then winked. "Kathy wants you right next to her."

The festive air and the happy vibes everyone gave off made her want to laugh. Still feeling giddy despite her breathlessness, she nodded. "Where else would I be? We pregnant women have to stick together."

"There they are." Kris waved. "They haven't seen us yet."

Though Lilly squinted, she couldn't make out where they were.

"Over there." Kane pointed. "See the sign that says Frunter's Shoes?"

As she stood on tiptoe to try to see over the sea of heads in front of her, she heard a boom, a crack, a loud explosion or something. The earth shook, a rolling wave of sound and pressure. Somehow, she found herself on the ground, her ears ringing.

Dazed, she lay there, trying to make sense of what had just happened. Gradually, she realized there was smoke. Fire? People were screaming. Shouting, crying and wailing. As she tried to push to her elbows, she saw her hands were scraped and bleeding.

What had just happened? Had someone set off a bomb?

Another pop, almost like a gunshot, immediately followed. The billowing black smoke stung her eyes. Disoriented, she heard more screams of pain and terror, faint as if coming from a distance. Weakly, she pushed up onto her hands and knees, trying to stand. Finally, she managed to do so, shaky and confused, her mouth dry with shock and tasting of ashes.

Kane appeared in her wavering line of vision. "Lilly." He reached for her, gently pulling her close. "Are you okay?"

Before she could answer, she saw Kris, staggering toward them. "What happened?" she asked, her voice weak and shaky. "What on earth was that?"

"I don't know," Kane answered, grabbing for his brother with his other arm. "It sounded like an explosion."

"A bomb?" Kris moaned, wiping ineffectively a trickle of blood running from his forehead down his cheek. "Damn." He squinted, trying to see through the smoke. "Debi and the kids are out there. And Mom and Dad and Kyle and Sharon."

Jerking away from Kane, he staggered in the direction they'd initially been heading. "Come on. We've got to find them and make sure everyone is all right."

Without waiting for an answer, he lurched away, trying to get to the spot where, moments before, the entire McGraw family had been standing.

Kane started after him, then hauled Lilly against him, his gaze searching the crowd. "Are you hurt?"

Numb, she looked down at herself. While she might be bruised, she didn't see blood except on her hands and both her knees, where they'd hit the concrete. Minor stuff. "No," she croaked. "Please. Let's go check on your family."

"Not you. I need to leave you with one of the Protectors," he said, soot-stained expression grim and desperate. "I've got to go help Kris and make sure my family is safe."

In the distance, sirens sounded. As Kane looked around them, trying to locate one of the Protectors, just like that, Bronwyn materialized. Despite the ash in her hair and on her clothes, with her big floppy hat and denim overalls, she looked as if she'd just come into town directly from the farm. Her disguise was so at odds with her true personality that Lilly could only stare in dazed wonder.

"Bronwyn?"

"Yeah." She grimaced. "I was pretty close to where it detonated, but I think I'm okay."

"Where'd it go off?" Kane stared at her, unable to mask his desperation.

"Over there." Bronwyn pointed. "Kind of in between the shoe store and the ice-cream place."

In other words, close to where Kane's family had been standing. Kane blanched, going pale.

"Can you guard Lilly?" he asked, balancing on the balls of his feet as if about to take flight.

About to protest, Lilly bit her tongue. She'd do whatever was needed to help ensure Kane got his family to safety. She could only hope no one had been hurt.

Bronwyn glanced at her as if she expected her to object. When Lilly didn't, the other woman nodded.

"I've got her," she told Kane, low-voiced. "Sly and the others are helping set up a triage area for the wounded. Go!"

Kane nodded, planted a quick kiss on Lilly's mouth, and took off. Lilly watched him go, her entire body aching.

"Come with me," Bronwyn said, all business and appearing completely unruffled by the chaos around them. The wail of sirens had grown closer, and then stopped. People were still shouting, weeping and running in every direction. The keens of pain and grief were the worst, cutting Lilly to the bone.

Bronwyn took a step, and her knees almost buckled. She grabbed Lilly's arm to steady herself.

"I want to help the McGraws," Lilly rasped, staring as she realized a huge bloodstain was spreading on Bronwyn's side. "You're hurt."

"It's nothing," the other woman said, her face pale but determined. "Come with me. Remember what Kane said."

Watching as Bronwyn's bloodstain grew larger, Lilly

started to protest, and then finally nodded and followed the Protector.

Weaving on her feet, Bronwyn led her around a corner, to an area where several police cars, ambulances and fire trucks were parked, lights flashing. "This is probably the safest spot right now," she said, using the brick wall at her back to support herself. "We'll wait here."

The instant she finished speaking, she slid to the ground in a crumpled heap, the bloodstain spreading from her to the concrete.

"Help," Lilly shouted, motioning to one of the ambulance workers. "We need help."

Two men came running over. Taking in the situation instantaneously, they lifted a now unconscious Bronwyn onto a stretcher and carried her off to one of the ambulances. A moment later, the lights started flashing. The siren whoop-whooped and the vehicle roared off, leaving Lilly alone.

Now what? The McGraws. She needed to make sure Kane's family was safe. Thankful for her disguise, Lilly turned and began staggering back the way she'd come. Though she didn't think she'd been hurt, she believed she might be in shock. It didn't matter. She needed to find Kane and his family.

As she rounded the corner, a third explosion went off. In the distance, flames roared toward the smoky sky. The acrid scent hurt Lilly's nose. The awful cries from the wounded hurt Lilly's heart.

"Help me," someone moaned, staggering out of the dusky cloud toward her. With a jolt of recognition, Lilly realized it was Anabel, holding her torn and bloody dress closed around her waist. Blood trickled from a deep gash on one arm, and part of her hat appeared to have been singed.

Forgetting her disguise, Lilly stepped toward her. "Anabel. Are you hurt?"

Raising her head, Anabel squinted at her with a bleary gaze. "You look familiar," she croaked. "Please, help me get away from here."

Thoroughly disoriented, nonetheless Lilly nodded. "Come on. Let's go find the McGraws."

Anabel stared. Covering her mouth with her hands, she began making a keening sound. "The entire McGraw family was there, right by where the bomb went off. I don't know if they made it."

As she looked at Anabel, Lilly felt bile rise in her throat. "No," she managed. "They have to be ail right. Kane and Kris went to go check." She gasped, trying to catch her breath. "Come on, Anabel. Let's go find them. They'll know."

Anabel didn't move. Despite her obvious injuries, she stared at Lilly as if she thought her insane. "Who *are* you?" Anabel asked. "Are the McGraws friends of yours?"

"It's me, Lilly Green. I'm wearing this because…" She waved her hands, wincing as she saw spots. "Long story. Now come with me. We ought to be safe together."

Slowly, Anabel nodded. "I thought so. I know a short cut. It will help us get away from the crowd and the wounded." She pushed herself forward, clearly hurting. "Follow me."

Suddenly, misgivings gave Lilly pause. "Anabel, you're hurt. Let's go talk to the medics first. Then we'll go and find the McGraw family."

"I'm fine." With a jerk of her chin, Anabel squared her shoulders. "You have no idea what I've been through. I'm strong. I can handle this."

That said, she staggered off, not even looking back to see if Lilly followed.

Debating for the space of two heartbeats, Lilly hurried after the other woman. She caught up with her as Anabel grasped the door handle of what was clearly a back door leading into one of the shops. "There you are," Anabel huffed, brushing an ash-coated strand of her jet-black hair out of her face. "Help me get this door opened."

"Why?" Lilly hesitated. "It's probably locked. And if it's not, it seems a lot like breaking and entering to me."

Anabel shook her head. "Whatever. A friend of mine owns this shop and the next four, which are being used as a warehouse now. If we cut through it, we'll come up on the other side of where the bomb went off."

This raised another set of questions. Chief among them, Lilly wanted to know if it was safe. Logic dictated any structures near the point of detonation would be shaky, at best.

She started to tell Anabel this, but the other woman continued to pull on the door handle. Finally, with a grunt, she managed to yank the door open. "Are you coming?" Without waiting for an answer after casting a backward glance at Lilly, she disappeared inside.

Lilly debated for half a second. She wanted to check on the wounded. If Anabel truly knew a shortcut, then she was wasting time by waiting.

She took a deep breath, grabbed the door handle, and went after her.

Chapter 17

Following his brother into the smoke brought Kane back to a mission he'd once gone on overseas in a war zone. The smoke, the chaos and the smell of charred flesh was the same. Ditto the rubble still falling and the panic.

With an explosion that size, he knew people had been hurt and killed. He could only hope his family wasn't among them.

Ahead, Kris disappeared into a crowd of first responders. Ignoring the stitch in his side where a piece of metal had struck, Kane hurried after.

When they reached the area where the shoe store had been, Kris stopped and stared, causing Kane to nearly run into him. A huge hole had been blown in the front of the building. An emergency triage area had been hastily erected in the street, and here the people with the worst injuries were treated and made as stable as possible before transport to the hospital.

"Come on." Kane grabbed his brother's arm. "Let's check over here first."

The scope and severity of the injuries boggled the mind. Missing limbs, gaping wounds, the kind of things one expected to see in a war zone. Not at the Labor Day parade in Leaning Tree, New York.

Moving quietly, Kane and Kris searched through the victims, both relieved and worried when they didn't see anyone they recognized. "Where are they?" Kris muttered. "We've got to find them."

Once outside again, Kane stood facing the shoe store. He tried to breathe deeply, to keep his hopes high. He tried to focus on what he did know—his family wasn't in the triage area among the wounded—rather than what he didn't.

"Over there!" Kyle shouted, lurching toward a crowd of stunned survivors being shepherded away by uniformed police officers. "I think I saw Mom and Dad."

Kane rushed after him. When he caught sight of his father's shiny bald head and mother's long gray braid, the relief that blasted through him almost sent him to his knees.

The instant his mother saw him, she cried out and opened her plump arms. Her gardenia scent brought him comfort, even as he looked past her for the rest of his family.

Kris had already located Debi and his children. A little ways beyond him, Kane spotted Kyle and Sharon, huddled together with their brood. At first glance, everyone appeared uninjured.

The police continued to move the uninjured away from the blast zone. Kane went along with them, keeping one arm around his mother's rounded shoulders and the other around his father's waist. "Where's Kathy?" he asked, realizing he hadn't seen his sister.

"Kathy and Tom already left," she said, still sounding a bit shaky. "Tom was frantic that the shock and stress might make her lose the baby, so he hustled Kathy away." Her smile wavered a bit, but she continued. "He says he's going to make sure she gets an evening of pampering."

"Good. She needs that." Kane dragged his hand across his chin. "You should consider having one of those yourself, Mom."

"I just might," she said, even though they both knew good and well she wouldn't. "This was a close call."

"What happened?" Kane asked. "How did you all escape without being hurt? It looked like the blast went off near you."

"I can't imagine how we were spared," his mother said again. "It was a last-minute series of events actually. If little Anthony hadn't chased after that puppy, and Kyle and Sharon hadn't gone after him, and we all hadn't rushed over when he was nearly run over by that bicyclist, we would have been standing right next to where the bomb was detonated."

Kane didn't even want to think of how things might have turned out if not for blind luck. Or fate. Either way, no McGraws had been injured. Once they were outside the temporary police barricades, they stopped moving. His mother smiled at him, and then turned and watched misty-eyed as his two brothers shepherded their individual families toward the area where they'd parked their cars.

Chest tight, Kane did the same. Glancing around him at the damage and destruction, the barely organized chaos of the first responders and the numerous wounded, he struggled to understand.

"Do you think it was terrorists?" his father asked, apparently thinking the same thoughts.

"I don't know." Kane shook his head, his mood grim. "But what else could it have been?"

"Good thing we've already got Protectors on-site," the

elder McGraw continued, wiping more soot off his bald head with his hand. "Though I imagine they'll be sending more."

"I'm sure they will. Pretty soon, this place will be crawling with FBI and ATF, not to mention the media." He couldn't help but think their planned attempt to capture the cultists was now doomed.

He hugged her again. "Now that I know the family is all safe, I've got to go check on Lilly."

"Lilly?" Wide-eyed, his mom did a quick search of the crowd. "What happened? How'd you two get separated?"

"It's okay." He gave her what he hoped was a reassuring smile. "I left her with Bronwyn. She's fine."

Exhaling, she fiddled with her braid. "Thank goodness. By all means, please go and find her. And then I want you to bring her to us, so we can all see that she's all right with our own eyes."

Kane hugged his mother again, and then his father. "I will." Then he turned and reversed direction, slipping past the police barricade and heading toward the ambulance area where he'd last seen Bronwyn and Lilly.

The instant she stepped inside the building, Lilly had to stop and allow her eyes a moment to adjust to the darkness.

"Anabel?" she called, coughing as she choked a little on the dust. "Anabel, where are you?"

"Almost to the door." Anabel's voice, faint and ghostly sounding, drifted back. "When I reach it, I'll hold it open for you so you can see the way."

"Thanks," Lilly croaked, coughing again to clear her throat. While the interior was dark, the dim light coming from the front room was enough to guide her steps. "But I think I can find my way to you, if you'll only wait."

Anabel didn't answer.

Lilly's wolf chose that moment to raise a ruckus inside her, snarling and whining. She paused. Her other self felt something was amiss, and barked a warning. For the first time Lilly wondered if she'd made a mistake following Anabel. Kane and Kathy both had said the other woman wasn't right in the head.

"Lilly?" Anabel's voice, perfectly sweet. "I'm waiting for you. Are you lost?"

Remembering the pain in Anabel's eyes, Lilly took a deep breath but regretted it as she doubled over coughing.

"Lilly?" Anabel sounded concerned. "Are you all right? Do you want me to come back for you?"

"No." Lilly wiped her mouth and made up her mind. She ignored her wolf instincts and moved forward.

As she rounded a corner, someone jumped her from behind, twisting her arms behind her. Remembering Kane's lessons, she fought back. She kicked, high and swift, hard to the groin.

It worked. Whoever had grabbed her let go.

Not waiting around to see who or what had assaulted her, Lilly hurried toward Anabel. She couldn't leave Anabel alone, especially with this danger. She didn't know if the other woman knew how to fight, so Lilly might have to defend her. Plus two were always better than one.

As if her thoughts had brought double danger, two shapes materialized in the dusty light. Willing herself to calm down, Lilly dropped into a battle crouch, ready to deflect and defend until she could attack.

They both rushed her at once. At the same time as the one she'd just fended off, jumped her from behind.

Lilly screamed. Not for help. No, to warn the other woman. "Run Anabel, run. I'm being attacked. Run and get help."

The man behind held her while the other two tied up her

feet and then her hands. They shoved her, still standing, into the cement wall. "No sense trying to get help from that one. She's been paid to bring you here to us."

As if on cue, Anabel emerged from around the corner. Her mocking laugh seemed to echo in the empty room. "I know you're being attacked, silly. I'm the one who arranged this."

She came closer, letting Lilly see her wide, toothy smile. She held up a shopping bag as if it was a trophy. "It's been a pleasure doing business with you, gentlemen and lady. I'll be taking off now."

"Not so fast." One of Lilly's captors, reached for Anabel. "You'll be staying with us. We can't have you leaving." And he snatched the shopping bag out of her hands just as the other two grabbed her.

That voice. Lilly's heart thudded in her chest as her blood turned to ice. She recognized that voice. He was one of the doctors from Sanctuary, one of the ones who'd held her prisoner and tortured her.

Anabel let out a snarl, the sound full of fury. "Don't you touch me," she screamed. And just like that, she began changing into her wolf self.

The instant Lilly recognized the brilliance of this, she too dropped to the ground and began to shape-shift. Her clothing ripped as her bones lengthened. As soon as the change was complete, she crossed over to stand flank to flank with the other wolf. Though Anabel had betrayed her, in this they were kin. She'd deal with the other later, if, no, *when* they got out of this.

The three humans, and now Lilly recognized them as Sanctuary doctors all, glanced at each other and began to slowly advance.

Both Lilly and Anabel crouched low, giving nearly identical warning growls. One of the men had rope, the same one that had earlier been used to bind Lilly's ankles.

The lone woman stood in between the two men, as if their larger size would protect her. Lilly exchanged a glance with Anabel, communicating silently that they should attack her first. In nature, the weakest always were the initial target.

Anabel rushed forward, powerful jaws snapping. The woman went down, screaming as Anabel tore at her flesh.

Taking advantage of the distraction, Lilly jumped the shorter of the two men, aiming her teeth for his crotch. She slashed, tearing at his clothing and ripping skin. He screamed, a high-pitched, terrible sound.

The third man raised his arm and metal glinted in the faint light. Lilly recognized his weapon, the same tranquilizer gun from Sanctuary that had been used on her too many times to count.

She twisted and went for his ankles. He shot her midstride, barely pausing as he pivoted and then shot Anabel, while the other two humans continued to scream.

As Lilly felt her consciousness ebbing, she struggled against it. She only hoped that the one who had the tranquilizers didn't remember how she'd built a gradual tolerance to the dosage, even as she prayed that was still the case.

While mentally struggling against the sedative, she let her entire body go slack and closed her eyes. Best if they thought she'd gone unconscious, like the slack-jawed Anabel on the floor close by.

As she watched through her lashes, Anabel's body shuddered and began to change back to human form. Lilly remembered how that had always happened to her as well, and that trying to stop this occurrence was one of the doctor's many experiments on her.

She realized she'd need to shape-shift back into a human,

too, or they'd know she was faking. Taking care to keep her breathing deep and even, she initiated her own change.

The hard cement floor hurt her human skin and joints. She hated her nakedness, wishing she had a way to cover herself, but knew she could not. She thought of Kane, wondered if he even knew she was missing.

"Now we've just got to load them up and get them out of here," the female cultist, a Dr. Menger, if Lilly remembered right, spoke.

"You know, that's why we set off that bomb," one of the men said. "Creates a hell of a diversion. No one will even notice."

Lilly tried to swallow past the sudden lump in her throat. *They'd* caused the explosion, callously injuring and even killing who knew how many people, simply to create a distraction?

Worse, they'd done it because of *her*.

She thought of Kane and his Protectors and their now useless plan. The doctors from Sanctuary had managed to outsmart them without even trying. They'd take her somewhere and finish the experiments they'd started.

Experiments. Suddenly she remembered what had happened to Kane when she sang. Was there some way she could use that to her advantage without getting herself raped?

Since they'd used the tranquilizer on her, her captives hadn't bothered retying her bonds. She tried to picture the scenario, feeling that if she could get a clear vision as to how she might fight her way free, she'd have a better chance.

She knew she had to try. It was better than just going meekly to her fate, which would be a fate worse than hell.

Starting out low, she began singing the same song she'd made up that night with Kane. She'd never forgotten it, because every note had come from someplace deep inside of her.

As her voice soared, she pushed slowly to her feet, testing out her balance, the strength of her limbs. She was ready. More than ready.

Her two captors paused. The woman froze. They all stared at her as if she was a demon emerging from the bowels of the earth. Which, to them, she supposed she was.

Drawing strength from this, Lilly sang with all her heart. She had a mental image of the evasive moves she would take when the men tried to rut with her, and she knew she'd need to avoid the woman at all costs. Lilly had no idea what her voice would do to a female.

But instead of lust, pain contorted their features.

"Stop it," Dr. Menger shouted, hands over her ears. "Stop it right now!"

Ignoring her, Lilly stared at the men. One of them had dropped to his knees. He, too, had his hands covering his ears and appeared to be shaking with pain.

The other man screamed.

Seeing her opportunity, still singing, Lilly ran. Back the way she'd come, knowing once she made it into the alley, she could find help.

To her surprise, she wasn't followed.

Only when she'd pushed into the outside air, did she stop singing. Since she was naked, she grabbed a discarded black trash bag from the ground and used it to cover herself as best she could. Then, gasping, she rushed away, screaming for help, her cries mingling with those of the injured and panicked.

When Kane made it over to the area where he'd left Lilly, he spotted one of Sly's men. Hurrying up to the other Protector, he asked about Bronwyn.

"She was wounded," the man said, his expression grim. "They took her by ambulance to some hospital in Margaretville."

Kane cursed. "What about Lilly? She was with Bronwyn."

"I don't know. Maybe she rode in the ambulance with her."

Jaw clenched, Kane considered punching the guy, but knew it wasn't his fault. "Find Sly," he ordered. "Tell him the asset— No," he corrected himself, "tell him Lilly's gone missing. He needs to mobilize the team and help me find her."

He hurried off without waiting for an answer. He knew Sly would do his best to help, but most of the Protectors had joined the other first responders in helping the wounded. He couldn't, in all conscience, pull his men away when they were needed to help save lives.

He had to find Lilly.

Taking off at a slow jog, he circled the area where he'd last seen her. He considered her viewpoint, asked himself what would she do? Once she realized Bronwyn had been injured and needed help, he knew she'd get the other woman to the medics.

And then what?

She'd try to find him and Kris and the rest of his family. She'd have headed in the direction of the shoe store.

Turning, he jogged in that direction.

"Kane!"

That voice. Lilly. He spun around as she came barreling out of an alley, covered in soot and dirt and wearing a filthy black plastic trash bag.

He held her while she sobbed out her story. Sly came up with three of his team, and they followed Lilly to the back door of the deserted shop.

Weapons drawn, they entered. Kane made Lilly stay

behind him. He planned to get her outside at the first sign of trouble.

But once they reached the room where Lilly had told him she'd sung, their footsteps were the only sound. At first, Kane feared they'd escaped, but once they rounded the corner he and the other Protectors stopped in shock.

The three cult members lay on the floor, immobile and unconscious, their frozen expressions still contorted in expressions of pain.

Next to them lay Anabel, still out from the tranquilizer. Kane found her torn clothes and gently covered her nakedness. The others were cuffed and prodded until they groggily came to.

As soon as they were able to stand, they were led away. Sly went to find a medic to tend to Anabel, hopefully to neutralize the tranquilizer or at least monitor her until she was back to normal.

"Come on," Kane told Lilly, gathering up her ruined sundress and taking her arm.

"Wait." She pointed to a shopping bag on the floor. "That's what they gave Anabel for helping them get me. I want to see what's inside."

He fetched it for her and they opened it together. Inside were neatly rubber-banded stacks of hundred-dollar bills. "There has to be several thousand dollars in here," Lilly said. "She sold me out for cash?"

"I guess she needed money," Kane answered, his heart aching at the bewildered and stunned shock darkening Lilly's expression. "Come on, let me get you home so you can clean up and rest."

Home. The last cabin on the lane at Wolf Hollow Motor Court Resort.

If Lilly noticed his slip of the tongue, she didn't comment. Instead, she simply nodded, slipping her hand into his.

Later, after Lilly had showered and he'd taken her up to the main house to let his family see she was safe and vice versa, he watched as she and Kathy, Debi and Sharon put their heads together over some magazine and then traipsed into the kitchen to attempt to make whatever recipe they'd found. With their hair all worn in ponytails of differing hair colors, brunette and blond and redhead, they looked like a hair-color advertisement straight from the pages of some glossy magazine.

Kane's brothers had taken Tom and the kids outside for a raucous game of tag football, leaving Kane alone with his parents.

"How'd she get away?" his mother asked, watching him closely, her light blue eyes worried. She fingered her braid as she caught him staring at the kitchen doorway through which Lilly had just gone.

He told her, not sure she'd believe the story.

"I've heard about that talent somewhere," his father mused. "I can't remember where, though. It sounds awfully familiar."

"The legends mentioned it," Kane's mother said, her voice rising with excitement.

"Really?" Kane scratched his head. "I don't remember ever hearing about anything like that. I remember learning about a Healer, but not any kind of singing skill."

"I do." Getting up, she pulled out her laptop and accessed the internet. "They call it being a Wolf Siren. Just one second. Here we are." She handed the computer to him.

"A Wolf Siren." he read out loud. "Every generation, a few selective females are born who can sing to determine which male is their mate. The sound of her voice beguiles and bewitches the wolf who is to be hers, but incapacitates any other male or female who hears her sing. In ancient times, these females were revered and became oracles, and their offspring were carefully monitored since it was likely one of their children would carry this gift."

Both his parents were smiling and nodding. At first, he didn't realize why, but then he understood.

"It only affected me." He swallowed hard, his throat tight. "That means I'm her mate."

"Yes, and once the mated pair acknowledge this fact to each other, the song no longer affects anyone in the same way." To his shock, his mother winked.

On top of that, next his father playfully punched his arm. "You're her mate. As if you didn't know."

Kane grimaced. He looked down, then at the kitchen doorway, before meeting their eyes. They'd all been through so much today, how could he be any less than honest now. "Yes. I know. I've known since the first moment I laid eyes on her."

"Then why haven't you talked to her?" his mother asked.

"I don't think Lilly is ready to hear anything about that. She claims she doesn't want a relationship. She has this idea that she wants to go off and be on her own."

"What?" His mother sounded shocked. "That girl spent fifteen years in solitary confinement. If there's ever been someone who needs to be with someone, she does."

He shrugged, trying to appear casual, when in fact every word his mother said had hope flowing through his veins and energizing him.

"Doesn't she realize how difficult it is to find one's true mate?" his father groused, still smiling, still watching Kane closely. "To disregard such good fortune would be such a waste."

"You need to tell her, son," his mother put in. "At least give her the option. Have you ever mentioned how you feel?"

"No." Kane swallowed. "I didn't want her to feel she

owed me anything, or that she had to be with me out of pity."

At this, his mother snorted. "Lilly? That girl's become a regular firecracker. She's really gained a lot of self-confidence since she's been here. Give her a chance."

Give her a chance? As Kane stared at his mother, wondering if she'd lost her mind, or he had, he realized she was right. He'd never actually told Lilly how he felt, and the only discussion they'd ever had about a future relationship, he'd had a sense she was telling him what she thought he wanted to hear.

At the time, he'd told himself that was wishful thinking. Now, he realized he'd never given her a chance to choose.

If she truly wanted to be alone once she knew he loved her, well then he had no choice but to let her go.

"You're right," he slowly told his parents. "And I know exactly what I want to do and how I want to do it. I'll need your help. But first, I want to test something."

In the days after the remaining cultists from Sanctuary had been apprehended, Lilly felt a lightness to her spirit that she hadn't felt since she'd been fifteen, before Jacob Gideon had caught her and Lucas shape-shifting and labeled them demons.

Kathy had taken her under her wing and Lilly suspected they might have become best friends if she'd been able to stick around Leaning Tree longer. Still, for the time she had left here, Lilly accepted the offer of friendship. Debi and Sharon, who seemed to defer to Kathy, appeared to welcome Lilly into their new circle of four.

Today they were cooking desserts. Since the Labor Day celebration had turned into a disaster, none of the law enforcement personnel or first responders had gotten to celebrate the final summer holiday. The women of the McGraw family, led by Kathy, had decided to remedy that. They planned to bake as many cakes, pies and desserts as possible, and then deliver them to those police officers and firefighters and EMTs.

Though Lilly had never baked a single thing in her life, Kathy had laughingly promised to teach her. "Watch and learn," she said. Sharon and Debi echoed the sentiment. They'd banned the elder Mrs. McGraw from the kitchen, telling her to enjoy her rest, and planned to spend the next several hours baking.

Without the shadow of the cultists hanging over her, Lilly realized she was truly happy. Kane's family had accepted her as one of their own and sometimes she caught herself wishing she could stay at Wolf Hollow forever. With him.

The thought caused her shivers. Kane had taught her so much, but more importantly, he'd shown her how to have faith in herself. She wondered if her irrational desire to be with him longer would invalidate all she'd learned.

Confused, she decided to take things day by day. Though Lilly had spoken to her brother, Lucas, about the cultists' capture, she hadn't yet told him of her tentative plans for the future. Of course she was going to have to stay somewhere until she could find a job. It might as well be with him and Blythe, but she needed to emphasize it would only be temporary. Again, even the thought of leaving Kane felt like ripping a hole in the center of her chest, where her heart was.

Kane hadn't yet given her a date when they'd be leaving Leaning Tree, but the darkening shadows in his amazing eyes told her he, too, had this on his mind.

Later, after all the baked goods had been delivered to their grateful recipients, Kathy dropped Lilly off at her cabin. Kane waited out on the front porch, his guitar on his lap.

Struck by the homey feel of the scene, Lilly got out of the car and waved goodbye, watching as Kathy smiled and drove off.

Feeling inordinately self-conscious, Lilly walked over to Kane. In the waning light, he watched her come, his silver eyes blazing with summer lightning. Her heart turned over in her chest as she drank in his masculine beauty.

"Hey," she said softly, stopping on the bottom step and looking up at him.

The slow smile he gave her made her feel warm all over. "Hey yourself. I'm playing around with a few songs. Remember that one we worked on together? I played the melody and you made up the lyrics."

Heart skipping a beat, she nodded. "That's when I sang and you…"

He nodded. "Yes. I want to try that again."

Chapter 18

Lilly recoiled, exactly as Kane had known she would. "You can't be serious," she said. "I know you don't remember what happened before, but—"

Setting his guitar down, he got up and crossed the distance to her. "You said you sang when you were captured and the sound of your voice incapacitated the cultists."

Slowly, she nodded.

"Yet when you sang to me, you said I wanted to jump your bones. I need to know if that's still the case."

She frowned. "Why would anything have changed?"

Giving her a deliberately casual shrug, he took her hand. "Come on, try it."

"Absolutely not." She jerked her hand away, gave him a look as if she suspected he'd lost his mind, and hurried past him into the cabin.

Dropping back into the rocking chair, he realized he'd gone about this all wrong. Deep inside, he believed she loved him. Getting her to realize this wouldn't be easy, but he thought he knew how he could go about it.

He had to go big or go home. With that in mind, he put down the guitar and walked a short way from the cabin. He needed to enlist help to pull off what he had in mind. He dug out his cell phone and called his mother.

Once the conversation was finished, he walked back inside. Lilly was still holed up in her room, avoiding him. Though every instinct inside of him wanted to go to her, take her in his arms and show her they belonged together, he forced himself to be patient.

Decision made, he turned and went back outside. He'd walk and clear his head, and then turn in early. Tomorrow would be another day.

The next morning when Lilly made her way into the kitchen, drawn by the mouthwatering smell of bacon frying, Kane smiled at her and handed her a cup of coffee. "Already made the way you like it," he said.

Relieved that he wasn't immediately going to rehash his crazy idea of having her sing, she accepted the mug and took a seat at the kitchen table.

"I've also made you breakfast," he continued, his silver eyes gleaming.

"Thanks." Should she be suspicious? No, this was Kane. He'd always been upfront with her. "So what's up?"

"What do you mean?" He set a plate in front of her. Scrambled eggs, toast and three slices of perfectly crisp bacon.

"This." She leaned over and inhaled the wonderful scents wafting from her plate. "Not that I don't appreciate it, because I do. But…"

His smile seemed a bit sad. "This is one of our last mornings here together. I wanted to make it special." He turned away, busying himself again with the stove and his own plate.

His words made her chest tighten. She let her gaze roam over the back of his head, his broad shoulders to his narrow waist, lingering on his amazing backside. Her entire body flushed as she remembered cupping her hands on his taut flesh when they'd made love.

Heart pounding, she forced herself to look away. Though her food had lost its appeal, she picked up her fork and dug in. She barely looked up as Kane carried his own plate over to the table and took the seat across from her.

"Do you like it?"

She nodded. "I do. Thank you very much."

To prove he hadn't wasted his efforts, she forced herself to clean her plate. When she looked up again, she realized Kane had done the same. He sat back, drinking his coffee and watching her. She shivered at the heat in his gaze.

"My mother wants to have a party," he said. "A going-away type of thing. She and Kathy are already deep into planning it."

Though Lilly could scarcely breathe, she took a deep breath and nodded. "That sounds lovely. When?"

"Tonight?"

Shocked, at first she couldn't react. "Are we leaving so soon?"

A shadow crossed his face. "Yes."

She knew she had to ask him when, even if she didn't really want to know.

As if he understood her dilemma, he told her. "I figured we'd pull out midday tomorrow. I know your brother is eager to see you."

"He is," she answered automatically, while mentally reeling at the short notice. "I...I suppose I'd better pack."

His hand covered hers. "No rush. You can do that in

the morning. I want you to thoroughly enjoy today, so I've made plans. We're finally going to take that day trip to Woodstock."

Now, knowing her time at Wolf Hollow numbered hours, she shook her head. "That sounds lovely, but I'd rather spend time here, with your family."

"Mom wants us out of the way so she can plan this party," he told her. "She specifically asked me to find us both something to do away from here."

That hurt. She knew it shouldn't have and, while it made perfect sense, she'd rather have spent time with Kane and his family here, in the place she'd grown to love and would always miss.

But none of this was Kane's fault. Slowly, she nodded. "I understand."

"Good." Sounding satisfied, he checked his watch. "Why don't you get ready while I clean up in here? We'll head out as soon as you're ready."

She fought hard not to allow herself to sink into depression at the thought of leaving. She bit her lip and then pushed to her feet. "I just need a few minutes," she said.

Once she'd closed her bedroom door, she sank down on the edge of her bed and struggled not to cry. What on earth was wrong with her? She'd known this day was coming, longed for it, in fact. She'd thought she wanted to test her wings and learn to fly solo, but now she realized there was greater strength in learning to forge bonds with others.

Hell, who was she kidding? She wanted Kane. Not just for a day or a week or a month. But forever. Clearly, he didn't feel the same.

Trying to locate the numbness she'd once used to cloak her heart, she went to her closet, grabbed an old T-shirt and a pair of khaki shorts. She brushed her hair into a tight ponytail, slipped her feet into her most comfortable flip-flops, and sighed. Once, she'd thought she couldn't wait to get out of Wolf Hollow. Now, realizing how much these people and this place meant to her, she didn't want to leave.

Squaring her shoulders, she told herself to suck it up and be strong. And then she opened the bedroom door and walked into the den where Kane waited, car keys in hand.

On the drive, she kept her gaze focused on the scenery, afraid if she talked too much, she might let slip how she really felt. Torn apart, hurting and wondering why she couldn't seem to regain her equilibrium.

Kane appeared to have no such problems. One beautiful, long-fingered hand on the wheel, he drove with his usual self-assured confidence, making her love him more. It broke her heart that he acted as if this day was no different than any other, as if this wasn't one of the last times they'd spend together before beginning the journey to reunite her with her brother.

As Lilly battled to keep her inner turmoil hidden, Kane sang along with the radio, cheerfully pointing out places of interest as they drove past. She alternated between wanting to snarl at him and weep. Instead, she kept her head held high, feigning interest in the landscape, and wondering when she'd become such a fool.

Her inner wolf wanted out, and his apparently did, as well. Several times, as she tried to keep her inner beast leashed, she caught Kane struggling to do the same.

The town of Woodstock was crowded and quaint, as though locked in an earlier time. They ate pizza in an outdoor restaurant and wandered in and out of various shops.

She bought a lovely natural stone necklace and earring set, the deep blue and green colors reminding her of a mountain stream. She thought it would always remind her of this place, and this man. The thought brought her melancholy back, though she managed to push it away.

Several hours passed. Attentive and solicitous, Kane also appeared nervous, judging from the numerous glances she caught him sneaking at his watch. He appeared in no hurry to go back home, despite the upcoming party.

Finally, after reading a text message on his phone, he asked Lilly if she was ready to go.

Relieved, she nodded.

As they got in his car, she again fought the urge to kiss him. Once again, she concentrated on the scenery while Kane drove.

As they approached the turnoff to Wolf Hollow, Kane pulled over. "I need you to do me a favor."

Crossing her arms, she waited.

"Mom has been decorating the backyard all day and she doesn't want you to see it yet. She wants it to be a surprise."

"I'll cover my face with my hands," she said.

He grimaced. "I promised her I'd tie this scarf over your eyes. Do you mind?"

Did she mind? Not really. What she minded was that there even was a necessity of a going-away party. If she was honest, she'd like to stay at Wolf Hollow, or at least in Leaning Tree, for the indefinite future. Maybe even...dare she think it? Maybe even forever.

"Fine," she said, holding perfectly still while he tied a silken scarf over her eyes.

Once he had it secure, she waited for him to put the car back in Drive. Instead, he kissed her, his lips touching hers like a whisper. Shocked, at first she couldn't respond, but then as he continued to sensually caress her with his mouth, she returned his kiss with reckless abandon. Surely now, he must understand how she felt about him. Surely now, he'd tell her he wasn't going to leave her.

Instead, his lips left hers, blazing a path down her neck, making her shiver. Finally, after one last kiss at the hollow

of her throat, he moved away from her and the car began to
go. She felt like he'd stolen her ability to breathe.

Luckily, she managed to get herself under control. The
sensation of driving without her sight was disconcerting, to
say the least. Even her inner wolf went quiet, as intrigued as
her human half. She kept wondering if he'd touch her, even
the slightest caress. The thought made goose bumps rise
on her skin and her nipples pebble. But, to her disappointment, he must have kept his hands on the steering wheel.

She felt when they left the pavement for the gravel road,
knew every turn and bend, and could tell when they'd
passed the main house. Nevertheless, Kane didn't tell her
she could remove her blindfold, and she couldn't help but
picture what it would feel like to make love with it on. Judging just from the kiss, every other sense would be intensified, magnified to compensate for not being able to see.

She barely hid her disappointment when, as soon as
Kane parked and cut the engine, he took the silken cloth
off. She blinked, dazed and disoriented, and glanced his
way to find him smiling at her.

Again, he looked as if he hadn't a care in the world. No,
more than that, she thought as she climbed out of the car.
His entire body practically vibrated with excitement, his
eyes bright and full of half promises. She didn't understand
this and even considered asking him, but knew whatever he
might reply would most likely decimate her pride.

Still, it really was a struggle not to let this put her in
a bad mood. And right before the big going-away party.

Once they were inside the cabin, he stretched and
grinned. "I'll let you have the first shower."

She nodded, fisting her hands to keep from crossing the
room to him, grabbing him by the shirt and making him
kiss her again. What the hell had that been? Another form

of torture? His way of saying goodbye, by letting her know exactly what she'd be missing?

"You've got a little over an hour to get ready," he continued, the warmth of his smile echoing in his voice. "Mom said we need to dress what she calls resort casual, whatever that means." He shrugged. "It makes me think of Hawaiian shirts and swim trunks, even though I know that's not what she means at all."

Puzzled, Lilly knew she'd better ask. "So what does she mean?"

"I think she wants you to wear something like you'd wear on vacation, like a cruise or at some beach resort. You know, like that sundress you wore the last time we were going to visit Woodstock."

Nodding her thanks, she hurried into the bathroom, glad to escape the constant temptation.

After a nice long shower, she felt a lot better. Confident even, certainly able to deal with the myriad of emotions she was sure to experience that night.

Back in her bedroom, she ignored the carnal images dancing through her mind as she heard the sound of the shower start up. The thought of Kane, naked and wet... Shaking her head at herself, she went to her closet, wanting to dress carefully for the party. Instead of the flirty little sundress Kane had mentioned, she chose the only maxi dress she'd brought with her. The slinky material clung to her figure lovingly, and the green and navy diagonal slashes of color went perfectly with the necklace and earrings she'd bought in Woodstock.

She even applied a little makeup, her mood improving as she laughed at herself for her ineptitude—it had been too long since she'd used cosmetics.

By the time she'd finished, she felt much better. Confident even. Surveying herself in the mirror, she thought she looked good, maybe even pretty. Her hair, usually the bane of her existence, fell in natural waves past her shoulders.

When she emerged from her room to find Kane waiting, she even managed to smile at him.

Staring at her, he slowly stood, his gaze traveling over her, as intimate as a caress. Her pulse leaped, but miraculously she kept her expression merely pleasant.

"Are you ready?" she asked, her voice cool.

"You look...amazing," he said.

"Thank you." Deliberately, she surveyed him in much the same way he'd done her, praying her rapid increase in pulse didn't show. Kane wore khakis and a short-sleeved, button-down shirt, along with deck shoes. As always, he carried himself with a masculine air of self-confidence. His stance emphasized the force of his muscular legs, and the well-fitting white shirt did little to hide his broad shoulders.

Her mouth went dry as she stared at him.

Smile widening, he held out his hand. "Let's go."

She slid her fingers through his and, at the contact, her entire body felt energized, as though his touch had delivered a powerful jolt of electricity.

Marveling at this, she wanted to ask him if he'd felt it, too, but she chickened out.

Dusk darkened to night as they walked outside. Kane drove the short distance slowly, and she gasped as they rounded the curve and she caught sight of the hundreds or thousands of tiny white lights decorating the trees and patio in back of the main house.

"It's beautiful," she said, stunned. "Simply amazing."

When they pulled up in front, all the other vehicles parked there told her everyone else had already arrived.

Inhaling deeply, she smoothed down her dress as she climbed out of the car.

"Nervous?" Kane asked.

"Maybe a little." But she wasn't, not now that the moment had actually arrived. She owed these people so much, and the fact that they cared enough to throw a party to say goodbye was humbling.

"Come on." Again, Kane took her hand, leading her in through the front door instead of their usual way out back.

The front room was completely devoid of people.

"Where is everyone?" she asked.

"Out back," he told her, with a gentle smile. "This way."

Feeling like a fairy-tale princess, she let him lead her through the kitchen, out the back door, and into the transformed backyard.

Everyone waited, smiling at her. A little girl broke away from a group of children and ran to her, shouting her name.

"Hailey?" Stunned, Lilly caught her niece midjump. "What are you doing here?"

Beyond excited, the five-year-old grinned and pointed. "Mommy and Lucas are here, too!"

To Lilly's amazement, her brother and his new bride appeared, gathering her close. Blythe wore white flowers in her hair, and a long champagne colored dress that appeared to be made entirely of lace. Lucas was still growing out his dark hair, giving him a slightly dangerous air. They both glowed with happiness.

Hugging them, Lilly struggled not to cry. She blotted at her eyes, glad she'd chosen waterproof mascara. "What on earth are you two doing here?"

Lucas grinned. "Kane invited us. He wanted us to see where you've been living, and to meet his family."

Still perplexed, she smiled back. She nearly gasped out loud as she realized what this most likely meant. She'd be going home with Lucas. This, then, would be her last night with Kane.

She wished he would have warned her.

As she tried to keep smiling, the rest of Kane's family surrounded them. Kris and Debi, Kyle and Sharon, Kathy and Tom. Not to mention their combined brood of children. Someone put on music, everyone talked at once, and Kane's mother began bringing out the food as Kane's father manned the grill.

There was steak and chicken and fish, every kind of protein a carnivore could desire. Head swimming, Lilly found herself being pulled here and there, as Kane's family all had brought her small gifts. Sharon and Debi gifted her with a bottle of their favorite tequila and margarita mix, Kathy with a box of homemade cupcakes.

She didn't think she could eat, but to her surprise as the meal was set out buffet-style, she found herself with a heaping paper plate. Kane sat next to her, his thigh touching hers. She tried not to let it affect her while she ate.

The celebratory air of the party made her wonder, but she put it down to the fact that the escaped cultists had finally been caught. Still she couldn't help but question all the smiling glances everyone cast their way. As if they all knew some big secret to which she was not privy.

Once everyone finished eating, the tables were moved away. Kathy's husband, Tom, set up a drum set on a brick area to the side of the large patio, and Kane's brothers appeared with guitars. To Lilly's surprise, Kathy joined them, carrying a guitar of her own.

"What is this?" Lilly asked Kane. "Are you going to play, too?"

Never taking his gaze from her face, he slowly shook his head. "Nope. They're making music so you and I can dance."

Stunned, she looked around. "I don't know how."

He laughed, lightly touching her chin. "It's instinctual. I'll guide you and all you have to do is follow my lead."

Still she balked. "In front of everyone else? I don't think so."

"Lilly, I'm sure Lucas and Blythe will dance, too. Even my parents will probably take a spin around the floor. It'll be fun, I promise."

"But—"

He silenced her with a quick kiss, right there for anyone to see. She felt her face turn to fire, but his tactic worked. "I'll try," she finally said.

Kane's mother appeared, carrying drinks. A beer for Kane and some orange concoction for Lilly. "It's a mai tai," she explained. "Try it. You'll like it."

Lilly took a tentative sip. Fruity and sweet, it tasted a bit like punch. "It's good."

Both Kane and his mother laughed. "Enjoy yourselves," Mrs. McGraw said, patting Lilly on the shoulder. "This is a special night." She waved to a teenager who was watching the children play on another part of the back lawn, and bustled off.

The band started playing, leading off with a catchy song that had Lilly inadvertently tapping her feet. She stood next to Kane, watching as her brother and Blythe began dancing.

"Do you want to?" Kane asked.

She shook her head and sipped her drink. "Not yet."

The next song was slower. Lilly couldn't get over the feeling that everyone was watching her as if they expected something to happen. But what?

Lucas and Blythe swayed to the music. A moment later, Kane's parents joined them.

"Come on." Kane took Lilly's arm. "Let's give it a try."

She couldn't say no to the beseeching look in his eyes. Setting her drink down on one of the small tables that had been set up with chairs on the perimeter of the dance area, she walked with him out to the center.

Lucas smiled with approval as Kane took her into his

arms. Then he began to dance and she forgot all about her brother and everyone else.

There was only Kane.

Slow dancing, body to body, he moved and she moved with him, stunned by the way they seemed to flow together. It was sensual and more. Gazing up at Kane's chiseled profile, her heart swelled, her throat ached, and she realized she'd never been as happy as she was at that exact moment.

This man...this wonderful, beautiful, rugged man. Dancing with him, she craved him. She ached to have him desire her, just this once, without any siren song compelling him.

The song ended and they stepped back to the side. Stepping to the mic, Kathy announced they'd be taking a short break.

Kane led her away from the others, to a little stone bench in between two towering oak trees.

They sat. Suddenly she found herself close to tears.

"Lilly?" Hand cupping her chin, Kane raised her face. "What's wrong?"

He needed to know the truth.

"I don't know how to seduce you," she said, her low voice vibrating with need. "I have no idea how to make you crave me the same way I do you."

"Make me?" Incredulous, he kissed the tip of her nose. "Lilly, don't you realize you merely have to be in the same room as me and I'm on fire?"

Gaping at him, she couldn't find words. Then, to her complete and utter shock, Kane stood and dropped to one knee in front of her. He took out a small box and opened it.

"Lilly Gideon, I've loved you since the first moment our eyes met, there in that horrible cell at Sanctuary." The tinge of wonder in his raspy voice made her smile. "I grew to love you even more in the time we've spent together. If I know anything, it's this. I don't want to go on living without you."

A warm glow began spreading through her, she tried to speak, and found her throat too clogged with emotion.

"You are my mate," he continued, his voice breaking with emotion. "Do you realize this, too?"

Raising her head, she took a deep breath and pushed aside the last lingering shred of fear. Her strength, deep within her, would never be lessened if she shared her life with Kane. Instead, she knew it would only be enhanced.

"Yes," she whispered. "I definitely do."

For an instant he closed his eyes, as though her words overwhelmed him. When he opened them again, the silver had become molten. "Since you know we're mates, will you marry me?"

Cocking her head, she decided to pay him back a little for his earlier torture. "Only because we're mates? Not for any other reason?"

He groaned. "Because I love you. You know that. Marry me, please, and let me love you for the rest of our lives?"

Joy bubbled from her heart. Blissfully happy, she nodded, finding words of her own. "I will, if you'll let me love you, too. For the rest of our lives."

He gave a glad shout, slipping the ring on her finger. As he rose, he pulled her up with him. He kissed her, a kiss of possession and promise, before tugging her along with him, back to where his and her entire families waited expectantly.

"She said yes!" he told them, holding up her hand so everyone could see the ring that sparkled on her third finger.

At once, everyone cheered.

Kane swung her around in his arms, kissing her cheek, her neck, before muttering in her ear the things he planned to do to her the instant they got back into their cabin.

She gasped, and then laughed, her entire body growing hot as Kane caressed her with his eyes. More laughter and clapping from the others, made her see where she was, and that there were others watching. And then she realized she didn't really care. She reached for him, feeling completely and utterly naked even though she still was fully clothed.

He met her halfway, claiming her mouth with his, the heat emanating from him making her melt against him. "Will you sing for me now?" he rasped. "Please, sing to me."

"Here?" she gasped, looking around at his assembled family, all of whom watched them with a combination of love and amusement and joy. "I can't."

"You can."

When she hesitated, he kissed her again, his mouth lingering over hers. "Do you trust me?"

Bemused, she nodded.

"You're what's known as a Wolf Siren," he told her, his handsome face full of a fierce, possessive love. "*My* Wolf Siren. And legend has it that once we've committed to each other, your songs no longer have any kind of power. Over anyone."

At his words, a quiet knowing filled her. "So it wasn't because of any of the experiments they did on me at Sanctuary."

Slowly, he shook his head. "No. Now please, will you sing?"

"Only if you'll accompany me with your guitar."

When he nodded, she took his hand. Completely without fear, she walked with him to the area where the band had been playing and stepped up to the microphone.

As if they sensed something momentous was about to happen, everyone drifted back to stand in front of them. They grew silent as Kane began to play the melody.

Lilly began to sing. She remembered the words, even though she'd only made them up that one day. Unknowingly, even then she'd sung their song, a song of love and finding the one who could complete her. Her voice rose and soared and she caught more than one of the women wiping a tear from their eyes.

No one fell to the ground and Kane continued playing, no longer driven by the compelling and immediate need to possess her.

Because, she realized, he already did and he always would.

* * * * *